LIGHT
COMES
TO
SHADOW
MOUNTAIN

Toni Buzzeo

HOLIDAY HOUSE  NEW YORK

The publisher would like to thank Rick Childers of the Loyal Jones Appalachian Center, Berea College, for his expert review of this novel.

Library of Congress Cataloging-in-Publication Data is available.

ISBN: 978-0-8234-5384-9 (hardcover)

On page 37, two lines from an American folk song "Lonesome Scenes of Winter" appear. These lines were sourced from Henry Marvin Belden's *Ballads and Songs Collected by the Missouri Folk-lore Society* (published by The University of Missouri in 1940), the text of which dates this version of the song to 1904.

To Kelly Loughman, who spotted the glint of this novel in a picture-book manuscript and had the grace and love to wait for me to see it too.

CONTENTS

ONE
In the News

When Miss Bentley rings the Friday dismissal bell, Ceilly and I slide out of the wooden desk we share and push past the eighth graders rising in the back row. We scramble for the coat hooks next to the door and hurry into the fading daylight.

"Do you have it?" Ceilly demands.

I pat my pocket. "It's like to burn a hole in here!"

I take off up the path after Ceilly. Behind us, kids large and small scatter in all directions—down, up, and off to either side—from our one-room schoolhouse perched midway up on Shadow Mountain.

As often as I can slip away for a speck of time alone, I follow this path far past all of the houses, to its very end. There, from the peak of Shadow Mountain, I catch glimpses of our homes nestled below. Each one is much like the others, from oak shingled roofs and weathered barns to stone springhouses and charred smokehouses, and always, sprawling gardens competing for sun among the towering trees. Beyond them, I can only just make out the mouth of the holler and the little town of Spruce Lick, with the general store, the boarding house, the building-supplies and feed store, the Presbyterian church, and the empty bank building, closed five years ago now, Pap says.

When I gaze straight out, I see more peaks stretching as far as forever, filling me full of love for these mountains.

Or, depending on the day and Mommy's mood, with a secret longing for what might lie beyond them.

At the moment, I'm having a hard time fixing my gaze on Ceilly. She might as well have been born a cottontail as a girl, so as much as I try to stay close on her heels, I lose all sight of her when she swerves off the path. But I've known her, and this path, for as long as I've known anyone, excepting my family. That's why, well before the fork, I veer off into the woods, past the sweet-smelling witch hazel, and head to the beechnut tree where I'm certain she'll be waiting.

A startled chipmunk skitters away at my footfall, its cheek pouches bulging with early autumn nuts. I hurry through fallen leaves in my bare feet, the beginning of October still too early for costly shoes. I'm careful to avoid the prickly burs on my way to the beechnut that's been our tree, mine and Ceilly's, since the day we scratched our names in the trunk when we were only five years old. We've traced the letters with our fingertips countless times in the six years since—a tribute to our friendship. I don't hardly remember why we chose this particular tree in a forest of them, but it's been special to us ever since.

Now, our beechnut isn't a practical tree to climb—silver bark as smooth as river rocks and no low-slung branches like the others nearby. And that's precisely why I reckon I'll spot Ceilly way above where I come to stand. Up in the air is her favorite location.

Sure enough, amid the leaves glowing like copper, she's hanging by her knees from a high branch. Her long brown plait dangles from her head, about as different from my ginger curls as hair can get. She's tucked her dress into her drawers, no doubt to assist in her climb. Her great-aunt Exie would surely be scandalized.

"C'mon up, Cora. The world looks a mite bigger from up here," she calls, as though we haven't had this conversation a million times or more.

Fact is, not a soul but Ceilly—or possibly her heroine, Amelia

Earhart, Queen of the Air—would ever dare to shimmy up such a towering trunk. But Ceilly says such stunts are good practice for a future aviation career.

"I will not," I holler. "You come down, instead. Mommy expects me home straightaway."

Ceilly's coat lies on the ground where she tossed it, an old copy of *Aviation and Aircraft Journal* rolled up and poking out of the pocket. In my own coat pocket, I'm carrying the copy of *Pollyanna* that Miss Dortha Fee, our pack horse librarian, lent me at school this morning when she came through on her twice-monthly visit. It awaits my hungry eyes the minute I have a chance to read. Right now, though, it's protecting the article from the *Courier-Journal* that Miss Bentley read to us today during our Friday newspaper review, which I love even more than our weekly spelling test. I slip it out from under the cover of the novel.

"I haven't got but five minutes to study this again before I need to race home," I say, shaking out the creases. "Imagine, Ceilly, electricity!"

That one word is enough to bring her scrambling down. Dust rises as she plops onto the dirt next to me, and we sit together, leaning against the gray bark of our tree.

"Go on, Cora," Ceilly says.

I smooth the article on my leg and set to reading it aloud.

ELECTRIC COOPERATIVE INCORPORATED
Electrical Power Finally Arriving for Southeastern Kentuckians
By Jewell Roberts

FRANKFORT—OCTOBER 4, 1937. ELECTRICITY IS COMING TO ONE THOUSAND SQUARE MILES IN SOUTHEASTERN KENTUCKY THAT WILL BE SERVED BY THE NEWLY INCORPORATED AND RECENTLY FUNDED

Southeast Counties Rural Electric Cooperative Corporation. Mr. Garnett Combs of Resolute Gap has been named president of the board and will provide oversight of electrical installation in the region. Mr. Combs accepted his appointment from the capitol steps in Frankfort on Friday with words that spoke to the future as he beseeched a surrounding crowd to "Think of all the folks still living in the unelectrified Kentucky dark. Does the new generation coming up not deserve the same modern conveniences as city folk?"

Currently, 90% of Americans living in cities have access to electricity, while only 10% of rural Americans enjoy its benefits. This discrepancy was a large impetus for President Franklin D. Roosevelt's support of the Rural Electrification Act, which passed last year and provides federal loans to cooperative electric power companies.

First-ever electric lines are expected to be strung later this month in areas where at least two houses per mile of wire, as required by the Rural Electrification Administration (REA), have signed membership papers. The initial cost of a household membership is $5, which qualifies the cooperative, as a whole, for a federal loan. Ongoing costs will be $3 per month, per member.

In his speech, Mr. Combs acknowledged the expense of electrification as well as potential disruptive effects on local landscapes, but struck an optimistic tone overall. "This is an investment in possibility. We've long since seen such possibilities play out in our cities, and it's high time our hardworking rural communities reap the same benefits."

I tap the article. "Just like Miss Bentley said, looks like we've finally got a corporation fixing to electrify us." My whole self sizzles with excitement.

"Which reminds me," I rush on, "did you know your uncle Eben came by on his ride back from the beekeepers' meeting in Williamsburg yesterday? He looked about ready to sting someone himself when he dismounted. Apparently, his mood was on account of the general store being closed. But late as it was, he said he couldn't just pass on by the turnoff to the Tipton house, because the twins always set him to laughing."

"They can be counted on for that," Ceilly agrees. "Wonder what he needed at the general store?"

"Wanted to pick up his mail, he said."

Ceilly nods. "Likely he was hoping for some honey orders. He was mighty quick to blame *you* for his lateness to supper when Great-Aunt Exie raised a ruckus. He said you asked him nigh on a hundred questions about his trip and scribbled out answers fast as lightning in that notebook of yours."

"Well, I surely did," I say, "with him having been out in the wide world and all. Did you know he rode in a motorized vehicle past Spruce Lick?"

"The wide world?" Ceilly teases. "Cora, he was gone not much more than seventy Kentucky miles from here."

"May just as well be ten thousand, Ceilly." I pause, wondering exactly how far one *did* have to travel from Shadow Mountain to start experiencing the glowing America that lucky Uncle Eben got to see. I should have asked him that.

"I wish Great-Aunt Exie would ever once let me skip school for a day to go over with him and see it all too," Ceilly says wistfully.

"I know," I say, feeling my heart beat a little faster. "Did he tell you he saw one of those machines that'll do the clothes washing *for* you?"

"He did," Ceilly replies, grinning. "Though maybe here on our mountain, Cora, if we got electric lines, we'd just start with lights."

I pause to rein in my enthusiasm an inch or two. "You're right," I say. "Even one light would surely be a worthy beginning."

Ceilly bends to study the article. "It does seem like this Mr. Garnett Combs is concerned about us kids out here in the unelectrified Kentucky dark."

I elbow her. "I believe he's concerned that these mountains need electricity to raise up the next aviation pioneer, now that poor Miss Earhart and her plane have gone missing."

Ceilly pokes me back. "Or to raise up the next Nellie Bly, Ace Reporter."

I think about how, way back in July when our mountain school always starts, I didn't even know who Nellie Bly was. Then along came our new teacher, Miss Bentley, fresh from college way over in Louisville. On her very first day, Ceilly and I stayed inside at the lunch hour, and I asked her near a dozen questions about herself and her schooling. It was a good long while before she could get a word in to compliment me on my inquisitive nature. And not long after that, she presented me with a reporter's notebook she'd made, saying, "For Cora Mae Tipton, future Nellie Bly of Shadow Mountain." Inside, she'd written a quote from Miss Bly on the first page to encourage what she called my "questioning mind and exceptional writing skills." Now I plan to paste this newspaper article in there, right next to my interview with Uncle Eben.

Ceilly points at the byline—Jewell Roberts. "Looks like a lady wrote this article, Cora. Just think, someday *you* could be the reporter writing in a paper like this!"

At that, my soaring spirits tuck themselves back into their nest. Miss Bentley told us the *Courier-Journal* was published way over in Louisville and only brought to us because she has a mail subscription. And if the two hundred miles of distance between Louisville and me weren't problem enough, Miss Bentley says to be a journalist I'd need high school, which we don't even have on Shadow Mountain, and then likely college too.

As usual Ceilly is mind-reading. "I might not be able to bear it when you leave for all that schooling."

I turn and look her square in the eye. "Ceilly, if Uncle Eben has his way, you'll be working toward *your* own dreams for schooling and then some."

"When does Uncle Eben ever have his way against Great-Aunt Exie?" Ceilly asks.

"There's a fact," I say, and I can't help but sigh for us both. "You know, Mommy's not likely to ever approve such a thing as me boarding at a high school off this mountain. Miss Bentley says I'd need signatures of both parents to even sit for the scholarship exams the settlement school offers, never mind Mommy approving attendance at college. She's still not forgiven my aunt Thelma for turning her back on our mountain ways and heading to big-city Detroit, and that was years ago."

I pause to take a deep breath. Then I whisper, "And with Ida gone…" My throat closes, and I spend a quiet minute thinking of my big sister. I suspect Ceilly does too.

Then I jump to my feet and nudge my spirits back to life. "Well, either way, whether we go venturing off someday or not, the least we can do is to take advantage of the president's proposal and improve life right here and now on Shadow Mountain."

When Ceilly doesn't respond, I pause to look at her. "You *do* think it would be an improvement, don't you, Ceilly? Electricity?"

Ceilly puts her hand over her heart. "Cora, I do. But *we* can't join the cooperative!"

"'Course not," I say. "It's for the grown-ups to decide." Then I smile at my friend. "But I reckon their decision would be easier if people knew what your Uncle Eben saw with his very own eyes. Maybe we need to spread the word about this opportunity and what all electricity can do for a place like Shadow Mountain."

Ceilly smiles back. "I'll be your willing and steadfast partner in that."

"Then I'll set my mind to figuring how we might do it," I say.

Suddenly the length of the afternoon shadows catches my attention, and I gasp. "Time to go." I reach for Ceilly's hand and pull her to her feet. "Mommy's mighty short of forgiving bones where I'm concerned."

Ceilly knows the truth of that—how Mommy's been since Ida died. We head back up the path toward home.

TWO
A Fox in the Chicken Coop

Most every day Ceilly comes to our house after school. She tells her great-aunt Exie that Mommy needs help with the twins and the chores. I can just about hear Ceilly piously tell her, "It is my Christian duty to offer help wherever it is needed."

Great-Aunt Exie doesn't push the argument either. It's obvious she isn't any fonder of Ceilly than Ceilly is of her, despite her grudging generosity in taking four-year-old Ceilly in when fire burned down her house and orphaned her. It always seems to me that it's people's *opinions* that Great-Aunt Exie cares about, more than anything else.

"Just think," I say as we walk so close that our flour-sack dresses brush against each other. "If we had an electric cooperative on our mountain, we'd have light in the winter dark."

"I'd wish for that light up in my bedroom," Ceilly says.

"For drawing?" I ask, already knowing the answer.

"Yep. I'd sketch airplanes to my heart's content—well out of Great-Aunt Exie's view."

I squeeze her arm. "You'll fly someday, whether she thinks you should or not."

Ceilly's eyes glisten for a moment, and I think about how it's *my* Christian duty to give her every bit of the encouragement she so rightfully deserves, living with Great-Aunt Exie as she does.

"As for me, I think I'd prefer a light right above our kitchen table where I study. Maybe I could keep it on long enough after dinner to prepare for those scholarship exams. 'Cause even if Mommy *did* some-day say I could go to the settlement high school, scholarship money is the only way I'd ever be able to attend."

Ceilly stops walking and smiles at me. "I just *knew* you hadn't *really* set aside that notion! So you think there's a chance your mommy might change her mind?"

"No…but I s'pose I haven't given up on trying to convince her just yet. Same as I hold out hope for Uncle Eben convincing Great-Aunt Exie to let him enroll you in that high school over to Williamsburg."

Ceilly laughs. "Only difference is, Uncle Eben's approach to con-vincing is like a mountain lion sneaking up on a deer while yours is like a fox causing mayhem in the chicken coop."

I can't help but laugh with her.

"Anyway," Ceilly continues, "Great-Aunt Exie *needs* me to stay right here on the mountain, as a constant reminder to every other soul around of her capacity for Christian charity."

"Hm. Seems to *me* Uncle Eben needs you to go off to school in Williamsburg."

"Much as I think he'd like me to," Ceilly says, "I can't think why he'd *need* me to go."

"Well, seeing as how his own dream of attending school there was lost to him…" I stop short, feeling so sorry to have spoken those words aloud.

Ceilly squeezes my hand. "It's okay, Cora. I don't mind you talking about it."

We walk on for a while before Ceilly speaks again. "If there's one thing I do understand, it's that losing Mommy and Pap upended things for all of us. Uncle Eben would surely have gone off the moun-tain to school himself except that Great-Aunt Exie couldn't bear to lose both her only niece and her only son at once, never mind being left *alone* with a four-year-old."

When we reach Clayton Fork, Ceilly drops my hand and turns toward her home.

"You're not coming with me?"

"Not today," Ceilly says. "Great Aunt Exie needs help bottling honey while there's still some light left in the sky."

"But Ceilly…" I say.

"I know. We'll surely talk about electricity more on Monday." Ceilly pauses, clamps her lips tight for a second, then says, "But we shouldn't ought to get completely attached to the notion, Cora."

"Because of the five dollars for a membership?"

She nods.

"And the three dollars every month after that?"

She nods again. "It *is* a lot to ask, Cora, especially in these hard times."

Then she glances up the hill toward my house, and I know that money isn't our only worry as concerns electricity on Shadow Mountain.

We both know that Mommy is also likely to be one of Miss Bentley's spelling words—an "impediment"—to any ideas I have about my life being any different than it is right now.

*** ✳ ✳ ✳ ***

The twins run happy circles around me as I head up the porch steps. But they don't follow me inside, where the stinging smell of vinegar greets me.

"Cora Mae Tipton," Mommy calls from the dry sink, her arms outstretched past her pregnant belly. I'm guessing she is straining the echinacea blossoms, leaves, and roots she has had soaking in that big jar for the past six weeks to make a tonic for treating winter colds. "What made you so late?"

I don't argue or explain. "Sorry, Mommy."

I drop *Pollyanna* on the table with the newspaper article tucked carefully under its cover. I try to remember what it was like to come home to a mother eager to hear about the book I'd brought home, even if my strong will kept the two of us from getting along as perfectly as she did with Ida.

I climb the stairs to change out of my school dress. I slide closed the curtain that divides the boys' side of the bedroom from my side. Through the single bedroom window, I glimpse the rim of the early October harvest moon rising above Shadow Mountain. Good. I resolve to read just a few pages before supper. That moonlight may not be an electric lamp, but when it gets full like this, I've found it can be just bright enough to read by.

Back downstairs, light from the inside lantern spreads around Mommy. At the other end of the room, I scoop up *Pollyanna* and glance down at the first page. If I keep standing by this window, it will soon be bathed in moonlight.

Mommy's voice interrupts my intention. "Don't make me ask you to shut that book. You should be setting the table right now," she says without turning. "Besides, you've got but one set of eyes, and you know your Pap doesn't have money to give for spectacles neither. Those stories of yours aren't the beginning nor the end of this world, Cora Mae, and hardly worth the cost of your sight either way."

I let out a small sigh, too quiet for her to hear. I know that's true for Mommy. But with Miss Fee's visits, books and stories of all kinds really *do* sometimes seem like the beginning and end of my world.

I snap the book shut and squeeze past Mommy to reach into the top cabinet and drawers of the Hoosier for plates and forks. As I set the table, bedtime hangs even heavier than usual in my mind. It's been pitch dark and desolate in that bed for the year and more that Ida's been gone. Under the lonely quilt, the quiet comfort of my sister's reassurances has vanished. Ida always knew just what to say after I'd had a tangle with Mommy. And Mommy used to remember to set things right with me in the morning, even when I was in the wrong.

I remember the last time, before Ida caught the fatal flu. Mommy was furious that I refused to weed the newly planted bed of beans to rid it of lamb's-quarters. I hated the blisters the hoe handle gave me, and I hated losing a day of spring sunshine after the long, dark winter. I hollered, "Someday, I'll live in a place where there *is* no garden, where all food comes from a store!" and stomped out the door.

Mommy called after me in a sour voice, "Well, Cora, until you do, you are a part of this family and you will do your best to be a generous, contributing member like your sister is."

In bed that night, I couldn't stop thinking about the argument with Mommy. Ida and I were so different. She'd never have even *thought* such things as I'd shouted at Mommy, much less said them aloud.

I grabbed my sister's hand under the quilt and gave it a squeeze. It was blistered from the hoeing I'd refused to do. While Ida weeded the whole bean patch, I'd kept her laughing by spinning a story of her, Rilda, and Hildy on a journey to the center of the Earth, taking my idea from the book by Mr. Jules Verne.

"Ida," I whispered.

"Hm?"

"Ida, you are generous down to your very bones. And your ambitions are so like Mommy's. I wish I hadn't been born with these selfish bones that make me hate to hoe and harvest, that make me dream of a different life someday. Crossing Mommy like that was a big mistake you'd never make."

"No, everyone slips up. I do too," she said. "You know that Mommy will be ready to forgive you in the morning. Besides, you don't have *selfish* bones. You just have *different* bones from mine—bones I happen to love."

And I drifted off to sleep with the comfort of her words, absolved of the selfishness I feared and with hope that I was lovable just as I was.

Now, though, in Ida's place on the feather mattress is an icy chill, cold as the rippling waters of the Resolute River. I'm not able to believe Ida's words anymore. And unless I can read a handful of pages now, I'll have to drift there awake, shivering, once again reflecting on my selfish bones, and wondering who Pollyanna is and whether she has them too.

✳ ✳ ✳

The twins bang through the door. Orrin scurries to my side, nudging my elbow over and over with the book of Jack tales he's retrieved from the shelf. Clint lurks behind him with hopeful eyes. If Ida had survived the flu as my brothers did, she and her generous bones would have occupied the boys while I snuck in those first few pages—or maybe the whole darned chapter.

I remember when I was four, like they are now, how I believed Ida had magical powers as she conjured the Jack stories from the little black squiggles on the page of our only book—the same Jack stories I read to Clint and Orrin now, when there's enough light and a moment's opportunity.

I reckon Mommy will sentence me to a month of Saturday nights spent scrubbing the twins from head to hoof in the washtub if I don't mind her now. 'Course, if Ida were still alive, she'd do that scrubbing without it needing to be a punishment.

"Read us a Jack tale, Cora," Clint says. "The one where Jack tricks the mountain giant!"

His sweet expression about breaks my heart. "It's too dark now," I whisper.

"Tell it, then," Orrin pleads. "We'll 'magine the pictures."

"And be sure you do all the voices!" Clint exclaims.

I finish setting the table, glance at Mommy for approval, then stretch out on the rug Aunt Thelma braided so long ago, long before she left Shadow Mountain to try life in Detroit, to work in an automobile factory, to birth my cousin Glenna and raise her in the big city, to do everything differently.

My heart refills a bit as the boys snuggle up close. Clint sucks on the knuckle of his thumb. Orrin tugs his fingers through my curls as he always does. In this moment of big-sistering, I am comforted by how like Ida I can be on occasion.

If only she could see me now.

THREE
Dark on All Sides

I've barely commenced telling the story I know by heart when I'm interrupted by the sound of boots on the porch steps.

"Pap!" The twins hop up, throw open the door, and wiggle into his dripping arms. As I gaze upon the three of them, my comfort blooms to near bursting.

Pap's face and hands shine pink from scrubbing at the water pump as he does every Friday after spending the week away building roads over at Laurel Falls State Park. As always, upon seeing him of a Friday, I thank the stars and God Himself that he's not returning from the coal mines down in Harlan County. Miss Bentley read us a newspaper article about their fierce union struggles there.

Pap's laugh rolls around the room. "Lordy, you two have grown an inch apiece these past five days!" His eyes find mine. "And how's my storyteller?"

As if she didn't hear Pap, Mommy says, "Everyone sit themselves at the table now, before this stew gets cold."

Still Pap keeps his eyes on me.

"Just fine, Pap." I settle in my seat, longing to unbutton my excitement about the newspaper article regarding the cooperative, but afraid of the consequences if Mommy hears it.

Pap reads my voice. Seated next to me, his eyes travel over my face, searching. He reaches out to give my shoulder a squeeze. There's relief in knowing *he* understands me. I vow to find a time later to talk to him alone.

After he says grace, Pap leans over his plate. "Ahhh, Mattie, this stew smells delicious! And is that one of your tonics I smell too?" Of course he's teasing, in his gentle way, because the scent of vinegar is still strong in the air.

He waits for Mommy's small nod, then turns back to me. "Wasn't there a spelling test today?"

I know he's poking gently at the edges of my life, looking for clues. "Yes, sir."

"And?" he raises a bushy eyebrow.

"Ninety-five percent." I can't help but grin.

Pap winks at me, but Mommy just keeps eating.

"Is that good?" Orrin asks.

"Good?" Pap sets down knife and fork and rubs his rough palms together. "It's pretty near perfect. There's a reason your sister has won the school spelling bee three years running. It's one of her God-given gifts. Why, Cora might be the best speller in Eastern Kentucky! She's destined for great things."

Mommy's voice is flat. "There is no point in speculating what she's going to do with that skill. She'll label her jars of canned tomatoes and butter beans after she plants them, weeds them, and harvests them, all while warning her children not to trample the garden while she's pinning the wash to the line. Same as every one of us does." She looks up at us with narrowed eyes. "And there's not one lick of shame in it."

My shoulders slump. There it is, Mommy's entire vision for my life as a mountain wife, exactly like her own. And why does she assume I think there's shame in it? I don't dare to ask that question, though. I just hold my breath, hoping Pap lets it go too.

He glances at me, then continues. "Well, I'll just say that you boys had best hope to spell as well as your sister when your time for school comes around next year."

"We already can." Orrin springs out of his seat. "O-R-R-I-N!"

"Yep, C-L-I-N-T!" Clint adds.

Both boys hop around in the shadows beyond the lantern light, repeating their five letters in a loud competing chorus of two.

Pap grins, but Mommy slices the joy with a single word: "Enough."

The twins slink to their seats and pick up their forks.

Pap sighs. He won't say anything else, though. As usual, he's careful of Mommy.

We eat the rest of our supper in silence.

✳ ✳ ✳

After Mommy and I dry the dishes and put them away, she takes up the lantern and scoots the jack-in-the-box twins off to bed. We won't see her again.

Now that the lantern is upstairs and clouds have blown across the moon, my last chances to read are gone. I scurry outside and gather Stormy, Violet, and the pigs into the barn and water them. I lock the chickens into the coop for the night and look up to see Pap on the porch. I go join him at the railing. With Pap beside me gazing out into the velvety softness, there's just a whiff of contentment that hasn't been here the whole week he's been gone.

The night is full of sound. Stormy whinnies and Violet moos below in the barn. A strong October wind rustles dying leaves all around. That same wind is what smothered my moonlight earlier and now has filled the sky with heavy scudding clouds. Pap and I stand shoulder-to-side, listening and looking down the mountain on pure dark.

Dark below us.

Dark behind us.

Dark on all sides.

And lingering dark in my heart too.

As always, Pap just knows. "You seem low, Cora Girl."

Much as I love that he notices, I suspect he also knows the cause. And I know better than to complain about Mommy. I understand the rules that keep our family peace.

Looking instead for some cheer, I turn to the newspaper article. "Today Miss Bentley shared news about an electric corporation newly arrived in these parts."

"Why, yes! What do you think about it all?"

I snug up into his side. "It sounds so exciting, Pap! Lights in every house—and maybe even some of those modern machines folks have everywhere but here."

Pap reaches his hand around my arm. "It *is* exciting, and electricity surely can make chores easier. For my money, though, just about the best thing about it is a connection to the outside world."

"You mean by radio broadcast?" I ask, remembering something Uncle Eben said.

"Yes," Pap says. "Radio listeners hear news of the wider world right as it happens. They can discuss what they hear and take opportunities to act on it."

"Pap, Miss Bentley says there is a radio at the house down in Spruce Lick where she boards," I say. "Even without electricity!"

"Is there, now?" Pap says. "Well, that's a consideration. But then again, so's the ongoing price. Those radio batteries are mighty costly, so one would have to have the means to pay for replacements—and the will to spend one's money that way." He pauses and squeezes my shoulder. I know whose will might be lacking here.

"Still," he continues, "I reckon I'd like a radio someday."

"I told Ceilly I'm wishing for a lightbulb above our kitchen table," I say.

"You'd surely have that." But then he sighs. "But don't go putting the cart before the horse. Getting enough members to join the cooperative up here on Shadow Mountain may be quite a mountain to climb in itself. Some folks have promised an early commitment, but—"

"Pap! What do you mean? What folks? How many? When?"

He ruffles my curls. "My live-in reporter, full of questions."

"Tell me, Pap!"

"Well, a letter went out late last week from the Southeast Counties Rural Electric Cooperative Corporation to all of us folks living up here on Shadow Mountain. And those who already got down to the general store for their mail and had their minds made up have made an early response."

My heart sets in to racing. So *that's* why Uncle Eben was mad about missing the mail yesterday—he'd likely heard tell of the letter and wanted to bring it home.

Pap continues. "Seems there are even some affirmatives up here where we are, above the school. I don't yet know who all, though I imagine Eben is a strong candidate, having been so often exposed to it when he's in Williamsburg. Why, he's told me that some city beekeepers have electric honey extractors to do the work of that hand-crank machine of his."

My mind zings with the thought that Ceilly's family might be members of the cooperative.

But Pap continues. "Still, Cora, for many people the cost is too dear. And beyond that, there are folks who don't see any need for changes to our way of life, regardless."

And in an instant the fizz of excitement that was building in me about Uncle Eben falls flat. I remember the newspaper article mentioning the opposition. And even though I doubt that Great-Aunt Exie will share Mommy's exact concerns, they are both likely to take offense at any changes to our way of life.

Pap seems to note my flagging mood. "Still and all, Cora Girl, I've got some news to share about all this when—"

"What news? Do we have the letter?" I rush to ask.

"Not yet," he says. "I was going to say, I want to share it when we're all around the table again." He pats my hand. "But for now, try to remember what my pap always said about darkness."

I think on my Papaw and Granny, taken with Ida by the flu that brought fevers, and coughing, and gasping for air. "What?" I ask, hoping for something to make my heart lighter.

"In darkness we can better see the stars," Pap says.

I turn my glance up to the sky and think that Papaw was mistaken. Even Pegasus, the Winged Horse constellation, is hiding behind the clouds tonight.

I pause to remember learning so long ago about Pegasus in that book of Greek myths that Miss Fee had carried to the schoolhouse in her saddlebags. Ida brought it home to me. When Ida found books she thought I'd especially love, it told me I lived in her heart and mind even when she left to go to school. Now my brothers just might be ready for me to bring those Greek myths home so they can learn about Pegasus too—and know how much I love them.

I determine to ask Miss Fee about that book when she comes riding up to the schoolhouse two weeks hence.

I determine to fill my reporter's notebook with stories of news, be it of Spruce Lick or the great wide world—just like Jewell Roberts.

I determine to find a way to bring light to Shadow Mountain, whether I live out my life right here or not.

FOUR
Mommy Has a Day

When I open my eyes, the sun is brighter than it should be of an October morning. In autumn, when the evening dark falls earlier, we're up at dawn to fit in all our chores. So my heart sets to pounding before I remember. It's Saturday. No school, and Pap is home. Mommy has early-morning help that isn't me.

I lean over the edge of the bed and slip my fingers quiet-like around the spine of *Pollyanna*. If I'm silent as a mama possum in a wood pile, I can sneak in the first few pages that I never did get to read last night. Then, while I wrestle all that Mommy has stacked up on my Saturday to-do list, I'll make the time fly by as I spin my imaginings of what the rest of the chapter might hold. Or, if luck shines on my day, I'll get an hour to myself, and I'll carry the book to the mountain peak to find out what really happens.

But before I even flip the cover open, four small fists pound on the bedroom door frame at the top of the stairs. The twins stand on the landing awaiting an invitation to enter.

"Cora," Orrin shouts. "The sun is up, up, up!"

Clint nods seriously. "Mommy said no breakfast for lay-abeds. We already ate."

"Anyway, it was just lumpy old grits without butter," Orrin reassures me. "We made some butter just now, though."

The boys set in to chanting:

Churn, butter, churn.
Churn, butter, churn.
Peter's at the garden gate
Waiting for his butter cake.

I let go the book and curl my hand into a tight fist on the sheet. If I pat the mattress next to me, those troublesome twins will be over here in a minute and despite my desire to tame my selfish bones, I can't abide the interruption right now. I want my privacy this morning before Mommy's list of chores owns me—to read while there's light. I ignore my impatient brothers and stay still.

"But Cora," Clint finally whimpers, "Mommy banged the spoon down on the table—hard."

With that, my hand opens all by itself and pats the bed. They pile onto me and wriggle themselves under the quilt.

Orrin pulls his fingers through my curls and points. "What's this book?"

Suddenly, I know what I'll do. "Let me read you two pages. They'll be just our secret before I get to work."

At long last, I read the beginning of the chapter and answer a dozen questions from the boys about what I think might happen next. Then I shoo the twins out. Lord knows, Ida would have been up at sunrise, stirring, scrubbing, shining. I rush to throw on clothes. I hope for chores that will at least send me out to enjoy the sunshine—stringing bush beans for drying or picking cabbage worms off the collard and turnip greens. And maybe I can even find time to paste the electricity article into my reporter's notebook.

But by the time I get down to the kitchen, there's only Pap, leaning back in a chair with a sprinkle of wood chips in his hair and possibly the spoon Mommy banged lying on the table in front of him. My eyes search the downstairs for Mommy, but I only spot evidence of butter making in the kitchen—the butter churn, a big jar of buttermilk, and the crock, likely full now. Knowing how Orrin and Clint squabble over who gets to have a turn at the churning, I'm grateful to have slept late.

The smell of fresh-cut yellow pine fills the air as the boys tote kindling in to fill the wood box. Between the butter and the wood, it looks to have been a busy morning so far.

"Pap, where's Mommy?" I ask.

Pap just points to the chair next to him at the scrubbed table. "Have a seat, Cora."

I slide in and scoot it close to Pap's. "Where *is* she, Pap?"

He looks straight into my eyes. "She's having a day," he says, "for herself."

The heaviness in his voice takes the light out of my own day, as though I need to reach for the lantern. I've never in my life heard of having "a day." Mommy has a list of tasks—for her, for me, for the twins. But she doesn't have "a day," leastways not as far as I know.

"With who?" I whisper.

After a pause, he says, "Alone."

Mommy, alone? Fear creeps up in me like a copperhead in the weeds. Now my heart starts to pound. "Why?"

He holds my gaze. "I think you're near old enough to understand this, Cora. Your mommy is in a mighty struggle with a demon as fierce as that giant catfish folks say pulls people underwater." He gives me some time to picture that. "She needs our help."

My chest tightens. "Help?" I squeak out.

"For today, we need to get every chore on her list done." Then he says, in a voice so hushed I can barely hear, "Your mommy is struggling to hold fast. We need to help her do that. With the baby coming, she feels like she doesn't control anything at all."

I can't imagine what he can possibly mean. Mommy controls *everything* here. None of us—not a one—can have a thought, a feeling, or a plan that she does not control. As I see it, aside from keeping house, controlling is her life's work.

"Hold fast?" I ask.

Pap hears the confusion in my voice and reaches for my shoulder. "Cora, she didn't just lose her parents and your sister to the flu. In her sadness she feels she's in danger of losing her very self to something heavy in her spirit."

My heart pounds while my thoughts chase themselves around. As much as I sometimes long to throw off her control, I know that a struggling Mommy is still better than no Mommy at all. I want to run from the room, from the house, across the porch to wherever she is—all the way to Spruce Lick if need be. I want to fetch Mommy back—for herself, for me, for all of us—so she doesn't lose herself as she's worried she might.

Instead, fear glues me tight to my chair. Pap waits.

Finally I speak, and along with the words, a sob escapes. "Where did she go, Pap? When is she coming back?"

"Coming back?" Pap asks. He jumps up from his chair, upsetting it. I feel his rough palms on my wet cheeks.

"Oh, no, no. I'm sorry, Cora Girl. Your mommy's right here—she's just gone up to our bedroom."

And then he's rocking me like I was his baby girl. Rocking and rocking and rocking me while I think about all he's said.

* * *

After the churn is clean and the crock of fresh butter is put away in the springhouse, Pap rallies us around the other tasks Mommy left for us to do.

Outside, I ask the twins, "Which would you rather do, dig potatoes or pick cabbage worms?" knowing full well the joy they take in plucking the worms and dropping them into the bucket of soapy water.

"I'll get the soap," says Orrin.

"I'll fetch the bucket," Clint adds.

So the twins pick the cabbage worms next to me while I dig enough potatoes to scrub and boil in the buttermilk for lunch. Afterwards we all harvest and prepare a load of cucumbers to pickle. The sharp smell of newly pulled and peeled garlic wraps us round.

Then Pap and I take turns working with each twin alone. Pap takes Clint to the pawpaw thicket down near the church meetinghouse to fill a bucket with fruit. They'll likely not be gone more than an hour and a half—twenty minutes to the thicket and twenty minutes back, plus gathering time. Of course, it depends on how many other people decide to make a separate trip today when they could just as well bring baskets for collecting after Sunday service tomorrow. That thicket at the meetinghouse is sure an autumn-Sunday advantage over being a member at the Presbyterian church way down in Spruce Lick.

When they set off, Orrin and I walk up Clayton Fork, not quite as far as Ceilly's house, to dig mallow roots and harvest fox grapes. No need to wonder where the viney grape patch is. That wild smell, like fresh-dug earth, alerts us as we get close. I remind Orrin near to a dozen times not to slip the fruit out of its thick skin except for the grapes he is actually eating. And in that regard, I also have to remind him that our job is to fill this bucket, not just our stomachs, with the sour fruit.

On the walk back home, I finally spot a patch of mallow weed. We find a sturdy stick to dig wide and deep for the long, tough, tangled roots that are almost impossible to harvest. Mommy will dry them and then make an infusion that she'll mix with Uncle Eben's honey to create a cough syrup. And though I'll be glad of that syrup should a cough come on me this winter, I wish I didn't have to struggle with these dang roots.

Pap and Clint beat us back home, so after Orrin and I drink our fill of water, Pap outlines the rest of our chores from Mommy's list. As I move from task to task, I know that my job is to help Pap get every bit of the day's work done. But I know my heart will only be truly at rest after I've had one glimpse of Mommy in her bedroom.

When I cover up Orrin and Clint for their naps, Mommy's door across the landing is closed tight. I read the boys "Jack and the North West Wind." That task isn't on Mommy's list, but Pap says they likely need the comfort of a triumphant story.

As I read, I remember Ida squeezing my hand in our bed when an owl screeched in the chestnut tree on the path, when a red fox screamed on the mountainside behind our house, when lightning struck right outside our window. I strive to remember the comfort I felt with her hand around mine, so that I can pass it on to my brothers.

After the story, I slip downstairs to brew some of Mommy's fire-weed tea. Whenever mountain neighbors come to the door to trade a tallow candle or a small hank of wool thread for this tea, I hear her instruct them about how to prepare it for its mood-lifting properties. So I pinch some out of the labeled jar in the pie safe Papaw built for Mommy when she married Pap. Then I add boiling water and let it steep. After I strain it and doctor it with honey, I carefully carry the steaming cup upstairs and stand on the landing outside of Mommy's bedroom door.

Silence.

I listen for a long time, trying to work up the courage to knock. At last, I do. But no one answers.

Was Pap mistaken? Is Mommy really behind that door?

I knock again. Still no answer. I drop my hand in defeat, clump down the stairs, still carrying the cup of tea, and head for the next chore on the list.

But on the kitchen table, I find a surprise. A magazine titled *Life* in big white letters on a red background. I remember the time last year when Miss Fee brought a similar magazine called *Look* to our school in her saddlebags, and we all pored over it. Pap must have left this one here for me, despite the risk that Mommy might come down and toss it into the stove. I wonder if this magazine has anything to do with the "news" he said he had to share when next we sat around the table. What could it be?

It isn't a shiny new magazine, but that doesn't matter a lick to me. As I sip the fireweed tea, I dive right into its curled and worn pages, filled with photographs, flipping them one at a time. Before long, my mood is lifted, and my mind is abuzz with the pictures and captions. As I begin each tiny article, I search for a byline, but there aren't any. I wonder who writes them then.

When I reach an article called "Today's Modern Schools," I suck in my breath as I study the photographs. These schools are nothing like my dim one-room schoolhouse. I see lucky city students filing through the doorways of classroom after classroom, which are all lit up like candles on a Christmas tree, radiant with light. Two neat rows of lamps with milky glass coverings are suspended from the ceilings of those classrooms. And I only see windows on one side of the rooms, as if the schools needn't worry about getting all the daylight they can, the way we do. Of course, with classrooms off hallways and lined up next to each other like train cars, there seems to only be one wall for windows anyway. My stomach clenches, though, as I read a caption that notes a brand-new scientific study about the importance of good schoolroom lighting to students' eye health, school success, and even lifetime success. I try to push that worry away for now.

As I lean in closer to the picture, I notice a clock hanging on the wall. It reads 9:25. I think of Miss Bentley winding the clock on her desk every morning just after the Pledge. Likely this newfangled wall clock works by electricity too.

I pause to wonder if electric light is hot, but the captions make no mention. I see no woodstoves in the corners of these classrooms. Does electricity take away the need for one, or is there some other heating miracle? Does electricity pop and crackle like kindling?

Miss Bentley told us about schools like these only yesterday when she shared that newspaper article. She said there are such schools in Kentucky's biggest city, Louisville, but also much nearer, which seemed near impossible to me before I talked to Uncle Eben about Williamsburg. Still, I didn't understand the full glory of those classrooms until now, reading this article.

Then again, just like Mommy, I haven't ever been beyond these mountains—not *yet*—but now I know that the near-impossible is closer than I thought. Maybe this is why some mountain folk, like Aunt Thelma, move away—to know such things for themselves, no matter that the ones left behind feel sad or even angry. The knowing is that important.

The fire to see that world glows even brighter within me too, now that I've seen these pictures. Surely I have reason to hope that even the settlement school will have electric lights by 1940, should I be lucky enough to attend high school there. I dare to imagine myself sitting at a desk on a stormy autumn day, rain falling in sheets outside the windows but the glowing lights hanging overhead casting a warm radiance all around and protecting my eyesight too!

Who wouldn't want to experience all that's on these magazine pages? I run upstairs to fetch my pencil and reporter's notebook. I pause to read the Nellie Bly quote Miss Bentley wrote on the first page:

I HAVE NEVER WRITTEN A WORD THAT DID NOT COME
FROM MY HEART. I NEVER SHALL.

I jot down so many notes—and my questions too—about these schools. Then I study an advertisement showing a father in fancy clothes checking a timepiece on his wrist as he opens the front door of his house, illuminated by lights on the porch. Through the window, I see a family of four smiling children taking seats at a round dining table. In another advertisement a mother with carefully styled hair and dressed in a fresh-pressed frilly apron is smiling beside a shiny white machine that scrubs clothes clean and wrings them too—no washboard in sight. Her children, dressed in fresh-pressed shirts and dresses, are laughing at something she is saying. It all seems miraculous to me.

Then I paste Miss Bentley's newspaper article into the notebook. As I do, an idea forms in my mind. What if I were to create a school newspaper for my classmates? The only real newspapers we see on Shadow Mountain come to Spruce Lick by mail subscription, like

Miss Bentley's. Besides, those papers aren't reporting on our local news. Maybe I could do some of that. And I could feature some piece of this bright-lit world in each issue too, to help my classmates learn the specifics of what life on Shadow Mountain could be like, if their families agreed to be part of the cooperative. I already know from when Miss Bentley read us the article that most of the kids are in favor of electrification, but a newspaper could give them facts to back up their opinions in family discussions. Then they could help spread the word about the good electricity can do.

I can't wait to talk to Ceilly. I want to ask her if Uncle Eben has plans for joining the cooperative like Pap said he might, and I want to show her the miracles pictured in this magazine too. Then I consider taking the magazine upstairs to show Mommy. Would a machine that washes clothes make her feel like she was having "a day"? Would she feel like she had some power if she could turn on a light as darkness set in?

But just as quickly, the memory of Mommy's closed door reminds me of the truth of it. Mommy won't look at those photographs of a future we could build, clinging as she does to this mountainside with its oil lanterns, its scrub boards, its gardens of vegetables and labeled canning jars of food and medicinal herbs. No, she just wants this life she's always lived—only with Ida still here.

And I can't bring my sister back.

FIVE
Pap's Big Announcement

When our rooster crows the next morning, I hop out of bed and try to decide. Should I wear my own flour-sack dress for Sunday service as usual or, for the first time, should I wear the Sunday dress Mommy made from store-bought fabric for Ida's twelfth birthday? It's still packed away in the trunk at the foot of the bed, but it might just fit me now.

I wonder, would the sight of that dress cheer Mommy today, or make things worse?

Either way, I don't expect her to laugh and sing "Noah's Ark" and swing me 'round as she so often did Ida and me. But Pap said she needs our help so as not to lose herself. When Ida was still here, Mommy *was* herself.

I decide to risk it.

The latches of the trunk open with ease, and after I dress, I follow the salty smell of bacon grease down the stairs. Mommy stands at the cookstove flipping the hoecakes sizzling in the iron skillet. She doesn't hear me behind her.

She doesn't look one bit worried. I notice she's already fetched water from the well and heated a first pan of it to wash herself up after milking Violet. Her bun is as neat as a warbler's nest. From behind, I can see that her dress, patched but crisply ironed, is stretched tight. I admire the way she shines like the morning light. Feeling rumply in Ida's long-folded dress, I try in vain to smooth it across my legs.

Then I speak up. "Shall I wake the twins?"

Mommy whirls around.

"Sakes alive!" Shock and then confusion wrinkle her brow. I hold still, but after a few seconds, she draws in a deep, shaking breath and just nods at me.

As I head back up the steps, I wonder if I made the right choice after all.

✳ ✳ ✳

I am taken by surprise when Preacher Jones includes the cooperative in his sermon. He mentions the letter some folks have already picked up at the general store. He quotes the newspaper article Miss Bentley gave me. It is a big decision, he says, for the families on Shadow Mountain. He even lifts his voice in prayer about it.

"Dear Lord," he concludes, "we lean on your wisdom and counsel as we each weigh a difficult choice concerning electrification. As in all things, we beseech you to guide us toward the path of righteousness that leads to eternal salvation. In your name we pray. Amen."

As we leave the meetinghouse, I see Mrs. Hudgins pull her letter out of her pocketbook and hear her trying to explain the cooperative to Granny Burris, who doesn't seem to grasp the concept of stringing the wires and apparently hasn't been to the general store to retrieve her own letter. I'd as soon have jumped right in to help Mrs. Hudgins, but Mommy has a tight grip on my arm and a mind-your-own-business look on her face. It makes me wonder how much she already knows about the announcement in the news article. Did Pap bring home a copy of the letter after all?

I give Ceilly a quick wave as we leave Pap behind in conversation with Uncle Eben and Miss Bentley and a few others. Though I am desperate to hear them, the expression on Mommy's face tells me she has no interest in joining in.

And I'm suddenly certain that everything that's been news to me in the past few days, Mommy's seen coming for far longer.

***

Back at home, I change into my own dress and set the table for noon dinner without Mommy asking, working hard to help.

Pap says the blessing, then clears his throat. When I look at Mommy's face, I catch her glowering at him, her lips pressed tight. A cold shiver passes over me. Mommy has returned to our table, but my fear about Mommy's "day" yesterday creeps back in.

I just can't help myself. I whisper, "Don't leave!"

Mommy's eyebrows shoot up. "Leave? Where in tarnation would I go?"

Pap rushes to say, "No one's going anywhere." He clears his throat before continuing. "Fact is, I'm coming home."

Orrin jumps up and dances a noisy jig. Clint follows and they sing, "Hi-ho the derry-o! Pap is coming home!"

Clint stops and climbs on Pap's lap for a minute. Placing his hands on Pap's cheeks, he says, "But you *are* home already, Pap."

"Yessir, and I'm aiming to stay." Pap turns to look at me. "This is the news I told you I'd share. I've left my job building park roads with the CCC. I reckon they'll get 'em built fine without me."

My head feels spinny. Pap was lucky to get that job with the Civilian Conservation Corps, even if some people thought it was charity to take a job from the government. Even if he *did* have to live away from us all week long, sleeping in a dormitory with other hardworking road builders like him.

Pap smiles my way. "I've accepted a new job with the Southeast Counties Rural Electric Cooperative Corporation right here in our county, and I start tomorrow. Most times I'll be sleeping under this old roof with you."

My brain scrambles to think. This is what the article was all about! My pap will be right at the center of it all—and home every night to boot.

"What's your work going to be, Pap?" I ask.

"I've been assigned to procure materials for the cooperative, contracting for poles and wire and transformers and such." He glances at Mommy before he adds, "But most importantly, I'll be here to take care of my family *every* day, not just on weekends."

I study Mommy's face before I say anything else. Might she be the smallest bit happy about this?

No, her face is dark and closed.

I jump out of my seat and encourage the twins to return to their places. We eat the rest of our meal in silence.

After Sunday dinner, I set in preparing the grapes to make jam without Mommy even mentioning it. And after that chore is complete and the jam is setting up in jars, Mommy goes upstairs to rest, Pap takes the boys off somewhere, and I'm suddenly alone, though I'm not sure how long the solitude will last. While I long to read at the top of the mountain, I dare not risk the time it would take me to get there and back, so I set that journey aside for another day. Instead, I stretch out on the rug to read *Pollyanna*, at long last.

✳ ✳ ✳

Tonight, after she wrestles the twins into bed, Mommy stays upstairs in her and Pap's room. Downstairs, Pap builds up the fire in the fireplace and sets a straight-back chair next to it. He lifts down his banjo and tunes it for a minute. I flop onto the sofa and prepare to listen.

The first notes of "Lonesome Scenes of Winter" are a match for my worry over the winter dark and chill headed our way.

Lonesome seems the winter,
the chilling frost and snow

But after just a bit, the music rests my soul.

When Pap finishes the song, he slides right into "This Little Light of Mine." I smile at the understanding between us. At the end I say, "That magazine showed lights and all sorts of other electric doodads."

Pap pauses, then returns to plucking softly. "Exactly why I thought you might like to give it a look."

"Mommy might not like it so much?" I say, with a question in my voice.

"Cora, I love your Mommy with all of my heart. And I love you too. Both you and your Mommy have strong ideas, and I reckon as both a husband and a pap I ought to listen to and support those for each of you when I can." He places his fingertips on the banjo strings but then pauses. "I don't know what the future holds for you, Cora Girl, but I see no reason you shouldn't at least have a picture in your mind of what all is out there beyond this mountain, if it's something that interests you."

Hope sizzles in me. "It does, Pap. I interviewed Uncle Eben as an eyewitness about electricity this past week. And now that you are working for the cooperative, I'll have you to ask questions of too!"

"I'd be pleased to answer your questions anytime, Miss Tipton," Pap says with a smile. I think if he had a hat, he'd tip it.

"All right, then." I consider running to get my notebook but decide to just turn on my remembering brain. Before I start questioning, though, Pap's expression turns serious.

"This new job of mine... well, Cora, as you can imagine, it is a bit complicated as concerns your mother. But if I keep in mind that demon like a catfish, I know that as hard as it may be for me to square my work with the cooperative with Mommy's opposition to it, taking care of her and helping her keep hold means being right here at home every night."

I chew on those words for a while as he plucks and strums. These are such big, complicated considerations Pap has put before me. I finally decide that I can depend on him to handle them. I shake my head clear. "So, will electric lights come all through our Eastern Kentucky mountains and hollers?"

Pap sets the banjo down next to him and rubs his scratchy cheek. "That's the plan. There's already a crew hired and being trained over to Stepdown Mountain because they have enough members paid into the cooperative to begin. I went over and met with those fellas a week ago yesterday after my trip to the general store."

"Did you already have the job by then?"

He nods. "Nearly so. The cooperative had come to me with an offer, but I wanted to talk to the crew there before I gave my final acceptance."

"How about electricity for Shadow Mountain?"

"Could be," he says. "Like I said Friday night, they've been getting folks signed up as members, area by area. I hear we'll be working toward next spring to start stringing wire to some buildings right down in Spruce Lick. The general store, for instance, and the Presbyterian church."

"Spring!" I cry.

Pap smiles. "As the ground thaws in March, some folks will start hearing the mule teams dragging those poles and spools of wire I'm procuring, shovels a-clanking in the dirt, and linemen hollering down from atop those poles."

He pauses while I imagine all of that joyful noise and commotion bringing light so close to us. But then a serious look shadows his face again. "But way up here at the school and above, sign-ups will likely be slower. Still and all, if my figuring is right since talking with our neighbors after church, we might only need three more members to join those already committed as a result of that letter."

"Only three?" My mind flits back to my newspaper idea, and I resolve to use my writing skills to bring the facts to my classmates. Then I suddenly remember the conversation I heard outside of the meetinghouse. I ask, "Wait! Is Mrs. Hudgins one?"

"That she is."

"And Uncle Eben might sign on soon?" I ask.

"This is private, adult business, Cora, but Eben tells me he and his mother haven't had that conversation yet," Pap says.

I can barely squeeze out a whisper for the next question. "What about our family?"

Then he says the words I've been both expecting and dreading. "Cora, it's best you know that your Mommy isn't one bit interested in us being one of those members."

My shoulders slump. "Not interested? Even with you going to work on it for other families?"

"Even with that," he says, rising to add another log to the fire. He pokes it to encourage the flames, but it doesn't flare up right off. "She's not agreed to the five-dollar cost of joining, which is most all of a man's wages for a week, should he be lucky enough to be employed as I am. Nor would she agree to a monthly three-dollar fee. Fact is, in all of our discussions, she's not been one bit happy with me taking this job working for the cooperative corporation, period. Not yet, anyway."

His "yet" holds a thimble of hope, but I think about Mommy's struggle with the demon-catfish and how she might not welcome one single other change for as long as her shoe leather treads Kentucky dirt, even if she had money to pay for it.

Pap's voice interrupts my thoughts. "Besides, our house would be near the end of the line. Earliest here would be next summer."

Summer! Only nine short months!

"What about the school?" I ask. "Could *it* count as one of the three members we need?"

"Wires will come near enough when the first houses below there are electrified." Pap shakes his head slowly. "But much as your teacher's in favor, born and raised up in an electrified city as she was, Miss Bentley says there is just no money in the budget beyond needed supplies and upkeep to the building."

Nevertheless, I sink down into a delicious well of imaginings, the kind Mommy tries to keep me from. "Unrealistic," she calls them. I imagine Ceilly propped up in her bed sketching planes while dreaming her high-flying dreams. And I see myself living in our house where lights on the porch extend a warm greeting to Pap when he arrives home night after night. As the cooperative expands, his procuring job grows too, so he stays right here with us. He finds me in the lighted kitchen, studying the subjects I need to learn in order to pass the high school scholarship exams—which not a single Shadow Mountain soul has ever taken so far as I know—all without Mommy objecting.

For just this little while, I leave behind worries about Mommy that might weigh me down like an anchor and cast myself into that bright future I want a part in creating. Tomorrow morning, I'll rise with the sun again and write the whole conversation down in my notebook.

SIX

A Surprise Visitor

At first light on Monday, I snatch up my notebook and try to record every word Pap said last night before I get dressed for school.

I don't hear Ceilly's usual *knock-knock-tap-tap-tap* at the front door after breakfast. That generally means that Great-Aunt Exie shooed her out the front door at sunrise, just about when the skunks go home to their burrows to sleep. So I set off alone under bright but chilly skies with the magazine tucked carefully under my arm. Of course, the first thing I do when I reach the schoolyard is search for her up high.

Now, I like trees well enough, but I'm not all-fired intent on climbing them like Ceilly is. It's why we're best friends, I guess. Each of us is missing the half of ourselves the other one has.

Turns out she's swinging by her knees from a branch of the chestnut oak just to the right side of the schoolhouse. I step into the litter of acorns and leaves below her and hold the magazine upside down for her to look at.

"Look at those rows of glowing lights in the classrooms, Ceilly."

"For certain," she says, gazing at the photos on each page as I turn them and peppering me with questions all the while. "The lunches on those trays might even be hot, don't you think? Do you think those little boxes hold milk? And if they do, is it cold milk? What's that room called, anyway?"

"What's the matter?" I tease. "Can't you read the word 'cafeteria' when you're hanging upside down? Must be a separate lunchroom."

I can tell that the pictures make Ceilly as hungry for it all as they make me.

"It's a world as different from ours as the Land of Oz!" she says, swinging wildly.

I explain to her about Pap and his new job and that my own house isn't likely to be one of three new members but that hers might actually be.

Her eyes shine like the stars. "Has your pap talked to Uncle Eben, then?"

"Yep," I say. "But he says Uncle Eben hasn't talked to Great-Aunt Exie about it yet. Keep your ears open!"

"I surely will." Ceilly reaches down from her branch and squeezes my arm.

"And Ceilly," I add, "I aim to make good on my promise to spread the word about the benefits of electricity to our classmates."

"How?" she asks.

"I'm fixing to start my very own school newspaper, and you're the first writer I'm hiring."

"Well, that's great news," she says, returning to swinging. "I'm pretty short of funds. How much are you paying?"

"Sorry to disappoint you, but I'm only paying in experience." I rush on. "But listen, I've got another idea too. What about the school as one of the three more cooperative members still needed? It'd be good for *all* of us kids. Pap says the school isn't likely to have money to join, but maybe *we* can help with that."

Ceilly's upside-down face grins at me. Her thumbs-up is upside down too.

I tuck the magazine back under my arm. "Well then, shouldn't we go talk to Miss Bentley?"

"Immediately!" Ceilly drops to the ground.

We smell the sharp, nutty scent of linseed oil even before we see Miss Bentley down on her hands and knees. With her black hair pinned off her face, she's finishing up her monthly floor oiling in the back corner under the art table she must have missed on Friday. Having seen those magazine pictures, I am reminded this isn't likely part of a teacher's job in the big-city schools, where Miss Bentley says there are professional people called custodians to keep things clean and orderly, and with tools like floor polishers you plug into electricity. We can tell she's rushing to get it done before the start of the school day, because she doesn't even stop to push her eyeglasses back up from the very tip of her nose.

"If the school got electricity, could we stay late to read and study past dark on winter afternoons?" I ask over her shoulder, noting spots she has missed. "That way I could prepare for the high school scholarship exams you mentioned."

Ceilly casts a hard questioning look my way over Miss Bentley's back.

I add, "I mean, in case I'm able to turn my mommy's mind around on further schooling."

Miss Bentley moves her rag to the back edge of the floor, gives it several circular swipes, and sets it down. She stands up and wraps her arms around our shoulders. "Good morning to two of my top scholars!" The smell of oil is stronger than her lilac toilet water. "Did your father not tell you, Cora? We do not have five extra dollars. I surely do wish you could study to your hearts' content here…even past dark. But do not worry. We will find a way for me to prepare you over the next two and a half years for all you will need to know, electric light or not. And I will make sure to keep your friend Ceilly here right up with you."

Ceilly sighs. "So no cold milk for lunch."

"True, that is another expense we do not have money for," Miss

Bentley says. "Refrigeration. Appliances that use electricity also cost money—to buy and to operate. But do not forget the advantage of having milk delivered fresh from your very own cows! There are always at least two ways to view a situation."

My mind scrambles for options like the grey squirrels outside searching for nuts amid the fallen leaves. "Miss Bentley, what if we were to *raise* the five dollars?"

"Cora, as we have discussed in our civics lessons, money is dear to everyone, especially now," Miss Bentley says. "And not just here on Shadow Mountain and down in Spruce Lick. Why, people all the way up to Canada and beyond are suffering in this Great Depression, with jobs lost and money scarce. Hardship is everywhere."

"But President Roosevelt has lots of plans," Ceilly reminds her.

"That he does." Miss Bentley smiles and squeezes our shoulders. "But no, girls, that particular world of electrical luxury is not for this school quite yet. Now come with me, and Ceilly, you can ring the morning bell."

Ceilly grins, despite the bad news. Most days Miss Bentley chooses someone else, because Ceilly just can't resist climbing up high on that rope and swinging while ringing. I s'pose this is Miss Bentley's way of saying "Sorry."

But "Sorry" surely isn't the end of this for Ceilly and me. We're not likely to let money stand in our way. We just need to hatch a plan to *get* the money. I pause to reflect on the fact that it will need to be a *secret* plan—one Mommy can't know about yet, not while she is still dead set against electricity. Despite changes to the landscape that I suspect will trouble her, I still can't entirely grasp why she objects. But she doesn't seem inclined to share her reasons nor am I inclined to insist on knowing them. Given her habit of completely forbidding any actions I might take, I won't risk that. The lie of omission pokes me hard, but I know I just can't stop, can't allow her to interfere and stymie a plan before we even get started.

After we recite the Pledge and Miss Bentley directs each age group to their reading and writing tasks, she calls my group up to her desk, one pupil at a time, to discuss our recent essays about the importance of awareness of current events. She calls me up last, which is good. She has a *lot* to say.

"Cora," she says, smoothing my essay with her hand, "this is truly excellent writing. As we were speaking of the settlement-school scholarship exams this morning, I want to follow up and say that I feel confident you would be able to pass the writing exam today, if you were not required to write about world history and science topics I have not yet worked into your lessons."

My heart races just thinking that I'm one step closer. Mommy aside, I mean.

"You would sit for the exams in April 1940. In addition to the writing exam, you must show proficiency in American history, world history, geography, biology and botany, and literature. I do not worry about the literature, so long as I guide Miss Fee in which books to bring for you and we discuss them together as you read them. But between now and then, I plan to incorporate more of those other topics into your lessons."

I gulp, thinking of all there is for me to learn. "And Ceilly's too?"

"Yes, of course! She will want to be prepared for the curriculum in Williamsburg, should that be what her future holds. And come next July when school begins, as I just told Ceilly, you two will have to make yourselves available either before or after school once or twice a week so I can tutor you."

Of course, I immediately set to worrying about Mommy letting me spend any extra time away from home studying when I could be helping out with the twins *and* the new baby. As for Ceilly, Great-Aunt Exie likely won't even notice her absence *now*. No, it's the thought of Ceilly's permanent absence off in Williamsburg that she'd be fretting over, wondering what all our mountain neighbors would have to say about it if the girl she took in with all that charity decided to up and leave the mountain entirely.

Miss Bentley continues. "If you pass the exams, you will be eligible to attend the settlement school and your room and board will be paid by generous donors." Her eyes shine with pleasure.

My heart beats out an alternating rhythm of excitement and worry as I slide back into my place next to Ceilly.

✳ ✳ ✳

When I open my bucket at lunchtime, I find a grape-jam biscuit and a note. I unfold it and read:

STRAIGHT HOME AT 3:00

in Mommy's writing. Ceilly reaches for it, reads, and raises her eyebrows.

My heart sets to racing.

What could it be?

The twins were fine when I left this morning.

Mommy's time for birthing is still weeks and weeks away.

But if she needs me, why didn't she say so this morning and keep me home from school? My mind scrambles for an explanation.

I give Ceilly a sharp look. She sees my panic and holds my gaze. She knows I will want to keep this private from the other girls around us. So she silently breathes in, lifts her shoulders up to her ears, and lets out a deep breath with a small whoosh.

Ceilly taught me this trick. She learned it when she was small from her own mommy, whom she still misses so much. I know to follow suit—one, two, three times—until my heart slows. Whatever Mommy needs, I prepare myself to do.

Of course, Ceilly will come right home with me at three o'clock. She'll not head up to Great-Aunt Exie and Uncle Eben 'til near suppertime.

That means Ceilly is right close beside my elbow after school when I turn off toward our front yard and stop dead still. Warning bells set to ringing in me.

There, sitting stiff on our front stoop reading a book, is my Michigan cousin, Aunt Thelma's daughter, Glenna Sue Huffaker, whom I haven't seen since June. She's wearing a pretty blue printed dress like those Miss Bentley wears. It's surely store-bought, with its white collar and puffed sleeves. Shoes peek out below the dress, and a wide-brim hat, suited to someone Mommy's age, sits on her head.

"What's Glenna doing here?" Ceilly asks.

"You mean why would a thirteen-year-old city girl suddenly show up on Shadow Mountain when it's not Thanksgiving, Christmas, or summer break?" I whisper.

"Right," Ceilly says.

"I haven't the faintest idea," I say softly.

"And why's she got that hat pulled down on the side like that?" Ceilly wonders.

That's when Glenna looks up at me. She slides her glance over at Ceilly too, without moving her head. Then she stares right back down at the page of her book as though she hadn't seen anyone at all.

SEVEN
Somewhere Dark but Safe

Not a minute later, Ceilly's hustled me around to the side of the house, wanting an explanation. "What was that all about?" she demands. "You don't seem the least bit glad to see Glenna."

"I'm not," I say.

"Why not?"

I pause to think. "You know how nice Ida always was?" I ask.

"'Course I do, Cora. Everybody does."

"Well, that was ninety-nine percent of the time. And I blame Glenna for the other one percent."

Ceilly wrinkles her brow. "Huh, Glenna has always been nice to me, bringing an extra of whatever little gift or treat she brought for you and Ida—a shell from Lake Erie or a Sanders chocolate. And I'm not even her cousin."

"But you remember before Ida died," I say. "Whenever Ida was with her, somehow quick as a jackrabbit I'd start to feel terrible."

"Yep—and mighty crabby too," Ceilly says.

I scowl at her. "It was even worse when you weren't there, Ceilly. I'm not exactly sure why or how, but Glenna and Ida had a way of shutting me out, as though I was too young, too silly, and just too not-worth-their-time. And there I'd be—all alone."

"Well, right now *she's* the one who's all alone," Ceilly observes. "I'll wager she must have been feeling that way at every visit since the funeral."

"Well, she never talked to me about it if she did. And I sure don't aim to start discussing it with her now. C'mon." I pull Ceilly over to the kitchen window.

Launching myself through, I land next to the pie safe. Ceilly squeezes in next to me. The sweet smell of cooked apples wraps us up, and I spot a pie cooling in the safe. It's not like Mommy to use our precious supply of flour on an ordinary weekday. This must be about Glenna's arrival.

We stop after only two steps toward the stairs. Ordinarily the kitchen would be empty at this time of day. But no. Here is Mommy sitting stock still at the table, staring at the front door. A pile of brussels sprouts from the garden is heaped in front of her. One hand holds a paring knife while the other hand makes circles on her belly like a pup looking for a place to land. She doesn't seem to hear us, despite our racket.

When I say, "Mommy?" she jumps. She turns to stare at me as if I were a ghost, and all of my earlier fear rushes back in.

"Mommy?" I say. "Is that baby set to come so soon?"

Mommy's forehead wrinkles. "Goodness no, it's too early for that."

"And the twins aren't sick?" I ask.

She shakes her head. "No."

I'm relieved—and irritated. The baby is fine. The twins are fine. That leaves Glenna. "Okay then, what in blue blazes is Glenna doing on our porch?"

"I reckon your cousin's come to stay."

"Aunt Thelma sent Glenna back to our holler to *live*?" I gesture around the room. "Does she *want* to live here on Shadow Mountain like...like all of us?"

"Cora," Mommy snaps, "I believe she does. And what, may I ask, is wrong with the way all of *us* live here?"

"Well, does she know how impractical those clothes she's wearing are going to be? Does she know how every single family member has chores from sunrise until sunset three hundred and sixty-five days a year? All the washing and ironing and growing, canning, and cooking food? Tending the animals and going herb gathering in the woods and cleaning and dusting and such? Does she remember we don't even have electric lights to read that book of hers by after the sun goes down?"

"Cora Mae Tipton!" Mommy's voice is sharp now. "Glenna's a child of Shadow Mountain, same as you, even though she was birthed and has grown up elsewhere. She knows our ways well enough. And I've told you this before. There are more important things than stories printed on a page."

Pap's words, telling me Mommy needs help to save herself, push forward in my mind. I rein myself in.

"Yes, ma'am," I say. Then I add, just as politely, "What things?"

"That's enough now," Mommy snaps. "You go upstairs, make your bed, and fetch the twins from their naps. Then you can go back outside. See if you can't make your cousin feel kindly welcome."

Mommy takes up the paring knife and sets to slicing the brussels sprouts.

Ceilly casts a questioning glance my way. I grab her hand, and we tiptoe up the stairs to my little room, divided from the twins' bed by the hanging length of fabric pulled closed.

My sheets, freshly laundered, are folded on my bed.

"Looks to me like she's sleeping in here with you," Ceilly whispers.

"I've only ever shared this bed with you—and Ida."

Saying my sister's name threatens to suck me back to the time when Ida and I shared everything. It's as though I can hear our voices from years gone, each of us holding a small doll Pap carved for us and moving them through adventure after imagined adventure. Then I hear whispers coming from the other side of the curtain.

Ceilly grabs up the sheets. She shakes one out and tosses it over my head. I squeal in surprise. She tosses the other over herself.

"Where are those twins?" she growls, and pulls back the curtain to their side of the room.

We each scoop up a boy and hurtle down the stairs. Since we can only see what's below our feet, I hope that Glenna has moved since last we saw her.

We stagger out the door. Orrin shimmies down from my arms to the porch and yanks my sheet off. I reach out and snatch it up before it hits the porch floor. There in front of me stands Glenna, sober and still, her book closed in her hand. Her hat is still pulled down over the one side of her face, but not quite as far. Beneath the edge, I spot a purplish-green stain.

I remember that color from the bruise on my shin after I fell from the tree Ceilly insisted I climb last summer.

From the corner of my eye, I see Ceilly throw her sheet over both boys. She chases them back inside, banging the door shut behind herself.

"Hi, Glenna," I say. "I hear you'll be staying."

She crosses her arms, head bent toward the ground.

I keep trying. "Did you ride the bus down?"

"What do you think?" she snaps.

I try again. "You must be plumb tuckered out, then."

When she still doesn't answer, I say, "Maybe you can write for my school newspaper."

Glenna doesn't respond.

"But you might ought to recall," I blurt, "we don't have electricity, for writing or reading your books after dark."

"I can do without," she says fiercely. She reaches for her hat and yanks it off her head. The bruise is bigger than I could have imagined. Purple all around her eye. Only faded to green at the very edges. Her eyelid is swollen and red.

I gasp. "Glenna, what happened?"

She ignores my question. "Better to be somewhere dark—but safe."

I hug the sheet close to my chest as a chill sweeps through me.

EIGHT
Pies, Pies, Pies

On Tuesday morning, right in front of me and with such a gentle tone of voice that I'm stung, Mommy tells Glenna she needn't attend school until her bruise heals some. Mommy doesn't say heals from *what*, though.

Twice under the covers last night I asked Glenna how she got hurt.

The first time, she said, "You're as nosy as a crow, Cora Mae Tipton."

The second time, she snapped, "Mind your own business." Then she rolled over to face the other way.

"You ought to be more understanding of your cousin," Mommy says when I grumble to her privately. "She needs time to get used to her new home and settle into this family."

I glance at the kitchen table, with six chairs now. The extra one's been brought in from the barn where Pap put it after Ida died. I wonder how long until we can put that chair back.

I surely can't imagine Glenna settling into our family with her silence and standoffish ways. Her only chore, so far as I can tell, is going to be fetching the rascally twins when they take a-wander. But at least it will save Mommy the work of chasing them while she's pregnant—and take away one of my chores too, when I'm home.

Truth is, I'm in no all-fired hurry to have Glenna at school. Ceilly and I need to focus on making a plan to raise the money Miss Bentley needs for our school to join the electric cooperative—and there's also starting the newspaper to consider.

If we can help the school to join the cooperative, we'll only need to add two last members to qualify for wires to come up here on Shadow Mountain. I smile just thinking that some other family, enlightened by advantages a classmate presents at the dinner table after reading my newspaper, might come on board. Then, just maybe, some near-impossible occurrence will soften Mommy's heart, and our family can be the third.

∗ ∗ ∗

At lunchtime in the schoolyard that day, Ceilly tells me about what she calls a rip-roaring fight between Uncle Eben and Great-Aunt Exie. Seems Great-Aunt Exie is cut from the same cloth as Mommy—opposed to spending money *and* opposed to any change to a way of life that suits her just fine the way it is.

"When he said the word 'cooperative,' Cora, she lit up like a fire burning last year's kindling, going on and on," Ceilly says, "hurling 'How dare you?'s and 'Ungrateful's and 'Over my dead body's. I hightailed it to my room where the volume was a mite lower."

"I don't blame you," I say. "Well, no surprise, I guess, that your household isn't going to be signing up anytime soon." I set my empty lunch pail aside and stretch out my legs. "So we're still needing three more members for the cooperative, and we want to make sure that the school is one of those three. Let's see about raising some funds."

"Got any ideas?" Ceilly asks.

I've been reflecting all morning on Mommy's efforts in the kitchen yesterday. "I do. I'm thinking... pie!"

Ceilly brushes biscuit crumbs from my shoulder. "Much as I love pie, I'm at a loss to figure what pie might have to do with electricity for the school."

"Well, to be more precise, a pie sale!" I say. "There's likely not a mommy nor granny around who isn't a pie-baker."

Ceilly considers for a minute. "So we'd get contributions...but where do you figure we could sell them so that your mommy and my great-aunt Exie won't catch wind?"

"Maybe right here in the schoolyard after school on Friday? Neither Mommy nor your aunt come near here. Bet we could charge twenty-five cents per pie and let the buyers know who to return the pie plate to."

"Hmmm, so we'd need twenty pies to earn the five dollars we need," Ceilly says, engaging her arithmetic skills so fast that I think Miss Bentley might be wise to assign *Ceilly* as my arithmetic tutor when beyond-school-hours tutoring begins.

"Do you have to be home straightaway after school today?" she asks.

"Not with Glenna wrangling the twins. Are you thinking we should get started soliciting right off?"

Ceilly nods, and we have a plan!

* * *

On the way down the path after school, the reds of the sourwood and sumac shout their glory. We kick our bare feet through fallen leaves on the path and set out to go a-calling at a few houses near the schoolhouse.

"Should we have told Miss Bentley about our idea?" Ceilly asks.

"Absolutely not," I say. "Won't she be surprised when we hand over the money we make on the pies!"

In my notebook, we've made a list of those folks we suspect might be sympathetic. We relied on comments we'd overheard before or after Sunday meeting, or on the level of enthusiasm we'd heard from their kids. Of course, sympathetic doesn't mean they'd have the money to join the cooperative, but even if not, they might be willing to bake a pie to at least get the school joined up. We also considered people who might have a little extra money, like Mrs. Milby, whose husband just sold those two weaned calves. We map out a route that starts at her house, right near the school, then follows the path over a ways, winds back up through woods and fields, and lands us at Clayton Fork, where we'll head for our homes.

We have our fingers crossed that we'll sidestep anyone who might have a chance to tell Mommy or Great-Aunt Exie what we're up to.

Using the lines we've rehearsed, we take turns asking.

"Hello, how are you this afternoon? The two of us are raising money for the school to join the electric cooperative. We're aiming to have a pie sale on Friday after school. Would it be possible for you to donate one of your favorite pies? We'd surely appreciate it."

"I'm all for electricity coming!" Mrs. Milby says. "I'll bake you up a molasses pumpkin pie. Friday just after school, you say?"

"Yes, ma'am." I note her down as a yes.

"Pie baking will be a good sight easier when I have an electric oven to bake in."

That fires up my curiosity. "What makes an electric oven better for pie baking?" I ask.

"No need to build a fire, for one," she says, and I reflect on that. No fire? I think about the awful stories I've heard all my life, of little girls in these mountains who've been tending a stove and whose aprons or dresses catch fire and burn them badly. And worse, I think of the fire that cost Ceilly her home and her parents. Ceilly's mind must go there too.

"And then there's even heat in the oven and on the cooktop,"

Mrs. Milby continues. "The temperature is reliable without having to constantly check and readjust the damper and the wood supply. Why, it's practically a miracle, and I can't wait to have one of my own!"

I write it all down in my notebook for future use in my newspaper and share her wish. Then Ceilly and I head down the path to our next stop, at Little Willie Burris's granny's house.

"I can manage a sweet potato pie," she promises us. Then she opens the door wide. "Do you care to stop and visit a spell? You can explain more about the 'lectric cooperative I've been hearing so much about."

"Oh Granny Burris," Ceilly says, "seeing as how we need the promise of twenty pies in all, we'll have to come by another day."

"Well, that will be fine then, girls, but just don't wait too long. The days are lonely, especially now that the autumn light fades so early of an afternoon, and Willie's mommy requires him to be home before dark."

I note down that we need to choose a day soon to come and explain it all to her as best we can so that maybe she'll join.

From there, we head off the path and through the woods, then over the stream on the rocks that one of Custer and Dewey Strickler's grandfathers planted generations back for easy crossing in all but early spring snowmelt and raging summer storms. But when we get to their house, their mommy deals us one heck of a surprise.

"Not only do I have nary a speck of flour to spare, you young'uns don't know a blamed thing about what all changes electricity will mean for us mountain folk," Mrs. Strickler practically barks. "Why, with those lines being strung on poles that require the felling of trees, we're like to lose many that give us food and wood for heating our homes and your school too. Those poles will also be raised on land that grows our garden plots and wild plants for feeding our families. How much will they take, in the end? Why, once it's all said and done, I suspect that our ability to pursue our whole way of life will be lost if those citified people get their way!"

I open my mouth to speak but shut it just as fast when too many questions suddenly flood my brain. *What does Mrs. Strickler mean? What* about *the trees? How many would be lost? How would Ceilly live without them to climb? And what* about *the plants and herbs in the garden and in the wild? Could Mommy even be an herbalist without them? Is* this *what Mommy's worried about?*

Mrs. Strickler continues, getting louder and louder. "It was the very isolation and the quiet darkness of Shadow Mountain that called to our Scotch-Irish ancestors, Cora Tipton. Ask your dear mother if you don't believe me. They longed for a new life away from government and separate from neighbors, so they crossed the ocean and found it *right here.*"

Then she slams the door.

I stop to consider these further comments. Somehow it's different, hearing objections coming from someone else's mommy, and spelled out too. More shivers of worry run through me. Would those ancestors, some of them my very own, not have shared my longing for light and connection and maybe even life in a wider-open world, if they'd only had the chance? Would those folks be just like Mrs. Strickler even today? Maybe they'd turn their backs on light and connection for the protected isolation and quiet darkness Mrs. Strickler mentioned. I think back to Papaw's words, *In darkness we can better see the stars*, and I imagine that thick canopy of twinkling lights I love to gaze up at on clear nights. *Will electricity change my view of them?* And I realize that as much as Mrs. Strickler's words sting me, they are powerful. I open my notebook and motion for Ceilly to stop and let me use her back for a desk.

"Mrs. Strickler sounded just like Great-Aunt Exie going on and on!" Ceilly says. "Why'd you want to write all that down?"

"Remember when we do newspaper study, the writers always mention both sides of things, if there are sides?" I ask. "Miss Bentley talks about that fellow Walter Lippman, who calls it being 'objective' when journalists say things like 'Despite the opposition's view' and go on to explain it."

As we walk back down to the road, I think some about Mommy's opinions and add, "I almost wish I had asked to interview Mrs. Strickler about that idea of stealing our way of life. What all do you reckon she meant?"

Ceilly ponders the question for several more steps. "I don't expect Mrs. Strickler has much time to think about what words she spouts, but seems she likes things just the way they are."

"Maybe so," I say. "I didn't ask her, though, because I got to fretting that if we talked any longer, she might find a way to tell Mommy or Great-Aunt Exie about the conversation."

"She won't," Ceilly says. "She's got her hands tied up with that passel of boys, all full of beans."

"That's surely true." But my spirits continue to flag. Fortunately, we come to Mrs. Hudgins's house next.

"Why, I've been keeping back a jar of blackcap raspberries for something special," she says, and I note it down with a lighter heart. "I signed up on that form a week ago Monday, the moment I opened the letter at the general store. Seems you girls are doing us all a fine service making the school one of the three additional members we still need. Though I wonder if everyone else has already made up their minds."

"Do you think they may just need time to think on it, though?" I ask.

"Some do, yes, of course," Mrs. Hudgins says. "But others plain and simple can't afford it right now or aren't willing to make the sacrifice it will require."

While that familiar concern worries me all over again, I resolve, for now, to concentrate on the school. At the very least, Ceilly and I can do something to bring the count of members still needed down to only two.

* * *

After two more afternoons of visits, we have twenty pies promised—including Mrs. Bertram's county-fair-winning chocolate walnut pie. And we're crossing our fingers tighter than ever that word doesn't somehow get back to Mommy and Great-Aunt Exie.

On Friday morning, with Glenna *still* not commencing school, I say, "Mommy, I won't be home directly today." Even though Ida never would have lied, I'm fixing to say that Great-Aunt Exie needs our help. I wait for her to question me.

But she only says, "That will be fine."

I'm glad not to have to convince her to let me be late. It's best for our pie sale, of course. And if it weren't for that demon-like-a-catfish, I would feel light and free, able to dance out the school door at dismissal without a care, like some of the other kids can. But since Glenna has no idea about it, I feel doubly guilty to be hosting this pie sale Mommy knows nothing about.

I think back on the mother I had when I was small, singing as she stirred the grits, pausing to whirl me around a time or two and pop a raspberry in my mouth when I came near. When I think of how happy she was then, I do have a bit of understanding about her not wanting anything to change. But that's an understanding of Mommy long ago. Now she doesn't seem happy with her life like she did then. She seems only angry in a way that weighs down a portion of my joy. So what is she even clinging to in her life today?

As we make our way out of the front yard, Ceilly says, "That was lucky. No need for a lie."

I sigh. "Lucky for the pie sale."

"Oh Cora, think! It's just a single week since we first read the cooperative article, and we're already raising money for the school to join." Ceilly grabs my hand and swings it. "Can't we just be glad?"

I pull my hand away and scowl. "Glad," I grumble. "That's easy for you to say!"

When she doesn't respond, I turn to look at her. I am stung by the hurt I see there, reminded of all the reasons Ceilly has *not* to be glad. *Selfish bones*, I scold myself.

"Okay," I say, reaching for her again. "Let's be glad."

✳ ✳ ✳

Ceilly and I wait through the whole entirety of the school day wiggling on our bench. Over and over, we jostle each other as we fidget, thinking only of our end-of-the-day pie sale.

Miss Bentley walks down the center aisle, then leans so near to me I catch a whiff of her lilac toilet water. She lays Ceilly's spelling test on the desk in front of Ceilly and then mine in front of me.

Ceilly's reads "90%" and mine "65%," with seven words marked wrong out of twenty!

"Cora, it is not like you to do so poorly," she whispers. "Did something prevent you from studying last night?"

"No, ma'am." I don't look up for fear she'll see the secret shining behind my eyes.

"We must take some time after school to talk—"

I hold my breath, thinking of the sale.

"Oh no," she says. "Actually, I have the Ladies' Holiday Fair meeting this afternoon." She straightens up. "We will not worry this one time. Still, we need to keep a watchful eye and not let your grades slip. When you apply for high school, the scholarship committee will look closely at your marks from your time in this schoolhouse, even before they consider the scholarship exam results." She lifts her gaze to include Ceilly. "And you, of course, will want to do the same, to be ready to compete with those students local to Williamsburg. So keep up the good work, Ceilly." She taps our desk with a neatly trimmed fingernail. "You two have lofty goals I would like to help you to achieve, but I can only do that if you put in every effort on your end."

"Yes, ma'am," Ceilly and I chorus together.

As she walks away, Ceilly lets out a whoosh of relief.

My mind is so consumed by the arithmetic of counting forthcoming pies and quarters that I don't hear a word of Miss Bentley's Friday afternoon read-aloud. I miss the whole next chapter of *Hitty, Her First Hundred Years*, where the doll is on her whaling-ship adventure. I'll have to sneak the book off Miss Bentley's shelf on Monday during lunchtime and catch up with the story.

Lucky for us, that meeting Miss Bentley mentioned has her gone in two flashes after the little clock on her desk reads 4:00 and the dismissal bell is rung. Everyone else is gone too—all except me and Ceilly.

And then, at exactly 4:10, from all directions, mothers and grannies march toward the schoolyard toting baskets covered in checkered cloths. I say the howdy-dos and thank-yous while Ceilly spreads the pies across a blanket she's laid out on the front porch of the school.

By 4:15, the final pie-donating lady claims she must hurry off to the Ladies' Holiday Fair meeting as all the others have.

At exactly 4:30, the first-ever Shadow Mountain School Pie Sale begins.

By 5:00, not one soul has come.

I look at Ceilly in the dim light. She looks back at me. We both realize the faults in our thinking.

"I…I guess I thought the bakers might stay to buy someone else's pies," she says. "But…why would they? They'd already done their part."

"And I thought they might have told their neighbors about the sale," I say. "But who would they tell, when we already spread the word as far as we could?"

"I was sure that we'd sell all of the pies," she says.

"Me too," I say. "So now what?"

Her face looks as sad as mine must be. "It's sure a lot of pies."

"Yep." I cast my eye upon the tempting sea of desserts. "Can we move them into the school for now?"

She manages a small smile. "You mean, did I jimmy the window?"

After Ceilly tumbles through, I carefully hand twenty pies to her, one at a time. We arrange them on the long table at the side of the schoolroom.

We don't say a word while we cover the crusts with paper torn from a long roll of newsprint Miss Bentley keeps in the cupboard.

This time, it's Ceilly's turn to ask. "Now what?"

NINE
An A+ in Gumption

Ceilly and I are quiet as we make our way along the mountain path, thinking. Just before we reach my house, Ceilly finally breaks the silence and says, "I have come up with precisely nothing. How about you? Have you got even one single idea for selling those pies?"

I nod slowly, as I shift my lunch pail from one hand to the other. "Just one," I say, "but I think it's a good one."

Ceilly grins. "So spill the beans."

"Pap told me there's a whole crew of hardworking men living in quarters over on Stepdown Mountain—getting trained up to set poles and string wires. I've been thinking, those men are probably missing home cooking and likely have a few spare coins in their pockets too."

"Oh, Cora, might your Pap be agreeable to telling them about a pie sale?" Ceilly asks.

"I think he might, but I'm not entirely sure," I say. "And even then, it's going to be a trick for Pap to get the crew here with them working Saturdays."

Ceilly wrinkles her forehead. "How much of a trick?"

"Maybe after Sunday noon dinner?" I say.

"But will the pies keep that long?" Ceilly says.

"I reckon they'll have to."

✳ ✳ ✳

I can barely wait for Mommy to take the twins up to bed and Glenna to head upstairs too so I can talk to Pap alone.

He rubs his whiskery cheek with his right hand when I finally get my chance to ask. "Pies, you say?" The soft rustling sound is familiar and comforting.

"Twenty," I say. "All kinds!"

"And given to you two girls freely by these neighbor ladies for the school to join the cooperative?"

"Yes, Pap." I hold out my open notebook with the first two pages of notes I'd taken about what each lady had to say about electricity. He leans over to study the comments. I wait only a minute, then blurt out, "It'd sure be an awful shame to let those pies go to waste after all their hard work."

"Well, you and Ceilly are an enterprising pair. I will say that." He continues to rub that cheek. "I know your mommy would have some trouble with this...."

I know that too.

He continues. "You realize, I'm sure, that I'll have to tell Mommy about this sale of yours."

"Pap, no—"

"Cora Mae, let me speak! Now, a marriage is an agreement between two people to respect each other. When those two people are raising children, the agreement extends to the decisions they make in regards to those children. Do you understand?"

I nod, but my heart sinks as I imagine those pies uneaten and awaiting Miss Bentley's arrival on Monday morning.

Pap interrupts my imaginings. "No, the question is not *if* I'll tell your mommy, but *when*. I see that demon-catfish threatening her right now, and I may wait until she is stronger." He is quiet a long time, and I hold my breath.

Finally, he sighs. "I'll watch for the best time to tell her. Meanwhile, I'll go to the general store in the morning and send a telegram over to the barracks. I'll invite the crew to come at 2 p.m. on Sunday."

He sees the joy on my face and holds up a hand. "You've got an admirable commitment to this project of yours, Cora. But *no more surprises* like this. I'm willing to join forces here because I know your mommy, despite her disapproval, would want those pies eaten in the end and all our neighbors' hard work not to be wasted."

I hold out hope that Pap's best time to tell Mommy happens to come after a successful pie sale on Sunday. Otherwise, I think, all is certainly lost.

* * *

Saturday is filled with Mommy's list of chores for all the rest of us, once Pap heads into town to do errands that include sending a telegram with our invitation. I can't help but fret between Mommy's many assignments, wondering if Pap is feeling as hesitant about telling Mommy about the sale as he seemed to feel yesterday when he finally offered to help, and then wondering if the crew will welcome the idea of buying our delicious pies.

Mommy eventually sends me off with the twins to harvest every last one of the apples that still cling to the rogue trees rooted in the cornfield, with instructions to be on the lookout for any spiked blazing star on the edges of the field. She says if I spot the flowers, I'm to dig up the roots for making snakebite poultices. Much as the twins are thrilled to pick apples with me, I'd rather have been sent off on this chore alone so I could have gone to the peak of Shadow Mountain instead, harvesting the spiked blazing star roots I know are plentiful along the path. I'd surely have welcomed a breath of time alone at the summit before picking the apples on my way home. But Mommy never asks what I'd prefer.

Meanwhile, she does ask Glenna, who chooses to use the afternoon and her crocheting skills to make the new baby a blanket. The soft woolen yarn arrived with Granny Burris this morning, spun from her own sheep and offered in trade for Mommy's rheumatism salve. *I'm* the only one Mommy trusts to recognize her medicinal herbs and dig their roots, but why can't she at least let me choose where I'll find them?

✳ ✳ ✳

Finally, Sunday morning comes. As my family approaches the meetinghouse for services, Ceilly rushes toward me, eyebrows raised.

"He said yes," I whisper before we get drawn apart to head inside. "Meet me at the school right after noon dinner."

Once again, Preacher Jones beseeches God to help us with our family decisions about electricity, but just like last week Mommy is in no mood to linger afterwards so that I can listen in on neighborly conversations that might involve the cooperative. I'm not especially bothered, though. I want noon dinner over and done with as much as Mommy does, even if I have my *own* reasons.

When the dishes are finally washed and put away, Mommy heaves a tired sigh.

I rush to seize the opportunity. "Mommy, maybe you could have a rest." Then I glance at my cousin. "Glenna, I aim to take Orrin and Clint down to the schoolyard to play. You can take a rest too."

Glenna gives me a quick nod, and Mommy just says, "Thank goodness."

I sigh with relief, but it stings me too. Before Ida died, Mommy might have said "Bless you, Cora."

I slip a knife into my pocket and herd the boys out the door.

As we get near the school, we hear *pee-a-wee*. And again, *pee-a-wee*.

"Ceilly!" Clint drops my hand and runs toward the sound.

When we were only six years old, Ceilly practiced that eastern wood-pewee whistle Uncle Eben taught her for a month until she had it perfect.

Now Orrin, who has been practicing with Ceilly, tries to answer her back with his own whistle before he sets out running too.

We send the boys to play nearby in the schoolyard, then quickly get to work, again passing the pies through the jimmied window and spreading them across our blanket laid out on the front porch. We warn the boys away from them and make them swear an oath not to tell Mommy. I wonder, then, if Pap has thought of that, the twins *and* me keeping a secret from Mommy. One more reason I'm glad he seems to have decided to wait to tell her.

Just after two o'clock, the second-ever Shadow Mountain School Pie Sale begins.

A round man in suspenders and a red bow tie shouts from the path, "Let me at those pies!"

I holler back, "Ready and waiting! Five cents for a generous slice."

More and more men follow behind him, talking over top of each other, telling us that they hitched a ride directly from Sunday services over to Spruce Lick. Telling us how they've worked up an appetite hiking up the path to get to us.

I open my notebook. For the very first time, I might have a chance to interview people who don't live on Shadow Mountain.

"Hello, sir," I say to my first customer. "Where do you come from?"

The young man brushes his sandy brown hair back from his eyes. "Is that walnuts in with the chocolate? Makes me think of my Sally. She does love walnuts. 'Course, she's too far away to share this pie."

"Oh, how far away is that?" I ask. "Where is home for you, again?"

An older man pushes past him, though. "That pumpkin pie looks like my mother's Thanksgiving pie back in Ohio."

"Ohio!" I say. "What's it like where you live in Ohio?"

"You can give me two slices," he says. "I've earned it after that hike."

"The three of us are going to split that there whole raspberry pie," says a black-haired man standing next to him wearing a porkpie hat.

"We'd sure rather be splitting it with our sweethearts, though," one of his friends says with a wink.

I don't even bother asking where those sweethearts are living. I see now that these swarming customers are only interested in getting their slices of pie before they're gone.

Still, I set to wondering something new. *Were Mommy and Pap sweethearts once upon a long-ago time? It seems near impossible now, with Mommy fighting the demon-catfish, with them on opposite sides of this electricity question.* I tuck these thoughts away to ponder another day when I'm not working next to Ceilly, slicing and serving pie on the sheets of newsprint we covered the pies with on Friday.

Those men open their jackknives and set in to feasting, smacking their lips and exclaiming their appreciation. I take a moment to jot down some observations about their clothing and their turns of phrase in my notebook while I have a chance.

Within thirty minutes, all the pies are eaten, leaving the twins scraping out the scraps from twenty empty pie plates we'll have to wash in secret and return. There's also a pile of quarters, dimes, and nickels. Ceilly and I count them up while the twins chase each other around the schoolyard.

"Cora! Five complete dollars and an extra fifty cents," Ceilly says.

Relief swells up in me, and I ask, "Where should we keep it?"

"Hand it over."

I do, and watch her climb back up on her cement block, shove the window up again, hoist herself up on the sill, and drop out of sight.

I meet her on the front porch. "Where'd you put it?"

"In Miss Bentley's top right-hand drawer. You know, the one that sticks a little?" Ceilly grins. "I put a note on top with a heart and signed our names."

"And the window and door are locked now?"

Ceilly nods. "Yup."

I clap her on the back. "You and your climbing come in right handy!"

We use up the rest of the daylight Sunday returning pie plates to their rightful owners.

✳ ✳ ✳

On Monday morning, Ceilly and I are as bouncy as short-tailed shrews while we wait for Miss Bentley to open that drawer. First there's roll call, then the Pledge, then a reminder about the penny drive for the Pack Horse Library Project.

Finally, Miss Bentley tells us to work with our seatmates on the new spelling lists she has written on the board. Then she tugs on that right-hand desk drawer until it opens. Ceilly and I watch so closely we don't dare blink. At first, she smiles when she sees our note. But then she frowns as she lifts the heavy bag of coins. She straightens up and looks back to our bench.

"Cora and Ceilly, please step outside with me." She heads down the aisle toward the door and we follow.

I can feel all eyes follow us.

Miss Bentley tugs the door closed behind her and sets the bag of coins on the step. Keeping her voice low she asks, "Girls, what is this?"

I follow her lead and say quietly, "Enough money to join the cooperative."

Miss Bentley's eyes open wide. "But where did it come from?"

"Sunday pie sale!" we chorus in a whisper.

"Cora and I arranged it all. We got donations from neighbors and sold pies faster than lightning can spark a steeple," Ceilly says.

"Well, girls, you both deserve an A in arithmetic and likely an A-plus in gumption," Miss Bentley says. "I am sorry, though. Even if this is the five dollars to join the cooperative, it is not enough. We would need three additional dollars for the first month of electricity and then three more dollars every month thereafter."

"There's a start there with the extra fifty cents, and we've only just got going on our plans," I say. "Give us some time."

"I am afraid it is not that simple," she says. "You know I want the best for all of my students. And I know that electricity would make some aspects of schooling easier."

"And safer," I add, "because of electric lamps helping vision and all."

She raises her eyebrows for a moment, then continues. "But I have to discuss your plans with the school directors down in Spruce Lick. While I can speak to the value of electrifying as it concerns your education—*and* your eyesight—such things are their decision, not mine. And electricity or not, we are all getting along here pretty well, I think."

Even the name, "school directors," makes them sound like a group of folks wanting to stand in our way. "Still, I'd like a chance to make my case with them!" I say.

"I am sure you would, Cora, but it is complicated further by the fact that they, in turn, must report to the county board of education. So girls, for now, I am going to let you keep track of this money. If it cannot support our joining the cooperative, it will make a handsome 550-penny contribution to the penny drive for the Library Project." She puts the bag of coins into my hand. Luckily, my dress has a pocket. The money seems to weigh heavy there, heavier than when Ceilly took it from my hands to place in the drawer.

TEN
The Quiet Dark

Ceilly and I rush up the mountain after school, zigzagging our way between trees well off the beaten path, looking for the perfect tree. And suddenly, there it is—a shagbark hickory, its leaves turning to gold. We raise our voices higher as we approach, to scare off the critters snacking on those hickory nuts.

When future aviatrix Ceilly is halfway up the tree with our bag of money, she calls down, "There's a perfect crotch in this trunk here for hiding the money, and not a soul likely to climb up to it but me."

She practically flies back down to where I'm standing, my lunch pail now full of fallen nuts I've collected for Mommy, who especially loves their sweet and smoky taste. I imagine her cracking the first nut open, then closing her eyes when she pops it in her mouth.

"Those school directors just can't refuse if we have the five dollars to join up *and* we manage to earn the first months of three-dollar payments!" I say.

"They surely *could* refuse," Ceilly says, "but I reckon they won't. Uncle Eben says those men got but one purpose to their job, and that's to keep someone employed to teach us."

We sit on a rock beneath the tree to think.

Coming up with a plan as good as the pie sale to make three dollars every single month is going to be a mite harder than it was for Ceilly to hide the bag of coins in this tree. Still, we have two strong brains, and our will isn't lacking either. But right now, we notice that what we don't have is much daylight left. We head home.

✳ ✳ ✳

I continue to chew on the need for a new money-making plan on the way home, which is why I don't at first realize that Mommy's waiting for us on the porch. She's not smiling.

"Ceilly, you'd best go home now," Mommy says. "You can see Cora tomorrow at school."

Ceilly scurries across the front yard. At the last minute I glance up to see her raise crossed fingers above her head before she disappears.

"Glenna." Mommy turns to my cousin, who is sitting on the porch, letting the twins drive the toy automobiles Pap carved for them over her feet. I think about how she's come from a world of actual automobiles to a place where my brothers have only ever seen a picture of one. "Please take the boys down to Mrs. Milby's house. Tell her our chickens are on strike. Ask to trade two eggs for this winter tonic she was asking after." She holds a small bottle out to Glenna.

Glenna doesn't reach for it. "I don't know where Mrs. Milby lives. Can't you just send Cora?"

I'm surprised to hear Glenna sass Mommy.

I'm even more surprised to see Mommy gently wrap Glenna's fingers around the bottle. "The boys will get you there and back."

The twins drag Glenna down the porch stairs and out to the path, and Mommy points me inside.

Before I can even get the lunch pail open to share the gift of hickory nuts, Mommy comes to stand over me. Her voice isn't loud, but it feels as though she is biting down hard on each word she speaks. "Thanks to your brothers, I know about this hear-tell pie sale your pap helped you plan without letting me in on it." When she pauses to

75

take a breath, worry for Pap rises in me. "*That* is between him and me. What's between *you* and me is this fixation of yours on electricity—"

"But Mommy," I interrupt, "it will be so good for all of us! And we'd finally catch up with the rest of the country and be modern, and I can—"

Now Mommy interrupts. "Listen to me, girl. This is not some *race*. This is very real change. Your aunt Thelma's told me all about electricity. In fact, she's told me all about life away from here: houses in rows and rows and gardens barely squeezed in, and nary a wild herb to be found. And I can't see that there's a thing we can do with electricity that we can't do without it, or any other *convenience* folks are so blamed eager to have."

Yes, there is, I think. *There's smiling and laughing at the end of the day because you're not so exhausted. There's watching your girl study at the kitchen table, even when the sun is down, and maybe imagining her life being different than your own. Maybe being proud of her for taking risks and trying something new.*

But she continues. "I've fed and clothed and raised up all my children…" Suddenly her voice breaks off, and I'm sure Ida's shadow just passed through her mind. But she takes a deep breath. "I've raised up you children and kept a comfortable home all without electricity or anything electricity can bring, just as my mommy did before me."

"But Mommy, Pap says in spring—"

"Yes, yes, it's coming to Spruce Lick," she interrupts again, "much as I'd rather it didn't come even that close. We don't need this new-fangled electricity taking over our mountain life, felling our trees that feed us fruits and nuts, digging up our land that provides plants for medicines, dirtying our water that runs fresh and clear—and all of this the mountain supplies *for free*. Did it ever occur to you, Cora, that the hills and hollers protect us, let us be who we are, leave us be in peace to live the life we choose with our children close around us?"

I cast my mind back to what I wrote in my reporter's notebook when we were collecting pie promises. Mommy sounds just like Mrs. Strickler when she said, "We're like to lose our ability to pursue our whole natural way of life if those citified people get their way." I open my mouth to speak, but Mommy holds up her hand.

"Cora, what I've got right now is a baby fixing to arrive in a short while and a great big girl landed on my doorstep filled with a world of hurt." Her voice grows louder as her words come even more slowly and forcefully. "I am asking you to take your mind off those electric wires, befriend your cousin, and," she practically yells, "be of *help* to me!"

I remain silent and think again on that demon-catfish Pap spoke about, making Mommy need help. And then that voice in my head starts right up again. *But Mommy, electricity* would *help you. You wouldn't have to hurry your chores in order to beat the sundown. You'd have light to see by whenever you wanted and a voice from the radio to keep you company. Maybe you'd even have an electric clothes washing machine someday, so you're not scrubbing on the washboard and wringing by hand. Most important, though, the electricity would shine a light on your life, Mommy. Give you time in your day to remember that even with Ida gone, you still have other children to love.*

I am poised to plead with her as I meet her eyes. But instead of the anger I expect to see there, I find only hurt. And then, without warning, and for the first time, that contrary voice in my mind gets quiet. Instead, I hear my reporter self asking: *What's the other side of the story?*

In the heavy silence, I replay Mommy's words and really reflect on her request. My stomach tightens as I realize that maybe I've been wrong all along. Maybe electricity can never be the fix-all for Mommy, because Mommy's life is more complicated than I've ever admitted. Even Mommy herself may be more complicated than I've put my mind to considering until now. Fifteen years ago, she lost her only sister to the bright lights of up-north Detroit. Now she's got that sister's daughter sent back down here to care for in the same house where she birthed and then lost her own first child, a half-grown girl like me. And soon she's fixing to do that birthing again, for the fourth time, right here in the shelter of the mountains and the quiet dark she loves and trusts.

I think Mommy truly doesn't want or need expanded horizons and new possibilities. Not now, and maybe, as she claims, not ever. Because, as we both know, there will never be enough light shone on her life to bring Ida back.

Humbled, I just whisper, "Yes, ma'am."

I stare at the floor, my mind and heart in a storm of conflict. I haven't promised to let go of the idea of electricity once and for always. But this new questioning has led me to an understanding about Mommy that has surely stolen every drop of joy and energy I had for thinking about it anymore right now.

ELEVEN
Ready for the Bee

Next thing I know, Orrin and Clint burst through the door with Glenna trailing after them.

Orrin grabs at the strings tying the neck of the cloth poke with the eggs inside that Glenna is carrying. "Give me one of those, Glenna!"

"We'll be mighty careful taking them over to Mommy, won't we, Orrin?" Clint says.

I think about how we *all* need to be mighty careful presenting things to Mommy these days.

Without a word, Glenna brushes them aside, marches to the table, and sets down the poke. The twins moan their disappointment.

Now the boys rush over to me. Orrin circles my chair while Clint climbs up on my lap. His gummy hands stick to my arms, and I catch the sweet smell of the molasses cookies Mrs. Milby surely gave them. The scent brings back a long-ago memory of Mommy baking Granny's sugar cookies. I would give so much if Mommy and I were ever to make cookies again.

"Read us a Jack tale," Clint pleads.

"Never you mind," Mommy says. "Your sister and Glenna are busy 'til dinnertime. You come out with me to bring in the animals."

I give Mommy a questioning look. Glenna heaves a sigh for us both.

"You girls are to finish preparing dinner tonight," Mommy says. "The soup beans are on the stove. Make the corn bread. Pap ought to be home soon."

When she's out the door, I fetch the eggs from the table and set to instructing Glenna in making the corn bread just the way Mommy likes it made, with bacon fat in the black skillet. She stays grim but follows my suggestions while I wash up the dishes and set the table.

All the while, I'm thinking on my conversation with Mommy. And I get to wondering whether Glenna might be able to help me understand even more of Mommy's side of the story. Since she's already agitated, I figure I have nothing to lose by trying to interview her.

"Glenna," I ask while we work, "I'm trying to understand Mommy's complete opposition to electricity. You've lived your life up there in Detroit, but now you seem content here in the dark of Shadow Mountain. Why?"

Glenna's reply is immediate, and given her mood, I'm actually surprised that she answers me in a reasonable tone.

"Because of electricity, life in Detroit is cursed with crowds and hustle and bustle that never slows down. Electricity is meant to keep things *going*. Some people love that, but not me. Sure, life is easier there in a lot of ways, when it comes to conveniences, especially. But here it's quiet, with space to wander, room to think, light *and* dark. Mountain living is a whole other way of life—and I like it."

There's the phrase again that I've heard from Mommy, Mrs. Strickler, and now Glenna—"mountain way of life."

I reflect on Glenna's words for a silent moment, trying to separate out electricity from Glenna's description of a crowded, busy city. I aim to write it all down in my notebook to see if I can figure out whether you can have electrification without the curses. But for now, I decide to change the subject.

"When are you commencing school?" It seems a safer question than the others rolling around in my head about what happened to her eye, how long she's going to stay, and why she is so all-fired cranky today.

"Aunt Mattie says tomorrow," Glenna grumbles.

Ahhh, that answers that last question I haven't asked.

Still, my heart squeezes down a bit when I think on how that bruise has been faded for days now but Mommy's let her stay home anyway. But I try to think of something cheerful to say. "There are two other girls about your age at school. Hildy is fourteen and Rilda is thirteen. You might remember them from services at the meetinghouse when you've visited other times. They're pretty nice."

"I don't need any friends," Glenna says, turning her back toward me. "I prefer being here at home with Aunt Mattie and the boys, nobody nosing around, and me left in peace."

It all adds up to me thinking Glenna might be more like Mommy than I even knew. But it sure shows how little Mommy knows about Glenna's need for friends.

✳ ✳ ✳

On Tuesday morning, I know Ceilly will be dying to hear why Mommy sent her home yesterday after school, but it's not meant to be. When her telltale knock comes, Glenna opens the door and steps through with nary a glance at Ceilly standing on the porch. I follow behind, and Ceilly raises an eyebrow at me. I shake my head and motion her to catch up with Glenna. How I wish we could send our thoughts out without needing to speak them.

Ceilly rushes through the foggy morning to walk beside my cousin. I zip over to Glenna's other elbow.

"Glad to have you join us at school, Glenna," Ceilly says over the musical trill of a dark-eyed junco up in an oak.

"Not my choice," Glenna says, her head low.

Last night, under the covers, I lay wondering about what Glenna was feeling. I whispered, "Are you nervous about starting to school tomorrow?" thinking she might be willing to talk to me again.

She just yanked the quilt farther up and stayed silent.

It brought back memories of long-ago bedtimes with Ida, her kneeling next to me to pray and then scampering around to her own side of the bed. She'd settle herself, then always reach over to pull the quilt up to my chin and brush my curls from my face. These days, I draw the quilt up myself and try mightily not to uncover Glenna.

How did Ida do it, I wonder? How did she manage to nearly always be so kind and caring and tolerant of me, in particular? My patience with Glenna runs out as quick as a timber rattler slips into a hollow log. Ida used to assure me I just had *different* bones, no better or worse than her own. But here and now, without Ida, I know the truth.

Even though I'm practically dying to fill Ceilly in on why Mommy sent her home yesterday and equally curious about what Great-Aunt Exie did when Ceilly showed up so early, I can't have those conversations in front of Glenna.

Instead, I say, "You ready for the bee, Ceilly?" I pat my pocket. "I've got my notebook to record every single fact you get right, like always. I may just assemble them into an article for that school newspaper I aim to start up. Imagine the headline! 'Ceilly Rose Shehan Continues

Her Winning Streak in October Current Events Bee.'" I feel a zing as my imagination fires up.

"I hope you get to write it, Cora," Ceilly chirps. "As to the facts, I hardly had a choice but to get ready. Great-Aunt Exie swept me out of the kitchen with her broom practically the minute I walked in early yesterday."

And even though she's not complaining about that, I'm struck by the memory of my selfish-bones words the other day, saying that it was easy for Ceilly to be glad. Truth is, living with Great-Aunt Exie isn't much different from living with Mommy, and it's surely a sight worse because Ceilly's great-aunt's only motivation for raising her appears to me to be Christian charity.

Ceilly continues. "So, I left the kitchen and climbed to the top of the woodshed with the fact sheet, questions on one side and answers on the other, plus a full bag of acorns and the secret slingshot Uncle Eben made me. I allowed myself to shoot one at the back door for each fact I knew."

And there it is—Ceilly's natural talent for turning hardship into honey. And I bet she shot every last one of those acorns. She's got a remembering brain for the when and what of things, and she hasn't lost a current-events bee in ages. My talent is for writing them down and gathering them up to tell an interesting story, like Miss Bentley says every good reporter does. But I never count on winning a bee except when it's for spelling.

Glenna, who has seemed to be ignoring us, finally asks, "What's the bee?"

"Just like a spelling bee but instead of a word to spell, you get a question," I say. "You good at remembering facts?"

Glenna shrugs.

"This bee is going to be about current events," Ceilly says. "I'm ready as I can be."

Glenna sinks back into her silence. I've lived with her for nigh on two weeks, shared a bed with her all those nights, and I still don't know a blamed thing about what makes her so glum. Not one blamed thing.

TWELVE

A New Champion

Just as Mommy instructed, Ceilly and I march Glenna right into the schoolhouse and introduce her to Miss Bentley.

"Glenna, this here is my—I mean *our*—teacher, Miss Bentley," I say.

Miss Bentley reaches out her hand. "Glenna, we have all been looking forward to meeting you." She glances at me. "I hope you will enjoy our school as much as your cousin does."

Glenna doesn't utter a word, so I fill in with "Yes, ma'am."

"You will sit with Hildy, Rilda, and Custer in the back row here," Miss Bentley says, leading Glenna to her seat. "Cora and Ceilly, go out to the yard until it is time for the bell. Glenna and I have some getting acquainted to do."

She doesn't have to ask twice. Ceilly rushes for the door with me quick on her heels.

As soon as we are under the chestnut oak in the side yard, Ceilly asks, "What did your mommy say to you yesterday after she shooed me off?" at the same time that I say, "We'd better hope that Miss Bentley isn't going to talk to Mommy about inquiring to the board of education on our behalf!"

Ceilly jumps in to calm me down. "Cora, there's no more a chance of your mommy talking to Miss Bentley than of a mud puppy swallowing a bobcat."

Of all the people in the world, Ceilly understands me the best.

Likely she's right about Mommy and Miss Bentley. Then again, I had high hopes that the twins wouldn't spill the beans about the pie sale and look where that got me. I commence to telling Ceilly everything Mommy said yesterday, concluding with the part that sank my spirits the lowest. "She was mighty mad about that pie sale."

"Well, I reckon we guessed that might happen if she found out," Ceilly says. "What's her major complaint?"

"Mommy thinks our whole way of life will be destroyed by setting poles to deliver electricity for one lightbulb or one appliance. She thinks the trees, medicinal plants, and gardens will be wiped out"—I snap my fingers—"just like that."

But hearing myself brings to my mind two truths. First, I hear the exaggeration in my words. Mommy certainly doesn't think *one* lightbulb will do all of that damage. But at the same time, I think on Mommy's true character, how she is not one to exaggerate reality—as I am. Likely she lacks my imagination for that. But that fact makes me wonder. Is it possible that bringing electric lines up Shadow Mountain with many, many lightbulbs and electric appliances truly might cost us trees, plants, and food, both grown and wild?

I don't share these thoughts aloud. Truth is, I'm afraid even to look too closely at them myself, and there's no one I can really ask. Everyone I know lives here or—I think of Glenna and Miss Bentley—came here from a city, not the country.

Instead, I carry on about Mommy. "All this while I've been hoping that electricity will make her life easier! That it will make *everyone's* life easier."

Ceilly nods. "'Course it will. Never mind that it will give you the extra light you need to study for those scholarship exams." But even though her voice is strong with conviction, I hear the underlying longing there, a wish for her future too, one she believes in less fully than mine.

"Even though it's two and a half years before I sit down to take the blamed tests," I say, "Miss Bentley says we can't wait much longer before we start preparing for our future education."

Ceilly pokes me. "Especially in arithmetic!"

"True. And there's another thing," I say. "You know how Mommy has been since Ida died? So sad and so... I don't know..."

Ceilly nods. "Sort of gone away."

A darkness passes over Ceilly's face now, and I'm reminded that when Ida died, Ceilly lost Mommy too. If Mommy seems removed from me, she surely is from Ceilly, which means that the person who was closest to being a mother to Ceilly since her own mother died has also disappeared.

My heart sinks. "Until yesterday, I imagined that lights could bring her back to us *both*. But now I know better. Only Ida could really bring her back to us." Once again worries bubble in me. *Could that light cost Mommy everything she's feared of losing?*

Ceilly surely detects the worries and changes the subject. "How are things with you and Glenna?"

"I've been trying mightily to make friends with Glenna, the way Mommy wants me to, the way Ida would have," I say.

"Is it working?" Ceilly asks.

"Not mostly. Glenna is about as different from me as a frozen stream is from a babbling brook. She says she likes being closed into this little world and its isolation. She sounds like Mommy, which gives me a further window into Mommy's thoughts." I sigh. "So there's every last scrap of yesterday afternoon and evening I can tell you about, Ceilly."

"Okay, then on to current events."

She quizzes me on my facts until school starts—for all the good that does.

* * *

When Dewey Strickler rings the bell, I spot Glenna at her desk reading *Hitty: Her First Hundred Years*. I suspect Miss Bentley is letting her catch up with the class, but I still feel a pinch of jealousy seeing her with that book right on her desk as if she owns it. If Glenna is being allowed to catch up, how am I going to do the same today like I'd planned?

Miss Bentley invites Glenna to participate in the bee just to get the feel of how it works, but it turns out that my cousin Glenna is smart too—at least current-events smart—and she gets the hang of it right away. I don't know if I'm surprised, but I *am* a bit nervous. One by one she knocks out the other students, as I note down each topic and both Ceilly's and Glenna's correct answers in my notebook. Finally, they are the only two left standing, and Miss Bentley invites them to the front of the room. When they stand facing each other, she snaps the next card over.

"Ceilly, what is a bank run?"

"A bank run is when a large number of people rush to take their saved money out of the bank," Ceilly says.

"Correct. Now Glenna, what is a bank pa—"

Before Miss Bentley can finish, Glenna barks out, "A bank panic is when lots of banks have bank runs at the same time."

It makes me wonder whether Glenna has firsthand experience with bank runs and panics, whether that black eye of hers had a bank connection.

"Correct. Okay, Ceilly, what is the most likely result of a bank panic?"

Quick as lightning, she answers, "The most likely result of a bank panic is an economic recession."

"Correct." Miss Bentley turns to Glenna. "Glenna, name one thing that President Roosevelt has done to intervene in what President Hoover first called 'our Great Depression.'"

Glenna looks at Ceilly. Then she turns to look directly at me before she answers. "Well, for one thing, President Roosevelt established both the REA and the CCC."

"Correct."

I hold my breath as I wait for Miss Bentley. She flips over the next card, then gives a tiny sigh.

"Ceilly, referring to one of these creations of President Roosevelt, what do the initials REA stand for?"

Ceilly pauses, which puzzles me. If anyone knows the Rural Electrification Administration, it's Ceilly and me. The room is so quiet, we can hear the seconds hand on the clock tick past each number, a full thirty seconds. Three through nine.

She squints her eyes at me, and then I understand that she has landed on a way to be generous to Glenna.

"R-Rural E-Economic A-Achievement," Ceilly says.

Miss Bentley looks up, surprised. "I am sorry, Ceilly, that's incorrect. Glenna, I will repeat the question. What do the initials REA stand for?"

Glenna glares, first at Ceilly and then at me. "REA stands for the R-Rural E-Electrification A-Administration."

"Correct!" Miss Bentley exclaims. "Class, give a round of applause for our new bee champion, Glenna Sue Huffaker."

I expect to see at least a small smile, but Glenna's face is tight. She walks toward her seat, head down, fists balled at her side as we clap for her victory.

THIRTEEN

Fire Under the Kettle

"Why'd you do it?" I ask the instant we take our lunches out.

Without a pause, Ceilly answers, "She needed to win more than I did."

"Maybe," I say, remembering Glenna's face as she headed back to her seat.

I look around. She isn't with Rilda and Hildy on a blanket in the side yard, though Rilda is about the friendliest girl you'd ever want to meet—short of Ceilly, that is.

I don't see her looking for me, but I'm pretty quick to stop searching. She must have gone off by herself somewhere.

For the remainder of the day, I don't see Glenna at all. And by the time we walk out into the schoolyard at the end of the day, we can't find her anywhere, so we head home alone. For a minute, I think about how mad Mommy might be if we arrive home without her. But what can I do? She's nowhere in sight. I reckon she knows the way home—or thinks she does.

The twins run to meet us as we turn off the path up toward our house. Orrin jumps into Ceilly's arms, and I open mine to Clint. For a shiver of a moment, I worry about that new baby coming so soon. With Mommy so distant, whose arms will he or she jump into? Will Glenna still be a part of our family when that little one takes to toddling and needing arms to jump into? And even if she is, will she act like a part of this family by then? Walking up the mountain with Ceilly and me, talking and singing and making plans? Reaching out in the front yard to receive a little jumping bean of a body?

We trudge into the yard with the boys in our arms. A fire has caught hold under the big black kettle Mommy uses for soap making. It brings to mind an electric stove I saw advertised in my magazine. No big wood fire in the front yard with one of those, and Mommy not needing to bend far over the pot with her big round belly.

"You'd best keep a tight eye on those boys and keep them *inside* this afternoon," Mommy orders.

The twins commence to complaining, but I catch the meaty smell of lard beginning to melt inside the kettle and nod. I know well enough that Mommy won't add the water and lye while the boys are running loose. Much too dangerous. So we carry the boys inside the house, promising stories in a little while, and shut the front door tightly behind us.

Upstairs, the door to my bedroom is closed. I guess Glenna really did find her way home without us. I set Clint down, then pause. Do I have to knock? It's my room, after all. But something about that closed-tight door sends a message that makes me feel I do.

I take the middle road and rap twice, then walk into the dim room without waiting for an answer. Ceilly and the boys follow right behind me. The boys head into their side of the room behind the curtain, and Ceilly closes the bedroom door tightly.

Glenna is sitting on the bed facing the wall, her back ramrod straight. She doesn't bother to turn around when I enter.

"You two think I'm stupid," she spits out.

"No, we don't," I answer, puzzled.

"I could have won that bee all on my own without you throwing it, Ceilly."

"I didn't—" Ceilly starts.

Glenna turns to glare at Ceilly. "You did too." She is practically growling now. "I've heard you go on and on and on about electricity and when it's coming and how it's going to improve *everything* in *everybody's lives* on your whole darned mountain. You certainly know what REA stands for."

"Well—" Ceilly begins.

"She was just trying to be kind," I say.

"I don't need your charity," Glenna snaps. "I can take care of myself."

"Oh, you can, can you?" I start out to say, thinking about that big old bruise on her face, but Ceilly grabs my arm and squeezes a warning.

"I'm sorry, Glenna," Ceilly says. "I made a miscalculation."

"That was not a miscalculation. You two planned a way to make me look a fool, and Aunt Mattie needs to know about it." Glenna stands and sweeps past us.

She flings the bedroom door open and heads down the stairs, leaving the door standing ajar. I gasp and leap to my feet. While the boys have been warned, many a time, about the dangers of an open flame, they are four years old and rascally.

Sure enough, in the next moment I hear Orrin shout, "Wait!" as he tears through the curtain. "I'm coming too!"

"*No!*" Ceilly yells, grabbing for him and missing.

And though I try to snare Clint, his giggles fill the air as he escapes too.

"*Glenna,*" I holler after her. "*Glenna, the fire!*"

Below, we hear the front door bang open.

But we don't hear it slam shut.

FOURTEEN
Without a Shred of Hope

Ceilly and I don't even have a chance to catch each other's eye. Visions of the kettle and the fire fill my mind as we sprint down the stairs after the boys, Orrin racing out the front door, chasing after Glenna, and Clint following close on his heels and through the open front door too, the wild giggles of both boys filling the air.

Daylight blinds me when I reach the porch. *"Orrin! Clint!"* I shout.

Right behind me, Ceilly's panicked screams echo mine.

The smell of hot fat rises on the air. In the light breeze, red flames snap under the black kettle.

"Boys, STOP!" I yell.

Mommy screams, *"Orrin, Clint, back inside NOW!"*

Still the boys follow close behind Glenna. Laughing, Orrin makes a beeline for Mommy. Clint runs blindly behind him.

"Glenna, grab the twins!" I shriek. *"Grab the twins!"*

Finally, Glenna veers from her mission to tattle to Mommy. She stops and turns. She squats and throws her arms open wide.

She snags Orrin with her right arm, just short of Mommy.

But Clint dodges around her, giggling. He veers around to the far side of the boiling pot, much too close, thinking about nothing but the game.

"NO!" Mommy wails.

In an instant, Clint's pant leg is in flames.

The flames lick up his skinny leg like kindling in the morning fire. I run for him.

I throw myself forward and drag him to the ground, leg down. Beneath me I feel the heat. I roll and roll him in the dirt.

His screams below me burn a hole in my heart as we roll.

From outside the nightmare, Mommy grabs my shoulder with one hand, then snatches Clint up into her arms. She lifts him above her round belly. Then she runs toward the house.

I stumble to my feet and chase after them to the porch.

Ceilly must have rushed to the well. She waits on the porch with a bucket of cool water. She grabs me tight.

Mommy thrusts Clint's leg into the water up to his knee.

His whole shin is swollen, the skin red and blistering. I hold his little hand tightly in mine while his screams fill the falling dusk.

In time, his screams turn to sobs.

"I need burn salve and clean rags—now!" Mommy barks.

Ceilly releases me, and I let go of Clint's hand. He whimpers but lets me loose.

Mommy's herbal burn salve is known throughout our holler. I'm the one who helps her gather wild plantain leaves in the summer, along with the St. John's wort and calendula flowers she grows.

We store the salve in a small crock in the pie safe. I dip a fresh spoon into the crock with a rush of gratitude for Mommy's skill and grab up some clean cotton rags from the bottom shelf.

* * *

When I return, Mommy snatches the spoon and rags from my hands without a glance at me. Her face is set hard.

Ceilly has taken over holding Clint's hand where he lies on the

94

porch. She wraps me with her other arm. It's then I realize that I'm sobbing. I try to stop. But there is no stopping. I glance down at the long flaming red oval with its angry white blisters.

Now my heart sets to pounding. *Where is Orrin?* I haven't thought about him once since Clint escaped Glenna's arm and the fire caught him.

I turn to the yard. There is Orrin, away from the pot, sitting in my cousin's lap, his face resting on her shoulder.

Anger burns in me. *How dare she?* I march over to where they are sitting. Glenna tries to resist, but I scoop Orrin up into my arms.

I stumble back to the house, leaving her sitting in the dust, arms empty.

I don't care one whit about what Glenna is thinking or feeling. I'd sell a hundred pies if I could raise enough money to send her back to Michigan on the bus.

Ceilly follows me inside, and Mommy calls us upstairs, where she has laid Clint on his bed. Clint's face is tear-stained and full of pain, but Orrin cuddles up right next him. I hope that is a comfort.

Mommy crosses to her room and beckons me. I leave the boys with Ceilly.

She starts in immediately, her voice dark and angry. "I told you to keep those boys inside."

"I *was* keeping them inside. Then Glenna—"

"I will *not* hear any excuses about your cousin," Mommy interrupts. "I asked *you* to watch your brothers."

And even though I'm flooded with worry, I snap, "You're wrong, Mommy. I did just as I was told. Why can't you see that it wasn't my fault?"

"You'll stop sassing this minute. I haven't time for it. There's barely daylight to clear up this mess."

I turn and stomp back through the landing to where my brothers are waiting. Because there's not a shred of hope when Mommy has made up her mind.

FIFTEEN
An Undelivered Apology

I thought Glenna would have followed us inside. I thought she'd find us now and apologize. But this is my cousin Glenna, and I'm coming to realize that what I think and what she will do never will match.

I push the curtain aside. The sweet green smell of Mommy's salve fills the small space.

I watch Ceilly with the twins on their bed. She and Orrin are playing with the wooden animal figures Pap carved. Clint lies watching.

"How are you doing, sweet brother?" I ask.

He only whimpers in response, which sets my blood to boiling. I turn and growl quietly to Ceilly, "Didn't she just tell us she's not stupid?"

Ceilly looks silently up at me with a small dog in her hand.

"And don't you go telling me about patience or Christian charity, Ceilly Rose," I snap.

"I wouldn't," she says.

Clint whimpers again softly, and Ceilly offers him the most treasured of the figures—the carved horse—to hold.

For a moment I know how selfish I am being, but I can't hold onto any resolve to stop. I think about Mommy saying a great big girl landed on her doorstep filled with a world of hurt. Mommy knows a lot more about Glenna than anyone is telling me. Still, Clint is badly burned and in so much pain—this little brother who fought so hard through the flu.

The anger in me bubbles over again at that thought. "How dare she take a risk with Clint and Orrin's safety? How *dare* she?"

"I know," Ceilly says softly. "She was just furious at me and wanted to get away."

"Yes, get away to tell Mommy on us," I say. "She's plain spiteful."

"But," Ceilly says, "she didn't know these boys would follow her."

"Why was she so mad, anyway? You gave that question away to her. *So what?*" I'm practically shouting at Ceilly, which is ridiculous. She's my best friend in the world, and it's not even her I'm mad at.

"Well, she has her pride. I truly made a mistake, doing that," she says. "And Glenna made a mistake rushing out of the house. Haven't you, perhaps, made a mistake or two in your life?"

She cocks her head to the side.

"Don't you try to calm me down."

"Okay." Ceilly straightens her head. "But really, can you just consider the question?"

Orrin and Clint are now watching me with wide eyes.

I grumble, "I s'pose I've made a mistake or two as concerns Mommy."

"And I've asked you to forgive yourself those times," Ceilly says calmly. She slides down flat next to Orrin on the bed.

With that, I lie gently down on the opposite side of the bed, careful not to bump or shake Clint, and cuddle up next to him. Before we know it, Ceilly and I set into quietly singing "Kitty Alone."

Saw a crow a-flying low, kitty alone, kitty alone;
Saw a crow a-flying low, kitty alone, a-lie...

Before long, Orrin joins in. Clint's eyelids drift closed.

As usual, I substitute each of the boys' names for "Little Pete" when

I get to the fourth verse. As we round out the song, my heart has finally slowed its pounding a bit. I'm grateful that Clint wasn't hurt even worse, but I'm still so scared remembering both twins running straight for that fire.

And at that very moment, when my heart is still, Glenna pushes into the room. Her shadow blocks what little light seeps in the window as she stops dead still and watches us. She draws a big breath and then her body sort of crumples.

But before we can speak, she spins around and walks away.

* * *

After a while, Mommy comes upstairs looking even more tired than before. "Ceilly, Eben is here for you. It's long past full dark, and Exie didn't want you making your way home alone. You go carefully, now."

"Yes, ma'am," Ceilly says.

In the hallway, I ask Mommy, "Is Clint going to be okay?"

"I don't know yet," Mommy says, "But I want you to go find your cousin. I saw her head off toward the woodshed."

"Yes, ma'am," I say.

Mommy asks, "Did you accept the apology I sent her to make?"

My mind scrambles to understand. "What apology?"

"Cora Mae Tipton, what have you done to that girl now?"

I realize that when Glenna came into the boys' half of the room, she must have come to say she was sorry for letting the twins out.

"Nothing, Mommy." My voice shakes. "She did come in, but when she saw Ceilly and me singing on the bed with the twins, she rushed out." But my thoughts spin as the astonishing truth spools itself out. If Mommy sent Glenna to apologize, then she didn't believe that all of the blame for Clint's accident was resting on my shoulders.

Mommy sighs but doesn't say another word.

In the yard, the air still smells of fire and smoke. I search everywhere near the house for Glenna, but I can't find her. She must have gone foolishly stomping off in the dark, despite hardly knowing where she is.

And to be honest, I don't even care if she loses her miserable way.

SIXTEEN
Another Monster Comes

Until the moon rises, I continue to burn with anger—at Glenna, at Mommy despite her asking Glenna to apologize, and maybe even a little at myself, imagining how I could have prevented everything— while I fill the water bucket at the pump. Before I am done, Glenna appears from wherever she's been, sliding behind me and into the house like a long-tailed weasel before I can speak a word to her.

Inside, I'm glad not to see her. I do as Ida would have done—set about making something to eat. I bring cornmeal, water, and a pinch of salt to boil and let the stirring calm me.

Orrin comes to stand next to me at the stove. He tugs my left hand. "Cora, how is Clint?"

I look into his big brown eyes, about to spill over with tears, and decide on honesty. "He's pretty badly hurt, Orrin. But after dinner, we'll go keep him company."

He nods.

By the time I help Orrin wash his hands and sit him at the table, red-eyed Glenna is standing at the bottom of the stairs. A small spark in me threatens to reignite, but my better self rises up.

"Eat." I motion her to the table and hand both her and Orrin a bowl of the cornmeal mush, each with a spoonful of butter on top.

I leave them there, return to the bucket, wring out a cloth, and bring it and a bowl of mush upstairs to Clint, to take over for Mommy.

When I get there, Clint is lying still as a possum, eyes closed.

I can't breathe as I watch to see if his chest is moving. I can't tell.

Finally, I come close and touch his shoulder. He doesn't stir, but he does open his eyes. My breath whooshes out.

Gently, I lift each of his hands and wipe it with the wet cloth.

"Let me prop you up," I say.

"No," he whines, "no, no, no." But as I suspect he will, he allows me to lift him.

I slide his little body slowly up against the pillows. But when he's upright, I can't interest him in his bowl or spoon.

I brush hair off his forehead, and my hand comes away hot. "Does your leg hurt badly?"

A tear slips down his cheek. He nods.

"Mommy will put more salve on it. I know that will help," I say. I give his hand a squeeze. "Think of all the neighbors who come to the door looking for a jar of that salve. And even when they don't have anything to offer in return, Mommy sends them off with a good portion, along with her wishes for the healing it will surely bring."

Another tear rolls down Clint's cheek, but again he gives a small nod.

After a long while, Mommy arrives with the lantern. "Let's see how the salve is working."

I briefly imagine how much better it would be if she could see his leg clearly with an electric light shining brightly. But then Clint clings to me, shaking his head, and I do my best to hold him still while Mommy carefully unwraps his leg. I can't bear to look as she washes the wound and applies more salve and a fresh bandage of torn cloth. Instead, I bury my nose in Clint's smoky mop of hair and close my eyes.

Later, when Mommy tucks the boys in, even the weight of the quilt makes Clint cry out. She leaves and returns with blankets that she rolls on either side of his leg to protect it.

Mommy kisses the twins and disappears downstairs with the lantern. In the darkness, I realize anew that nearly all thoughts of electricity, its arrival on our mountain, and my spreading the word in a class newspaper have been chased from my mind in this emergency.

We don't have light for bedtime stories, so instead, I invite each twin to choose a song for me to sing. Orrin chooses "The Old Man in the Woods" right away. Clint stays quiet and still, eyes closed again. I miss the usual jostling between them to see whose song I'll sing first.

When I'm done with Orrin's song, I touch Clint's hand.

It feels so warm.

"Clint?" I say in a voice too loud for the darkness around us.

"Kitty Alone," he finally whispers.

He must just want the little bit of pleasure that comes of hearing his name in a song again. That's good, I think. Maybe he'll fall off to sleep without reliving the terror of that fire burning up his pant leg. Maybe they'll both sleep full up with comfort.

After I finish the song, Mommy comes to take my place with the boys and sends me downstairs to eat. I pass Glenna sitting on our bed, hands folded, head down, but I don't speak to her as I walk by.

***

When at last Pap walks through the door, Mommy comes down to meet him and says, "To bed, Cora."

I imagine she wants privacy to talk through all the ordeals of this day with him.

As Glenna and I silently pull nightgowns over our heads, I glance at her. Her face is a mask, no expression at all. But I guess that's better than mad.

"It was a terrible afternoon," I say in a flatter voice than I might have used. I wait, expecting she'll finally offer the apology Mommy sent her to make earlier.

But she just nods.

I don't know what that means. Anger flares up, hot, inside me again. I try to untangle what all I'm angry about, trying to keep the blaze from leaping in Glenna's direction. I lie down at the very edge of the bed, longing to just grab up the whole quilt for myself and stomp down to sleep on the sofa. Instead, I clench my jaw to keep my lips sealed and let the flames burn me into sleep and nightmarish dreams.

✻ ✻ ✻

Twice Clint cries out in the night, and each time I hear Mommy and Pap's soft voices soothe him on the other side of the curtain. In the dark, I think back on the time Ida and I were little and peppered with measles, calling out again and again for Mommy and Pap— *Come quick!* and *I'm burning hot!* But that was the fault of a sickness, not the fault of a careless girl who saw a fire burning in the yard when she returned home and should have known better than to endanger little boys.

The third time Clint cries out, there's a tiny glow of morning light. I slip out of bed and rush to him first. When I touch his forehead, my stomach turns.

"Mommy, Pap, come. Clint's burning up!"

Mommy lumbers into the room and bends over Clint. "The fever-few tincture isn't working," she whispers. My breath catches as I remember harvesting the plant under her watchful eye in July, then tying the stems into drying bundles.

Pap appears two minutes later, pulling his suspenders over his nightshirt. "I'll ride for a nurse at the hospital."

Then he's gone.

I imagine Pap on Stormy in the dim light of dawn, riding those long dark miles south, down the mountain, through other hollers, picking his way across rocky streams.

I reach to touch Mommy's sleeve. "Mommy, can I help?"

She turns, and on her face is the same expression I saw when Ida's flu was the enemy she was fighting. I remember my sister lying in bed, pale and hot, coughing so hard she'd like to choke while Mommy waited with a spoonful of her soothing cough syrup next to her. She picks Orrin up and places his sleeping body in my arms without a word. I carry him to my bed, lay him down next to Glenna, and crawl in next to them to wait.

Daylight is full-on when Pap and the nurse ride into the yard, climb the stairs, and push past the curtain. Clint cries out, and I imagine her unbandaging that skinny little leg with its knobby knee. I get up to watch.

She pulls a thermometer from her bag and puts it under his arm. After five minutes, she removes it and carries it to the window.

"You were right to come for me," she says.

Back at the bed, she presses on a swollen area up on the inside of Clint's thigh, making him cry out again.

"That is a lymph node," she says. "The swelling and the high fever make me worry an infection is setting in."

A chill runs through me. I remember that the flu was a kind of infection. *Not another infection!* I plead in silence.

The nurse continues, "I know it would be a long and arduous trip off the mountain and over to the hospital for your boy. That would make any parent hesitant. So I'll leave the thermometer, and you will watch him for the next twenty-four hours." She places the thermometer in Mommy's hand. "Mrs. Tipton, I know you'll continue to administer your elderberry tea and feverfew tincture and sponge him with cool calendula water. But if the fever goes past 103 and cannot be brought down, or if that node swells any further, you must ride him straight to the hospital."

My head swirls as I imagine little Clint on the big horse in front of Pap on the jarring trip down the mountain and along roads winding up and down to the hospital.

Before she speaks another word, I run downstairs and out the door.

I lean against it, shuddering. *No, no, no!* I want to scream. *Not another monster come for my brother!*

And then the door pushes against me. Glenna steps out, tears running down her cheeks, chest heaving.

A thought burns in my mind, and this time I can't contain my fury. "Those tears are a small price to pay for this suffering you've caused, Glenna Sue Huffaker."

She doesn't say a thing in response.

SEVENTEEN
Terrifying Memories

I turn my back on the silent, stewing Glenna and head inside to dress. Upstairs, I kiss Orrin, still asleep in my bed, and rush downstairs to the kitchen. My fury fuels me. I aim to forget Glenna. I'll take up Mommy's chores and help her get through this day the way Ida would have. First, I stir up the hot ashes in the stove and add kindling. But when the kindling catches, and flames begins to crackle, it's all I can do to banish the memories of Clint's pants on fire.

Quickly, I close the stove door and turn away. With the bucket in hand, I head out to fetch water from the well. Back inside, I set a pot of water to boil like Mommy does every morning. I slide two big logs into the stove on top of the kindling.

When Mommy walks into the kitchen, she stares at the stove. I know for a fact she didn't sleep at all last night. So likely she is confused—trying to remember coming downstairs herself to relight the fire and boil this water.

"How's Clint?" I whisper.

She blinks. It's as though she hasn't seen me right in front of her. "You and Glenna get ready for school."

"No, Mommy, not today!"

"You are most certainly going," she says, her voice flat.

"But Mommy, Clint—"

"There's no reason for you to stay home. Pap'll help with Clint and Orrin."

"But he'll lose pay after only a week of work—"

"Your cousin has been to school but *one day* since she arrived. And you are meant to make her adjustment easier there. I'll not have her miss her second day with you there."

My cousin is the reason anyone might have to miss a day of work or school, I think. My cousin is the reason we could all miss my brother for the rest of our lives.

I run from the room and up the stairs to find Pap. He's sitting on the twins' bed, stroking Clint's hair back from his face, over and over again. Each time he lifts his hand, Clint's brown mop flops back down to his eyebrows.

"Pap?" I say as quietly as I can.

When he turns to look at me, his eyes are red.

"How is he now, Pap?"

"Holding his own, I reckon."

"Mommy says I have to go to school with Glenna, but I can't go to school. I can't leave Clint, and Orrin, and you...."

Pap sighs. "Do as you're told, Cora Mae. This isn't a day for arguing with Mommy."

I plod over to my side of the room and find it empty. Seems Glenna has gotten herself off to school without me, so maybe I can stay put.

Just then, I hear Ceilly knock at the front door. A ripple of relief travels down my spine. Ceilly will know what I should do.

"Coming," I call at the window, before running down the stairs.

I find Mommy at the table staring past the stove as the pot of water boils hard, Orrin playing with his automobile at her feet. The downstairs is as foggy as an April morning.

"Mommy, what about the water?"

She doesn't answer.

I wrap a towel around the nearly empty pot and move it to the front of the stove where the fire is less intense. Then I grab my sweater, slip it over my outgrown dress, and head out to the porch.

I sink down next to Ceilly where she waits.

"How's Clint?"

My words rush out into the cold morning air. "He's got a big fever, and Pap rode for the nurse, and he maybe has an infection in the burned leg, and he might have to go to the hospital, and Mommy is making me go to school, and I can't go." I let out a deep breath. "I just can't. What should I do, Ceilly?"

"What's your pap say?"

I shake my head back and forth, staring at the worn wood of the porch.

"Seems like you have only one choice, then." She squeezes my hand. "Do you have a lunch pail?"

I shrug.

"Never you mind, we'll share. C'mon, we're late." She pulls me back to my feet and toward the path down the mountain.

* * *

We don't pass a living soul except for scampering chipmunks on our way down. Sure enough, the schoolyard is empty when we get there. We head straight in. Glenna is in her seat next to Rilda. Miss Bentley nods at us but doesn't scold. Maybe Glenna explained the circumstances and took responsibility for it all when she did, but I suspect she did no such thing.

The morning drags, and I can't concentrate on any of it, neither reading nor geography. After lunch, I fix on a way to focus my brain.

I pull out my reporter's notebook and flip past pages covered with notes about electricity, words and ideas from Uncle Eben and Pap, from all the ladies who baked the pies and from Mrs. Strickler, who refused, from the article in the *Courier-Journal* and from the *Look* magazine—electricity that seemed so important only twenty-four hours ago. Now, I open to a new page and write down every single thing that the nurse said—about the infection, the lymph node, the temperature, and the thermometer. I write on every other line so that there's room to squeeze in more details as they come to mind. I don't hear a bit of what is said around me, listening as I do to the nurse's words and warnings replaying in my mind.

When it comes time for arithmetic, Ceilly pokes me. I sit staring at the long-division problems Miss Bentley has put on the board for our group. I copy them out but can't remember how to use multiplication and then subtraction to figure the answers. Miss Bentley likes to see a neatly written cascade of numbers and the correct answer.

But today, it's a plain and simple fact that my brain won't remember the times tables—so there's not a thing to subtract. Instead, I just scribble a guess on the top line of each problem. Then my brain starts playing yesterday's nightmare over and over again. Fire burning beneath the black kettle. Flames racing up Clint's pant leg. Cries piercing the silence of the night. The only thing that helps calm me at all is to look at the pages of notes I've just written about the nurse's visit.

I get every single problem wrong while I study the notes. And that's when it hits me hard. Maybe electricity could have prevented all of this! With an electric stove, there'd be no fire beneath a kettle on the bare ground of the front yard. No screaming little boy rolling under me. No infection, no nurse, no hospital. Instead, Mommy could regularly make smaller batches of soap in a safer, easier way.

A day ago, I'd have pointed this out to Mommy in hopes of changing her mind about electricity, but right now I know better than to do
that.

Doesn't mean my own thoughts about it won't keep churning,
though.

EIGHTEEN
A Ride Down the Mountain

At last, Miss Bentley rings the dismissal bell. I rush for the door with Ceilly so close behind I can feel her breath on the back of my neck.

"Wait! What about Glenna?"

I ignore Ceilly and continue my dash through the schoolyard and up the path.

Twice I slip on small rocks beneath my feet, pitch forward, catch myself with my hands, and just keep going. Ceilly follows right behind.

Out of breath, we stomp onto the porch and throw open the front door.

Silence.

An empty kitchen.

I run up the stairs and through my open bedroom door, and pull aside the curtain. There, huddled in the corner with two whittled automobiles, his own and Clint's, one in each hand, sits Orrin.

My heart catches. Where's Clint? Where's Mommy?

Orrin sees me and lunges up.

I dodge his outreached hands. "Stay with Ceilly for one minute. I'll be right back."

Ceilly slips forward to scoop him up as I cross to Mommy's room.

She's lying completely still in her bed, her eyes open wide, seeming to stare at the ceiling.

"Mommy?"

Not a muscle moves. Even her chest is stone still.

I grab her shoulder and shake her.

"Mommy?"

My heart hammers. At last, her chest moves the slightest bit, and relief runs through me.

"Mommy?" I squeak again.

She blinks once and shifts her eyes to me. "Orrin's in his room waiting for you." Her voice is raspy.

I stand still, my hands balled up at my side.

"Mommy, is Clint alive?"

"He was when they left."

"You should have let me stay home!" I cry.

Her unblinking stare silences me.

"Close the door behind you when you leave," she whispers.

I do. I rush back to Ceilly and Orrin. He launches himself from Ceilly's arms to mine and wraps his around my neck.

"Cora, I miss Clint! Pap took him for a ride on Stormy."

"When?"

He shrugs.

I have to put it to him in a way he'll understand. "Did Pap and you have some lunch before they left?"

He shakes his head and whines, "I'm hungry for some lunch. I looked and looked for something to eat, but I couldn't reach anything."

I'm hurt and angry and scared. Why didn't Mommy send for me at school if she couldn't take care of Orrin? But really, who could she have sent?

Ceilly chimes in. "Well, then, let's just get you some lunch, my little friend."

And we march him down to the kitchen just as Glenna flings the door open and rushes in.

"How's Clint?" she asks.

"Down the mountain to the hospital on Stormy," I mutter.

Glenna slumps into a kitchen chair. Orrin climbs from my arms into her lap. Ceilly sets cold hoecakes in front of him, and he grabs them up in both hands.

I take a deep breath and steady my voice. "Where was Mommy when Pap and Clint left, Orrin?"

"Clint was too hot. Mommy cried and cried in her bed." He blinks at me. "Cora, I want to be too hot and ride on Stormy with Clint."

"Oh Orrin, no!" Glenna cries out. "No one should be too hot."

Tears trail down Glenna's cheeks and they open my heart a sliver. Still, I aim a pleading stare in her direction. Those tears will only scare Orrin more.

She swipes her face dry with her fingertips, seeming to understand.

"When Pap comes back, will it be my turn to have a ride on Stormy with him?" Orrin asks.

"We'll see about arranging that," I say.

That seems to satisfy him.

"Read us a Jack tale, Cora! How 'bout the one with Jack and the ox and the dog and the cat and the rooster?"

There's nothing to do but fill in the time, so I read "Jack and the Robbers" in the fading afternoon light.

✳ ✳ ✳

It's late when Stormy's hooves sound on the last stretch of path to our front yard. Orrin is long tucked into bed asleep.

I rush out with the lantern, hoping to see Clint in front of Pap on the saddle blanket. But it's just Pap and Stormy alone.

Pap dismounts and gathers me in his arms for a tight hug.

"Where is Clint?" I whisper against his jacket.

He pulls back and says, "He's being cared for, Cora."

Then it's Stormy's turn to be cared for after a long day of riding. I bite back my questions as I help Pap get Stormy settled, then follow him inside and up the stairs. My heart pounds as I bite back my questions.

"Mattie?" he says into the darkened doorway of their room. "Mattie, listen."

Moonlight shines through the window and onto the quilt. Slowly Mommy sits up.

"I left Clint at the hospital," Pap says. "He needs care we can't provide here at home. They say he may need to stay as long as a week."

"Why?" Mommy squeaks.

"They are doing something called deep wound cleaning that is mighty painful. And they've got him connected to medicine that flows straight into his body, to help with the pain but especially to fight the infection."

"We don't have money for all that." Mommy's voice shakes.

"Mattie, they don't turn anyone away."

"But how can we pay for that hospital stay? I thought they'd dose him with medicine, and you'd bring him right back to me!"

I see Pap's jaw working. Finally, he says, "Without that treatment, Mattie, they say our boy could die."

At Pap's words, Mommy turns away and a terrible, mournful sound fills the room. I hold my breath and wait.

Finally, she turns back, nods, and reaches her arms out for Pap. He cradles her in the moonlight and whispers, "We'll work out the payment someways."

NINETEEN
A Big Sacrifice

I climb into bed and struggle to stay stone still. I do not want to talk to Glenna about what's troubling me. I wish, more than ever I have since the very first week after my sister died, that it were Ida next to me there in the dark. She'd be holding my hand, and she'd be the oldest. It'd be her job to come up with a solution to get that money for the hospital, a solution that Mommy would approve.

Of course, lying there, I know plain as day that there *is* a solution—just one single solution that makes sense, but it's not one that would put Mommy at ease.

Ceilly and I have a bag full of money up in that hickory tree. Money from pies donated by our neighbors for electricity at the school. Money meant for step one to make our dream come true.

I'm shamed that I have to struggle one bit against my selfish bones to think of giving up that money for Clint's care. My brother's lying in a painful fever in a strange bed away from everyone who loves him. And he might not survive.

Cora Mae, I say to myself, *you'd give your own life for him. What on God's earth does that money matter to you?*

It matters, a voice inside me argues, *for so many reasons—and not every last one of them is selfish. Because even beyond the hopeful ways electricity might change my life, I long for it to change most every life on this mountain if folks will let it. And someday, in the faraway future, that might even include Mommy's life too.*

As the sleepless hours wear on, I wish the blanket of night would suddenly lift, allowing me to slip outdoors and climb the path to the peak of the mountain where I would sit quietly alone with my tangle of feelings. One at a time, I'd gently tug the strands free as I let each one have its say.

But mountain paths aren't safe when the creatures of the night are about, no matter how bright the moon and the stars.

And so I close my eyes and let my mind paint the vista my eyes long to see. Slowly, I set to separating my jumbled feelings. When the barest bit of light shows at the horizon, I step into my clothes and creep down the stairs. I'll be back before a single soul knows I'm gone.

My breath puffs out in front of me as I walk. I smell a telltale hint of winter hovering near. Leaves crunch under my feet. Male wood frogs call out from the leaf litter as I head up past the woods and over toward Ceilly's house on the fork.

The long, dark winter, with its sky the color of ashes, is coming now without the promise of electric light. I had settled my heart on having light next year. I push that thought away and concentrate all of my energy on a picture of Clint, healthy and making snow angels under the bright winter sun.

At Ceilly's house, I take care to creep quietly around to her bedroom. Great-Aunt Exie's admonishments would raise the dead were she to find me here at dawn. I've gathered sticks on my walk—big enough to clunk against, but not to break, glass. I begin to toss them one at a time at Ceilly's window until she finally slides it up.

She stands shivering in the cold. "Is it Clint?"

"Yes, *saving* Clint," I whisper. "Get dressed."

Ceilly meets me in front, and I start walking before she's even had a chance to raise a question. But it's not long before she seems to understand where we are heading, and to her credit, she steps up the pace and says not a single word.

When we reach the hickory tree, she sets to climbing.

I wait below on the same rock we sat on not so long ago. That day, our spirits soared as high as a red-tailed hawk. Our hearts were full of determination and hope that we'd devise a plan to earn money enough to light up the whole holler with lines that would someday help lead us off into the futures of our dreams.

Now I've got but one hope.

When Ceilly drops down next to me and places the bag in my hand, she finally asks the question. "How will the money save Clint?"

The words rush out. "Pap left him at the hospital. They say it may take a week or more to clear up the infection *but only if he stays there.* Mommy says there's no money for that, and Pap says that doesn't matter right now. But there *is* some. And I know it will rest Mommy's mind if she doesn't feel indebted to anyone." I lift up the bag and look straight into her blue eyes. "May I take half?"

"Oh, Cora Mae, you may not!" Ceilly yelps. "You'll take the whole entire amount."

The bag plops back down into my lap.

She doesn't even hesitate, and I feel tears welling up. "Oh Ceilly, I'm a terrible person. I lay in bed last night, and I struggled—actually struggled!—to decide to give this money for the hospital. How could I even think twice about it, Ceilly? I'm selfish and horrible, not like you at all. I can never forgive myself."

Ceilly shifts over on the rock so that our bodies touch from shoulder to ankle. "Stop measuring yourself against people so harshly. You do it with Ida's memory. You do it with me. You think I'm entirely wise and generous and loving. I'm not, you know."

"Yes, you *are*," I squeak.

Ceilly rolls her eyes. "Fine, we can discuss my faults another time," she says. "But you are *not* a horrible person! You're full of dreams and aspirations, just like me, and it's all right to want Clint to get better *and* still hope for electricity." She shifts way around to look me straight in the eye. "So we won't give up on Clint, and we won't give up on electricity either. We're giving this money to your mommy and pap, and we'll start a brand-new plan today."

"We will?" I whisper.

"Yes," she says. "We will."

For the first time, a little flicker of hope for more than Clint arises in me.

✳ ✳ ✳

I leave Ceilly at the fork in the road and run up the path to home. Pushing straight through the door, I hold the bag of money tight in my right hand.

Pap is slumped against the kitchen counter, holding a steaming cup in his hand. His head snaps up when he hears me.

"Where have you been this early in the morning?" His voice sounds rough.

I set the bag down on the counter next to him. "It's from the pie sale, and it's for the hospital."

He picks the bag up and shakes it out onto the counter. "Lordy!" He reaches out to stroke my hair. "This is a big sacrifice for your brother, Cora Mae."

Suddenly, I realize it's even more complicated than that. What about the ladies who gave those pies to us for one purpose—electricity? Do we owe them that money or can we figure out how to replace it at no cost to them? But I don't ask Pap. He has more than enough worries. No, this is mine to figure out.

"You and Glenna will get yourselves off to school this morning." Pap's eyes are shining. And I wonder, deep in my heart, if that's because giving the money for Clint is what Ida would have done.

Not until I turn toward the stairway, with the empty bag in my fist, do I see Glenna. She is standing in the shadows in her nightgown. I say, "School," and climb past her. And just for my own comfort, I pull *Pollyanna* out of my school bag and read the final chapter one last time.

TWENTY

A Gift to Warm a Heart

Orrin hears me changing into my school dress on my side of the room and yelps from the other side of the curtain, "Clint?"

I rush past the curtain to his bed and gather him in my arms, but he swings his fists at me hard.

"Clint! Clint!" he hollers.

I grab his little arms and hold them firm. I look straight into his wild eyes. "Orrin, listen. Clint has to stay at the hospital while his leg gets better."

Now he's crying hard, and tears fill my eyes too. "Make him come home!"

"We don't know when he can come home," I say. "But Pap will go see him today." I know that is true because he has money to deliver.

That slows his tears. He turns to the shelf above the bed, hiccupping, and reaches for Clint's carved wooden automobile.

"Will Pap carry this down to Clint?" he asks.

"He surely will."

Downstairs, Pap dabs at Orrin's tear-streaked face with the handkerchief Mommy embroidered with his initials for their wedding day and he keeps always in a pocket. He assures Orrin that Clint will be happy to see his automobile, that the hospital will make Clint better, and that Mommy will stay with him all day.

I'm especially glad for that last news that Mommy will stay out of bed today.

With my heart more at rest about Clint, my brain takes over. I might have an idea for a new money-raising plan, and I can't wait to fill Ceilly in.

However, Glenna is with us on our walk down to school. I wish she'd just move ahead of us or behind. As soon as I have a chance, I pull Ceilly off the path into a chokecherry thicket, scaring off the feasting jays. I wave Glenna on. Her brow wrinkles, but I can't explain, so I swallow my feelings that I'm being unfair to her.

When I'm sure she isn't going to wait for us, I whisper, "I might have an idea!"

"Already?" Ceilly asks.

"I've been thinking on those pie customers from the electric crew," I say. "You know how they were all men away from their wives and families and all?"

"That's a fact."

"Remember how that one fellow said his Sally loved walnuts and the other man said he and his friends would rather be splitting the raspberry pie with their sweethearts?"

"Yep!" Ceilly says. "I was surely hoping that when I'm grown one of my sweethearts will get *me* some delicious pie."

"So, don't you s'pose they'd like to send a gift home to their beloveds, reminding them of their continuing affections?"

A donkey-laugh bursts out of Ceilly. "You read too much! Their *continuing affections*? Did you get that phrase in a novel Miss Fee brought?"

"So what?" I grin and duck back out to the path.

"How the heck are we going to mail *pies*?" Ceilly asks.

"Not pies, silly! What if we sell the men some hand-embroidered handkerchiefs? Simple to make, easy to mail, the perfect gift to warm a heart, and we can make them ourselves to replace what the donated pies earned."

"Well, Great-Aunt Exie won't complain if I want to embroider, that's for sure." Ceilly twirls on the path. "Give me the details."

"I figure a yard of fabric will make sixteen hankies, plus we'll need some of that colored thread and needles. At a quarter apiece, that would leave us only a dollar short of the five dollars for the school to join, but at fifty cents, we'd have that plus three dollars for the first month payment."

Ceilly is plumb shocked, I can tell. "You did all that arithmetic?" she finally exclaims.

I take a slight bow. "It kept my mind off worrying over Clint once I'd finished reading *Pollyanna*."

"Why, I bet Great-Aunt Exie will give us fabric and needles and floss, all while praising the Lord that her prayers for a ladylike great-niece have finally been answered," Ceilly says.

* * *

After school, we walk home with Glenna. When we walk in, Mommy is sitting near the stove, not chopping, not mending, just staring straight ahead.

"Mommy, has Pap returned and gone off again?"

She shakes her head no.

"Then did he call from the hospital to the general store and ask them to send up word to you?" I ask.

She shakes her head again, and I give up trying.

Orrin is playing nearby with his automobile. "I built a barn for mine and for Clint's too." But then his bright expression crumples. "But Clint can't put his automobile in it. I want Clint to put his in it!"

But Mommy is quick with her words. "Hush now, Orrin."

Silently, I vow to comfort him as soon as we have him alone.

"Ceilly and I need to go see Great-Aunt Exie." I glance over at Glenna. "Mommy, Glenna can help you get supper. May we take Orrin with us?"

Even before Mommy nods, Orrin slips his hand into mine and tugs me to the door.

The three of us head back over to the fork and up toward Great-Aunt Exie's house.

"Is Pap bringing Clint home today?" Orrin hollers from up ahead.

"Probably not today," I say.

He stops still in the road.

"But Pap thinks he'll be well sooner than soon," I say.

That seems to satisfy him, and he runs a circle around us with his usual energy.

"Will Uncle Eben be at your house?" Orrin asks Ceilly as he passes by her. "He's our favorite uncle, right, Cora?"

"He's not our actual uncle," I tell him. "He's Ceilly's uncle, Great-Aunt Exie's son."

Ceilly hops in. "Eben's not my actual uncle either. He's my cousin. But seeing as how he was like a brother to my mommy, I like to call him uncle."

Orrin stops. "Well, who's *our* actual uncle, then?"

"None here on the mountain, but one of them is Glenna's pap in Detroit," I say.

"Mommy said not to talk about him," Orrin says.

"She did?" I ask. "What else did she say?"

"Nothing," Orrin says.

Ceilly is quick to say, "You can borrow my uncle Eben for one of yours."

"Yay!" With that, Orrin tumbles down the path like a fox kit. No doubt the possibility of a lollipop from Uncle Eben has erased his sadness about Clint.

"I wonder why your mommy told Orrin not to talk about your uncle," Ceilly says when he is out of earshot.

"Maybe it has to do with that bruised-up face she came with," I say as we pass by the many fenced and roofed cages Uncle Eben has built around his hives to keep bears and skunks from the bees. A low buzzing hum surrounds them. "But she sure as winter frost won't talk about it."

At Great-Aunt Exie's door, we remind Orrin to sit quietly on the porch swing and mind his manners if she comes out to greet him.

Ceilly and I creep into the dim house, filled with the smoky smell from a pot of soup beans simmering. From the outside, it looks much like my house, but inside it's different. No signs of children's clothes or toys. Everything in order. And embroidered antimacassars and doilies on all the furniture.

We find Great-Aunt Exie at the table dampening laundry to iron tomorrow. She's so tall—as tall as Pap—that when she shakes the dampening bottle, it's like it's raining.

"Embroidery, you say?" she asks after Ceilly introduces the topic. "And you suddenly have an urge to keep an embroidered handkerchief in your pocket?"

Ceilly tries to work around the need to lie. A bit of silence hangs in the air until she pipes up with "I just think they are so pretty."

"Well then." Great-Aunt Exie smiles. I never knew that her two front teeth overlapped. "I'd say it's about time you left off your tomboy ways and took up stitching. Shall I teach you the basic stitches?"

Ceilly answers fast as all get out. "Oh no! You did that way back when I was eight, remember?"

"Why, yes," she says. "Did you ever finish that sampler about God's graces?"

"Not yet," Ceilly says. "But I will!"

Great-Aunt Exie fetches a length of white cotton lawn, a packet of embroidery needles, and a small wooden box full of bright little bundles of thread. We stuff everything inside a poke and escape as quickly as we can. As we head toward the front door, I offer to take all of the supplies home, cut the fabric into sixteen hankies, and work on a sample. Ceilly is mighty quick to agree.

Out on the front porch, we find Orrin happily licking a lollipop next to Uncle Eben, who keeps the creaky swing rocking beneath them. He's as short and round as his mother is tall and rangy, and neither of them would ever put you in mind of Ceilly. It comes to me that, like me, Uncle Eben's out of step with his mother and her wishes. We have that in common.

"Why, hello, Cora! I haven't seen you since my trip home from Williamsburg." He lays his hand on Orrin's head and looks at me somberly. "I hear tell that this little one's matching pair is down to the hospital?"

A sudden rush of sadness at the mention of a pair of boys swells my throat closed, so I just nod.

"Well, you tell your pap that if he needs any help at all, just to let me know." Then he chuckles just a little. "I s'pose you've already got a page of notes about Clint's treatment."

I don't yet, of course—just the notes from the nurse's visit—but I do have a list of questions in my mind. I resolve to get answers to some of those questions soon.

I find the voice to say, "I will soon, Uncle Eben. Time to go now, Orrin."

On the walk home with me, Orrin pulls a second lollipop, wrapped clumsily in paper, from his pocket. "I got one for Clint too! I'll save it 'til he comes home from the hospital."

His kindness sets shame running through me again as I remember my struggle in the night about the money. Am I the only one on this earth with selfish bones? And then I remember Ceilly saying that she's not as wise and generous and loving as I claim her to be. Whatever she meant by that.

TWENTY-ONE
Too Much Cora

Walking next to Ceilly and Orrin, I continue fretting my way silently down to Clayton Fork. I've allowed myself to think past my selfish bones for the moment. Now, I'm pondering my handkerchief idea plus the two additional electric cooperative members that will be needed after we have the school on board. My mind swirls with thoughts.

Finally, I blurt out, "Ceilly, what about plans for getting the last two members of the cooperative signed up after the school?"

"Cora Mae, you haven't even cut out the hankie fabric, nor have we sewn them," Ceilly says. "Slow your worries while people consider their options."

"Okay," I say. But I don't stay quiet long. "I overheard Viney telling Belle her parents are in favor but don't know where they'd find the money."

"See?" Ceilly says. "They need time."

"But then Belle said her mommy is totally opposed," I add. "Do you think *Belle* needs to be persuaded?"

"Belle? Not at all. I know she's on board, like most of us kids. Your plan about a newspaper might do the trick with Belle's mommy, though. Give Belle all the information she needs to get the rest of the convincing done by herself."

Ceilly's words are just a reminder that no convincing on my part will make *my* house one of the members.

"Anyway," she adds, as though she were listening in on my thoughts, "my house absolutely will *not* be joining. Out of the blue this morning, Great-Aunt Exie told Uncle Eben, 'I don't care if I go blind sewing in the dark.' And he hadn't even brought it up!"

"Poor Uncle Eben," I say.

On the last bit of the climb home, Ceilly takes to reciting multiplication facts past the twelve-times even though we've never had a multiplication table for those.

"Join in on the ones you know," she says in a breath between thirteen times nine and thirteen times ten. "I'll help with the ones you don't."

And even though thirteen times ten is easy enough, I stay silent. It takes all of my brain power to sort through my worries, but once I do, I know where I actually want Ceilly's help, and right now, it's not with arithmetic.

When Ceilly finally says, "Thirteen times twelve equals one hundred and fifty-six," we're home.

We immediately poke our heads in the door, and I ask Mommy, "Still no word?"

She is still in the same chair we left her in. She just shakes her head no, so I duck out quick, leaving Orrin behind. I point across to the woodshed roof. Ceilly knows it means some serious talk when I offer to climb. She scampers up, and I follow her in my clumsy-cautious fashion.

"What?" she asks. "Handkerchiefs again?"

"No. It's Glenna. I'm doing a terrible job with her."

"Really? I think you're doing fine," she says with a pull on one of my curls. "You're still working hard to get used to Glenna being here. And I reckon you're also working hard to get your brain to accept what your heart already knows."

I feel my shoulders creep up an inch or two. "Knows about what?"

"About Glenna. And what happened. That Clint's burn really *was* an accident."

I don't say anything.

"It's just…"

I see she is struggling for a way to say what I already think.

"I know, I know," I say. "Ida would've understood just what to do for Glenna. She'd have coaxed her into this family with a big old heap of love. But when I first saw Glenna in that front yard, any hint of the kind bones Ida left me were wiped out of my being as fast as a mudslide in spring. I really *am* working to get them back."

Ceilly seems about to ask a question, but I rush to interrupt. "Ida would have made Mommy proud without needing to be asked." I blink fast.

As awkward as it is on the edge of this roof, I lean sideways and put my head on Ceilly's shoulder. She puts her arms around me.

I can't stop the tears then. They turn to all-out crying, the kind with sobs and shudders and gulps, all while we are balanced on the edge.

Ceilly knows better than to reason with me when my floodgates open. She waits until I slow down to ragged breathing.

At last, she lets me go and looks into my eyes. "You are every bit as loving as Ida was."

And despite my resolving to do a better job with Glenna, I know Ceilly is wrong. "No, I'm not. You've got to remind me when I'm being too-much-Cora."

Ceilly stares at me, her grey eyes steely. "Cora Mae Tipton, I *won't*. You weren't put on this earth to be Ida."

She holds my gaze until my anger burns out. Then she says quietly,

"Who was it who came up with the pie sale? And who was it who decided we could encourage membership sign-up with a newspaper? What about *that* person?"

I smile. "What about her?"

She smiles back. "I'm darned sure that *wouldn't* have been Ida."

"That's a fact," I reluctantly agree. "Can I ask you something?"

"Anything at all."

"What did you mean when you said you weren't entirely wise and generous and loving?"

I can see her working out her reply in her mind, so I wait patiently.

Finally she sighs. "I think I have two sides, really. There's the side of me that knows what I want from life."

"Like adventure," I say, nodding.

"Yep. Adventure, and learning…and right now, electricity. That side of me wants to gobble up the world. But the other side of me is sad sometimes. And mad. And sour." Ceilly meets my eyes and I know she sees the questions in them. "It's plain to me why, Cora. I lost my home and parents who loved me and would have done anything for me when I was so small. I don't remember everything about them, but I remember that much. And in their place I got Great-Aunt Exie." She pauses. "I try not to dwell on that unfair exchange, but sometimes…sometimes it hits me so hard I cry myself to sleep."

Ceilly's words freeze me to the roof. At last, I manage a small gulp. "You—you've never told me that Ceilly, and I'm your best friend!"

"I know, Cora. I don't mean to keep secrets. It's just easier to keep that part of me tucked away. Besides, I love the way you depend on the other side of me. It makes me feel…necessary, I guess."

"You aren't just necessary, Ceilly. You're essential."

At that, her eyes shine. "Thank you, Cora," she whispers. "I love so many things about you too. You are brave, you are curious, and you are dedicated to your many plans."

"Well," I say. "Sometimes I feel like the juggler on that poster Miss Bentley uses to teach the new little ones their colors the very first week at school. I can't keep all of my little colored balls in the air."

"That's okay. I'd probably be the better juggler anyway." Ceilly giggles as she stands, then stretches one leg out straight. Rising on the remaining toes, she tosses imaginary balls into the air.

I hold my breath even though I believe that girl could balance on a pin—or take to flight. Still, when she collapses back to sitting, my breath whooshes out in relief.

"Stop worrying about what Ida would have done," she says as we climb down. "You've got just-right-Cora plans that need juggling."

TWENTY-TWO

An Artistic Heart

I don't get much sleep. Once Orrin is tucked in, Glenna, Mommy, and Pap head upstairs too. I ask whether I can stay up a while longer and keep the lantern downstairs with me. I hold my breath, expecting Mommy to object to the cost of the oil I'll burn, but she is too distracted to care, and luckily, though Pap raises a questioning eyebrow, he decides not to pursue his curiosity.

I lay the fabric from Great-Aunt Exie out on the table and set one of the irons on the stove to heat. Then I carefully fold the fabric and press along the folds, giving me lines to cut along. I use the scissors Mommy keeps on the top shelf of the pie safe to cut sixteen squares, then set in to hemming two as samples for Ceilly. With slow, careful stitches, I sew my way around the four edges of each hankie. As I do, I think of Pap saying at dinner that when he brought the money to the hospital the doctoring folks said Clint might "turn a corner" tomorrow. Pap explained that means that the infection-fighting medicine might show strong signs of working. But that word "might" worries me a good deal as I pull the thread in and out through the hems.

When I finish my stitching, I slip up to my bedroom and fetch my notebook back downstairs. I turn my worry into words on a new page that I title "Treating Bad Burns." But other than noting what Pap said about "deep wound cleaning" and the medicine that flows straight into Clint's body to fight pain and infection, I know nothing I can write. So instead, I write down my list of questions.

* Why does a fever come after a burn?
* What does it mean?
* What makes the fever dangerous enough to need to go to the hospital?
* What do they do for the fever there?
* What is "deep wound cleaning"?
* How does it help?
* What else do they do to treat the burn?
* What does it mean to turn a corner?
* How do they know when it's healed enough to go home?

I'll have to let Miss Bentley know that I need Miss Fee to bring me some sort of medical book, if they have such a thing at the Pack Horse Library, on her very next visit so that I can learn more, and maybe there will be a chance to ask Pap. For now, I try to tuck away my worry over Clint for a while and sleep just a few hours. Then, having hardly slept three winks, I head off to school just after dawn to meet Ceilly as we planned.

✳ ✳ ✳

Ceilly and I settle under our usual tree, and I am quick to hand over a stack of squares and show her my first two sample hemmed hankies.

Ceilly's eyebrows rise just about even with her hairline. "Cora, whenever did you find time to do all this work?"

"Give me a lantern and a night full of hours and I make do, but it sure would have helped to have an electric light shining."

Ceilly pulls a rumpled square off the unhemmed pile I've handed her. "I think Great-Aunt Exie would iron this first before hemming."

"She would, and they *were* ironed when I cut them, but I can't figure how to do that again in daylight without Mommy knowing, and I don't want to take any chances."

So we settle in to hemming our wrinkled squares, me leaning over to offer encouraging advice as Ceilly tackles her first hankie. But before long, I feel I must comment on her wobbly hem. "Ceilly, we need to keep our hems narrow—and *even*."

She shrugs. "Sewing's not one of my talents."

"It best become one quick." I poke her. "How're we going to decorate these handkerchiefs anyway?"

"Well, who's the very best artist in our school?" she asks.

"I was thinking *you* might qualify," I say.

Ceilly laughs. "Only if you want monoplanes on every one of these hankies!"

"I take your point," I say.

"It's Bobbie Clyde Hudgins," she says—Rilda's little sister, who is only nine but has a God-given talent for drawing.

"Maybe Bobbie Clyde could make some drawings for us that we can trace on our handkerchief squares," I say.

"Don't worry, I've already got it all figured out." She reaches into her pocket and pulls out a thin sheet of tissue paper. "Great-Aunt Exie uses this tissue paper for patterns," Ceilly says. "If Bobbie Clyde were to draw on this paper, we could sew right on her lines and then rip the thin paper away!"

"Let's have her draw warblers and violets and those sorts of things," I say just as the morning bell rings.

"And naturally, we need hearts, but we can draw those ourselves," I whisper as we slide into our seats.

∗ ∗ ∗

On my way to the privy, I drop a note on Bobbie Clyde's desk asking if she'd be willing to join us in a secret project. By the time I return, Ceilly has passed her the tracing paper with instructions about what to draw. She's also sworn her to secrecy except for telling Rilda.

Bobbie Clyde gets busy drawing a whole stack of designs for us, working behind her reading book so Miss Bentley won't see.

At lunchtime, Ceilly and I rush out to our tree. We gobble our lunches as quickly as spring peepers swallow flies in April, then begin our work. My heart remains lighter with Pap's news about Clint possibly turning that corner soon. It makes it easier to lose myself in the stitching.

At first Viney and some of the little girls beg to join us. But we tell them we have a secret project and can't have company. Seems as though Bobbie Clyde is honoring her sworn secrecy.

Not long before lunchtime is over, Ceilly holds up another hemmed square. "What do you think?"

Not only has she hemmed a little stack of them with much less wobbly stitches, but on this one, she's embroidered a pink heart in one corner that she is now surrounding with tiny daisies in purple. Great-Aunt Exie would be proud, actually. Ceilly shows signs of becoming a more careful stitcher than I expected from a girl who favors tree climbing over all else.

"Better?" she asks.

"Not just better," I say. "I think you've been hiding a talent!"

"Don't get too used to it," she says. "Once this project is done, I'm

136

never going to embroider again. Fact is, I'd rather lie in a ditch with my back broke."

"You say that now," I say, "but when Great-Aunt Exie sees—"

She interrupts. "She *isn't* going to see one stitch of my embroidery on these."

"But won't she be asking you about how you're using all these supplies she gave us?"

"You know we stay out of each other's way." Ceilly licks her finger and thumb and runs them down two strands of green thread as if she's been doing it her whole life.

"What I also know is that Great-Aunt Exie has a surplus of nosy bones. She's bound to want to know what's become of her supplies."

Ceilly ignores that and stabs her needle through the cloth. "I wonder whether Amelia Earhart has time to stitch, what with all of the flying over the Atlantic and all."

I laugh. "Maybe she does—wherever she has disappeared to. That article Miss Bentley read to us didn't mention her packing supplies for a hobby."

No matter what Amelia Earhart's hobbies are, I'm finding that I like embroidery. Ceilly says that's because it appeals to my artistic heart. I like that. *My artistic heart.* And coming from Ceilly, who draws beautiful monoplanes and could sketch a lot more besides if she were of a mind to, that's quite a compliment.

As I pull the knot tight at the end of my next thread, I remember Mommy's birthday's coming up in November.

"Ceilly, must we sell every single one of these handkerchiefs?" I ask.

"'Course we must. Why?"

"I was wondering about giving Mommy one for her birthday," I say, thinking about how Ida would have made one for Mommy.

Ceilly gives me a sly grin. "Well, do you have twenty-five cents?"

I smile. "No discount for the stitcher?"

"No discount," she says. "A quarter."

"Remember that leaves us a dollar short of the five dollars for joining. You don't s'pose those men would have *two* extra quarters to spare? That would give us the full five dollars along with the three dollars for the first month payment," I say.

"I don't imagine they do, Cora. Let's just work on getting as much money back in that bag as we can."

"Okay," I agree. Right that minute, I want to set aside the handkerchief I'm working on and start in on Mommy's. I imagine her opening a package from me on her birthday and finding the handkerchief with her initials on one corner:

MJP

surrounded by a ring of flowers she uses for healing—chamomile and feverfew and mallow and others. I imagine how I'd feel if she were to look me in the eyes and say thank you. I imagine her happy just for that one moment. I choose one undecorated square and set it aside for last. I'll worry about how to get the quarter later.

Just before the end-of-lunch bell rings, we hurry to divide up our supplies and the remaining squares, which, of course, takes longer than we planned for. We rush for the door after the bell's done ringing and arrive at our seats out of breath.

"Cora, Ceilly, you two know how seriously I take tardiness after lunch break," Miss Bentley says. "Do not let it happen again."

"Yes, Miss Bentley," we chorus.

Viney pipes up, "They've got a secret project, Miss Bentley."

"I am not interested in uncovering secrets, Viney," she says. "I am interested in teaching each of my students as much knowledge—and respect—as I can fit into a school day. I am sure Cora and Ceilly appreciate that."

I'm not used to Miss Bentley being frustrated with me, yet I can't help but smile thinking of her being this stern with those grumpy old school directors. They'd surely have to agree to sign on to the electric cooperative if so!

TWENTY-THREE
The Faith of a Four-Year-Old

When we reach the fork on the way home from school, Ceilly says, "Great-Aunt Exie claims she needs my help today. She says now that you've got Glenna, I can dedicate my after-school time to helping her instead of your Mommy. I can't figure why she suddenly wants me underfoot."

"Ha, now that I've got Glenna?" I sigh and reluctantly wave good-bye to her. Her afternoon will likely be a challenge. When I look over my shoulder, I see Glenna straggling behind me. I decide to wait for her, but when she catches up, I don't have the heart to talk and talk and not get a single answer. We walk home in silence.

Mommy greets us at the door. Before I can ask whether Clint has turned a corner, she says, "I've pulled out the baby clothes and blankets and whatnot and washed them all. They're hanging on the line out back." Mommy swipes a strand of hair off her cheek that has escaped from her bun. "You two will iron and fold them into this basket. The cookstove is hot, and the irons are ready on top for you. Be careful, Glenna. They're heavier than they look and can cause a mighty burn."

And *there's* another thing that would make life easier. That advertisement in the magazine said electric irons that plug into something called an electric outlet are lightweight and get hot quickly. But I don't dare say that to Mommy.

Glenna trudges toward the door. "I'll unpin what's on the line."

When she's gone, Mommy says, "You've got *two* jobs here, Cora. Talk to Glenna while you work on those clothes."

"She won't talk to me, Mommy. I've tried from the very first day. And since Clint's accident, she's been even quieter."

"Keep trying. I've told you—she's in a world of hurt. I won't say much more than this, but it was a sorry, sorry situation with her father up there in Detroit. She is still in need of your friendship, maybe more since what happened with Clint."

I take a few moments to chew on this advice. But surely Mommy sees that Glenna is closed inside some sort of box. And yet, there's something that feels real and true about what Mommy says. Glenna is *choosing* to lock herself up, but only Mommy knows why.

I lay layers of worn towels on the table. When Glenna comes in, she drops the basket on the floor next to me. The little baby gowns smell fresh when we lay them on the towels. The smell sets my heart to aching before I realize that it's a memory of the twins when they were tiny rising up in me. And now, one of them is lying in a hospital bed.

I shake off the memory and fetch an iron, and Glenna follows suit. I sprinkle the gown with water from the bottle Mommy keeps on the windowsill and hand it over, even though it would be better if the clothes had been sprinkled and rolled up overnight. With the baby not due for weeks and weeks, I wonder why Mommy is in such an all-fired hurry.

Glenna copies my actions. I can't help but wish I had the stack of hankies to iron too. The two of us work together in silence through two gowns each, steam rising when the hot irons slide over the damp cloth. I think on how she's her mommy and pap's only child. Did she ever want sisters and brothers? Would that have made things easier or more difficult with whatever happened to her?

I ponder those questions and imagine asking them out loud. They seem too personal to ask, but Mommy instructed me to talk to Glenna. I imagine she meant me to do it in some kind and generous way, but I can't puzzle my way through to how to ask those questions, so I simply say, "How do you like school so far?"

Glenna shrugs.

I try again. "I saw you talking with Rilda at lunch yesterday."

She only nods.

I take a deep breath and say, "Well, it's nice having you there." I glance at her, wondering about the secrets she's carrying. Then I decide to take a risk. I fetch my stack of nine hankies from my schoolbag and begin to press them flat, one at a time.

Glenna looks over and finally speaks. "What are those?"

"Hand-made hankies. They're the secret project Viney was yapping about to Miss Bentley after lunch," I say.

"Pretty," Glenna murmurs.

"You won't tell anyone, will you?" I ask

"'Course not," Glenna says. I see a tiny, satisfied smile drift across her face.

Then we return to our work and complete the baby clothes in silence.

Now, though, I find the quiet doesn't trouble me.

※ ※ ※

Because Ceilly spent the entirety of the afternoon and evening with Great-Aunt Exie last night, I'm not surprised to practically trip over her on the porch steps this Saturday morning when I carry the laundry basket loaded with overalls to pin to the line. I sure can't figure why Mommy is doing Monday laundry today, but I motion Ceilly to help with the hanging as October clouds scud across a blue sky.

I hold a pair of overalls high up to the line, and she hands me a clothespin. "Well?"

"Since Great-Aunt Exie was pleased to see me with a needle in hand, I managed to hem the rest of my pile and decorate a few. She seemed to have no idea it wasn't just a single hankie I was working on." Ceilly says. "What about you?"

"I ironed them yesterday afternoon. Then Mommy kept us busy all evening, but I got up early, and Glenna said she'd read to Orrin while I finished hemming my pile."

Ceilly looks alarmed. "Glenna?"

"I made a judgement call, Ceilly," I say. "She promised we can trust her with the secret."

"Well swell," Ceilly says. "Can she embroider?"

"That's not a question I posed," I say. "So, let's just figure out the work we have left to do."

She dips her head as though she has something to apologize for. "Cora, one of mine is too sloppy to sell," she admits. "I tried pulling out the stitching, but I made a big mess of it."

I stop pinning. "Oh Ceilly, how big of a big mess?"

"Don't worry. I waited until Great-Aunt Exie was snoring in her chair last night. I snuck her tiny snips out of her sewing box." Ceilly pats her pocket. "I have that hankie for you to work on while I start the next one of your pile."

"Think we'll be ready soon?"

"For the sale?" she asks. "Pretty soon, yes. Have you talked to your pap?"

"No, I want to be able to show him the full pile of completed hankies."

Ceilly picks up Orrin's wet overalls. "Let's get these hung so we can get started!"

We make quick work of pinning up the clothes. But just as I grab Ceilly's hand to leave, Glenna comes out. She picks up the empty basket from the ground and says, "Aunt Mattie says to stay put. I'll be right back."

As the door bangs shut behind her, I groan. "Saturday isn't even Mommy's laundry day. What happened to Monday?"

"Likely it's too much work to do this all alone of a Monday," Ceilly says. "I mean, when you're getting closer to having a baby and all."

I duck my head. Of course.

Before the sun is directly overhead, we've pinned up four baskets of laundry and chased Orrin around the yard at least a dozen times.

When Glenna comes out on the porch with the basket full for the fifth time, she offers to pin those clothes up. Instead, I lift the basket from her and wave that we'll do it.

Ceilly squeezes my arm and smiles. "Generous bones."

Warmth spreads from that place on my arm through my whole self. I wonder if a person can actually grow new bones on the spot.

* * *

Once all the clothes are hung. Ceilly and I gather up three big pieces of corn pone, our embroidery, and Orrin. Ordinarily, Orrin would be skipping ahead. But not today. I reach for his hand, and he hides it behind his back.

"I don't want to go," he whines.

I keep my hand outstretched toward him. "Why not?"

"What if Clint comes home?"

"Oh, my little friend," Ceilly says. "Clint still needs all of the help the hospital nurses and doctors have saved up just for him."

I admire how reassurance trips off her tongue. I squat in front of him. "Don't worry, Orrin. He's going to be back with us sooner than soon."

I hope that's not an exaggeration.

"Clint and me like the schoolyard best," he says with only a bit of a whine left in his voice.

Even though walking that far will take up another chunk of our time, I say, "Well then, let's go!"

Once we arrive and gobble down the pone, I set to cutting and pulling out the stitching on the start-over hankie. When all of the stitches are out, I try to smooth the bunched fabric over my knee, but it doesn't work. I sigh and say, "This needs an iron."

I set that hankie aside, and Ceilly hands me an undecorated one.

Twice, I set down the square to play with Orrin on the school steps. Once he even asks me to turn on on an imaginary lightbulb. When I laugh, he proclaims, "But 'lectricity is coming to our house."

I open my eyes wide. "It is?"

"Yep, Pap'll make sure of it."

Oh, how I long for the faith of a four-year-old—and the innocence about who is the boss of what in our house.

TWENTY-FOUR
A Change of Sunday Plans

By the time we head for home, Ceilly's last two hankies are finished. We part ways at Clayton Fork and just as we'd hoped, Glenna is outside unpinning dry clothes when I get to the yard. I carry one of Pap's shirts inside, silently rehearsing the words that Ceilly and I practiced.

I find Belle's mommy sitting with mine at the kitchen table talking about the cough Belle's little sister has come down with. Mommy is leaning over vegetables on the chopping board while she asks a dozen questions. It seems to me that her round belly might soon make it impossible for her arms to reach.

"I'll get a head start on the ironing," I say.

She doesn't turn but only says, "That's work for Monday."

"Monday is a school day," I remind her.

She turns to me, brushing the loose hair off her face. She looks worn to a nubbin.

Shame washes over me at my selfish desire to iron that last hankie. "Please, Mommy." I point to the vegetables. "Let me help you."

"Well, then, that'd be fine." She hands over the knife she's been using. "This okra needs slicing. Toss it in that cornmeal when you're done."

Then she gets up, spreads a small clean cloth on the table, and ties up a scoop of her lemon balm and elderberry tea. She hands it to Belle's mommy. "This will set to work on that cough mighty quick.

146

I've added a pinch of valerian root too, so maybe you'll both get some sleep tonight."

"I'm sorry not to have anything to give you in return," Belle's mommy says.

Mommy lays a hand on her arm. "Just take it and get that little one well. We won't worry about payment."

When her visitor is gone, Mommy practically collapses into a kitchen chair and worry prickles in me.

As I slice up the whole pile of okra on the counter, I fret—over Mommy and the baby, over Clint alone in the hospital, and now over the iron-and-hankie predicament. And even if I solve that last problem, I'll still somehow have to find time to hide myself away and embroider it again.

When we hear Pap ride into the yard, Orrin runs out to greet him. Pap enters the house with a big ole grin on his face, carrying Orrin on his shoulder. Orrin is clapping and chanting "Clint! Clint!"

It seems Pap stopped by the general store and placed a call to the hospital. He says Clint's fever is down, he has turned that "corner" for good, and he's finally on the mend. They will disconnect him from the medicine that goes straight into his veins tomorrow, Pap says, and then he'll come home Monday. Two more days! A nurse on horseback will ride to the hospital to collect Clint and fetch him home so that Pap won't miss another day of work.

Relief sweeps through me as one of my worries flies away for a moment.

As Pap sets Orrin down by Mommy, I see him pull a package from under his jacket and set it on the sofa, but before I can ask about it, he starts talking about Clint again.

"Mattie, they tell me our boy is going to need some extra care this next week," Pap says. "He'll have to stay abed and only get up for trips to the privy."

I pipe up. "I'll stay home from school and care for him."

"There's no need of that, Cora," Mommy says. And before Glenna can offer too, she adds, "No need for *anyone* to stay home from school."

"Now Mattie..." Pap begins.

"A nest of Granny's quilts on the sofa will suit his needs just fine," she says in her end-the-conversation way. But the tiredness in her voice makes me decide to ask about the ironing again. It *would* be a solution to both my hankie problem and my worries over Mommy.

"Mommy, I know you are planning to iron on Monday. But I think it would be best for you if you didn't have to iron the day Clint comes home. Couldn't we, just this once, iron clothes of a Sunday?"

At first she shakes her head no, but before I can argue further, she thinks it over. "Well, I don't s'pose God would mind this *one* time." She pushes herself up off the chair. "'Specially if we aren't also cooking on the Sabbath."

"Then Glenna and I will iron those clothes tomorrow." I glance over at my cousin. "Won't we, Glenna?"

Before she can answer, Pap interrupts and nods toward the sofa. "Glenna, when I stopped in to the general store, I picked up that parcel. It's from your mommy."

Glenna rushes to it, grabs it up, and hugs it hard to her, but she doesn't rip it open like I would. Instead, she heads up the stairs with it in her arms.

As soon as I can shake Orrin loose, I follow her up to our bedroom. She sits on the bed dressed in a soft blue sweater.

"Oh Glenna," I say, "it's beautiful!"

She smiles and whispers, "My mommy knit it for me."

I realize, of a sudden, that while I've wrangled with my mommy nearly nonstop, Glenna's been missing hers just as much.

"Was there a note too?" I ask, but she doesn't answer, just sits there smiling. It's the first big smile I've seen from her within the walls of this house since she got here.

* * *

The next morning before Sunday services, Glenna and I sort the clothes into piles for dampening. I give Glenna the overalls, aprons, and underdrawers. I take the shirts and dresses.

Glenna looks at her pile. "Aren't these all the easy ones?"

I smile. "Well, how many shirts have *you* ironed in your life?"

She just shakes her head.

Keeping my Glenna-friendship goal in mind, I try for a bright and cheerful tone. "Mommy'll be watching like a sharp-shinned hawk. This way, she's more likely to be satisfied."

Glenna wrinkles her forehead. "Okay, whatever you say."

I wonder what she really means. For a strong-willed girl, sometimes she seems entirely too willing to just do what someone says. I wonder if that has to do with the sorry situation with her father up in Detroit. Could it be that just going along was a way to cope in her house?

But that is absolutely nothing I'd feel comfortable to ask her, even now when we are friendlier. Instead, I fit the sprinkle top into the bottle of water. We dampen our piles of clothes, roll them up and put them into pillowcases, and leave the irons warming on the stove.

All through Sunday worship, I barely hear the singing, the praising, the preaching. Instead, I study on the challenge of sneaking that hankie under my iron. After service, I whisper my plan to Ceilly and make apologies to Mommy and Pap for rushing off. Tugging Glenna along with me, I head home. On the way, I explain that I have a hankie I need to iron in secret just in case she spots an opportunity to help me.

We tie on aprons and set out a noon dinner of cold roasted potatoes and leftover fried okra that's ready to eat when Mommy, Pap, and Orrin arrive. But before they do, I slip the hankie into my pocket.

After dinner, Glenna and I set to ironing.

It's a cold, damp day, and the heat of the stove is welcome at first. But Glenna and I are soon dripping from the hard work of pressing out the wrinkles while standing over the steaming fabric. Mommy always says that Tuesday's ironing is harder than Monday's washing. Now that I'm facing all of the ironing in one day, I know why—and *I'm* only doing half the work.

While Glenna is distracting Mommy with a conversation about the sweater Aunt Thelma knit for her, I pull the wrinkled hankie out. I lay it under one of Pap's work shirts. The steam from the damp cloth of the shirt and the heat from the iron should do the trick. I fold the shirt up with the hankie inside and wait for a chance to smuggle it back into my apron pocket.

When Glenna heads out to the privy, I say that I'll take a short break too. I risk Mommy's curiosity and race upstairs to hide the hankie in my school satchel. I'm back lifting a hot iron before Glenna returns. But Mommy doesn't let it pass.

"What sent you up those stairs?" she demands.

I struggle not to lie outright. "I needed to check on something Ceilly lent me."

"What did Ceilly lend you? You know I don't hold with borrowing. It's likely to leave you in a place of owing what you cannot repay."

My mind scrambles for a way to get out of answering. Then I do something I never imagined I'd purposely do. I glance down at the school dress I'm pressing, the one that's gotten tight lately. And I leave that hot iron too long on the hem. The smell of scorching fabric rises up to my nose. I yelp.

"For heaven's sake, Cora Mae!" Mommy scolds. She lumbers over to lift up the dress. As she runs a finger over the brown mark on the hem, Mommy sighs. "Stitch a patch on it."

It can't be much harder than hemming those hankies, I think.

✳ ✳ ✳

After the last of the ironing is done and as the daylight is fading, Pap climbs to the back of the hayloft and fetches down the cradle Papaw made when Ida was born. I wash the cradle clean, and while it dries, I melt some of Uncle Eben's beeswax on the stove in a pot of water. I carry the pot outside to cool just enough to scoop the soft wax off the top of the water and drop it into a cup, then add some black-walnut oil. I spread the warm beeswax polish on a rag and rub that cradle to a beautiful shine.

As I do, my mind ranges over memories of my Papaw, such a skilled and dedicated woodworker, and the twin babies cradled head-to-feet and feet-to-head inside this lovely wooden bed when I was seven years old and they were new to the world. I wish I'd had Papaw for more years than I did, but today I am filled with hope for Clint's recovery and grateful that at least we have many beautiful reminders of Papaw in the sturdy, useful furniture he built—this cradle, the pie safe, the table we eat our meals on.

I end my Sunday by the fire with Pap, sitting at his feet as he strums his banjo. And finally, I ask him the questions in my notebook about Clint's treatment. But he doesn't have answers to many of them at all, except the very last one: How do they know when it's healed enough to go home?

"That one's easy," he says. "When the fever goes away and stays away for two days and the burned tissue starts to look dry. Like it does right now."

TWENTY-FIVE
Where Is Clint?

I wake up early on Monday hoping that the nurse on horseback will trot into the yard before Ceilly comes to fetch me for school.

It's as though Glenna hears my thoughts because, as we dress, she whispers, "Maybe she'll come before we have to leave."

I'm surprised at how much like Ceilly this seems—Glenna knowing what I'm thinking. Maybe my job of making friends with her is actually working.

But the nurse doesn't come before Ceilly knocks at the door. We leave—in pouring rain under our oilcloth—without seeing Clint.

All morning, in the dark and gloom of the blustery day with the branches of the chestnut oak battering the side of the schoolhouse, I think about how different this day would feel if electric lights were shining overhead, casting a warm glow like in the magazine.

At lunch it's too stormy to go outside, so the hankie stays in my satchel. I can't sew a stitch, and I don't care a whit. I'm itchy and restless and very nearly dying to get home. I think hard on how I might make use of that restlessness. Of course, my thoughts immediately land on the other cooperative members still needed up here on Shadow Mountain, which leads me back to my newspaper idea. With Clint coming home and our hankie plan in motion to raise money for the school's membership, I reckon I can finally think about the school newspaper with a clear head. And the little spark of excitement I feel inside lets me know that it's the perfect thing to do.

I turn to Ceilly. "Today's the day, Ceilly."

"For what?"

"Why, that newspaper I've been hankering to start up," I say. "Want to start planning?"

When she yelps, "Sure!" I pull out my notebook, and we ask Miss Bentley whether we can work on a special project at the art table. Ceilly posts a sign reading DO NOT DISTURB.

We sketch out a plan for a one-page first edition. I will write the lead article for the center of the page about what electricity could mean for the families on Shadow Mountain, leaning heavily on the pictures, captions, and advertisements in that *Look* magazine Pap gave me. Ceilly will write a short article for the left-hand column of the page about the Southeast Counties Rural Electric Cooperative Corporation, reminding everyone of what was in the newspaper article Miss Bentley shared. And we speculate about asking Glenna whether she could write an article for the right-hand column describing her personal experiences of living somewhere with plentiful electricity. We decide to ponder that for a bit.

After an afternoon of studies, at last the clock reads four o'clock, and Miss Bentley sends us home in the cold, driving rain.

The dark gray sky is so low I can feel the weight of it on my shoulders, slowing me down. Wind whips wet leaves around the three of us, covering the path up the mountain. Even though we try to rush, we can't.

Three quarters of the way up, soaked through to my skin, my foot slides out from under me on a slab of shale slick with leaves. I fall—hard—and land on both knees. The rock slices them open, and blood runs down my legs. But I barely notice the pain because I'm so anxious to get home. Ceilly and Glenna lift me up, one on each side, and I hobble the rest of the way up the path.

When we finally arrive, I break away from the girls and practically throw myself through the front door, but the sofa is empty.

"Where is Clint?" I yell.

Orrin appears from under the table. He hurls himself across the room toward me, sobbing, "He didn't never come, Cora." But he stops short when he sees my dripping hair, sodden clothes, and blood-soaked socks. "Mommy!" he screams. "Cora is wet and bleedy."

Then he falls across the remaining distance anyway, grabbing me by the waist. I lean forward to pull him into the drenched skirt of my dress and pat his back.

My heart pounds as Mommy arrives downstairs carrying the lantern and Ceilly and Glenna push inside behind me, closing the door. We all four stand before her, three girls dripping puddles and one little boy standing in them.

"Where is he?" My voice rises. "Where is Clint?" I search Mommy's face for clues.

"Cora," Mommy says evenly, "be sensible. I'll get towels and dry things for you three to put on—and some salve and dressings for your knees."

My hands shake as I unwrap Orrin's arms from around me. I struggle to peel my soaked dress off my wet skin and over my head. My heart beats a rhythm: *Where is Clint? Where is Clint?*

Mommy brings Glenna's nightgown, my nightgown, and an outgrown one of mine too, along with the towels. When our skin is dried and our hair no longer dripping, Mommy silently attends to my knees. For a moment, as she bends over them, I think how lucky I am to live with the person who knows the most about healing herbs of anybody on this entire mountain. It stings when she washes the scrapes with her calendula tincture, but her healing salve soothes and makes up for the sting. She ties on bandages of cotton cloth, and my thoughts turn back to my brother.

At last, I dare to repeat the words my heart has been beating out. "Mommy, where is Clint?"

"We surely don't know," Orrin cries out before Mommy can speak. He crawls into my lap.

Mommy sinks into the big chair and motions us to sit on the floor.

I raise my eyes back to Mommy's face. There's a line of worry between her brows, and the little blood vessel on her temple that pulses when she's upset is fluttering like a hummingbird's wings.

But she looks at us sitting on the floor beneath the lantern, and says briskly, "If you were a doctor, would you let a healing boy leave his hospital bed to go out in this weather? And if you were a nurse on horseback, would you dare to ride up our path with him on your saddle?"

Still, the drumbeat of fear continues inside of me. "But Mommy, what if…"

"Cora, there are no what-ifs we can know the answer to." She leans back into the cushions and closes her eyes. Seems she is plumb worn out from talking and worrying. But then she opens her eyes and continues. "If there were news we absolutely had to have, it would have gotten delivered to our door one way or another."

She stops talking and so do I. We sit quietly as the darkness deepens outside the windows. The five of us are silent except for Orrin's leftover hiccups.

After a while, Ceilly rises to her feet next to me and leans down to lift my sleeping brother off my lap. She lays him ever so gently on the sofa in the nest of quilts Mommy prepared for Clint's return.

Watching her, I think on how lonely my ever-cheerful friend must be when she isn't here. When she is alone in her house with Great-Aunt Exie and Uncle Eben. Where she doesn't have us to love. Where she doesn't have us to love *her* either. And my heart that is already so sad and afraid slides deeper into the dark.

For a few more minutes, I hold that darkness—inside and out. Then I get up and turn up the lantern wick. It does the best it can, but it's not nearly enough.

TWENTY-SIX
Taking Up Hope

It's late and darker than dark outside when my dripping pap finally arrives home. I hear him speaking softly to Stormy as he leads him toward the barn before coming in the house. I know that he was expecting to see Clint, same as we were when we walked through that door hours ago.

He throws a questioning glance at Mommy, but she just shakes her head no. When she does, Pap's shoulders slump. He drips his way across the room toward the stairs.

"Put the stewpot back on the stove for your pap, Cora," Mommy says, as she slowly rises to follow Pap. "And for heaven's sake, keep stirring it!"

I think of the burned hem of my dress, and my bloody knees, and know Mommy thinks I am more careless than ever. I leave Ceilly and Glenna playing beanbag toss with Orrin and head to the stove.

My parents' concerned voices rumble above me, but I can't make out a word. When Pap comes downstairs in dry overalls, he sends Glenna and Ceilly upstairs to put Orrin to bed.

After they leave, he sits at the table and waits for me to carry a steaming bowl over to him.

He wraps an arm around me. "I reckon you're worrying over Clint."

My throat aches so that I can't speak. I just nod.

Pap squeezes my waist. "Cora Girl, you need to set those worries down and take up your hope instead."

I lean sideways into him.

"We all want your brother home, but we want him safe too. And as Mommy surely told you, riding up our path today wouldn't have made one lick of sense. I'm certain the doctor knew that. I'm certain the nurse knew that. And we know that too, don't we?"

I nod and he shovels several spoonfuls into his mouth before he adds, "Why, I had a terrible time riding Stormy over from Stepdown Mountain just now. Took us nigh on two hours."

Then Pap runs his big hand through my tangled curls. "I wonder whether Ceilly should stay warm and dry here in your old nightgown. Will having her here help you to wait out the hours until tomorrow when Clint comes home?"

I nod my head hard.

"Well, then, after my supper, I'll head back out on foot and hope Noah's own flood is receding. I'll tell Exie and Eben that we're keeping her."

I throw my arms around his neck. "Thanks, Pap."

He smiles. "Feels like it's been some time since you and I have talked. How are you and Ceilly keeping up with new plan-hatching?"

"Good, Pap. Mighty good. We're starting a school newspaper."

"You two have more schemes than a scurry of squirrels in fall." He chuckles. "Speaking of, with the hard frost likely to come any day, isn't it about time you and Ceilly harvested some beechnuts for us from your special tree? Otherwise, those thieving squirrels will get them all. You two ought to head out there soon."

"Maybe we can go tomorrow," I say, "once Clint is bundled up on the sofa."

I keep the hankie scheme to myself for now.

* * *

When Pap heads over to Great-Aunt Exie's, Mommy, Glenna, and Orrin are all upstairs, and Ceilly is back down with me. I slip upstairs with the lantern to get the hankie.

That's when I spot the letter. Along with the beautiful blue sweater resting under her hand, it's lying open, on top of the quilt, as though Glenna fell asleep reading it. For a moment I consider doing the right thing, but my curiosity burns too brightly for that. I slowly lift it up and read.

Dear Glenna,

My work friend Hattie came across skeins of this beautiful yarn in her mother's closet recently. She offered it to me, as her mother can no longer see well enough to knit, and she herself doesn't know how.

Every evening I've been sitting near the radio, knitting my love and thoughts of you into this sweater while I listen to my programs. I hope it will keep you warm as the autumn days grow chill there on the mountain. As much as I miss you, I am happy to know you are safe there with Mattie. I am so sorry I didn't send you away sooner, before he turned his anger on you.

As always,

Your loving Mommy

I blink back tears, and with shaking hands I set the letter on the floor next to Glenna's side of the bed where it might reasonably have fallen. Guilt burns in me, that I've read something I wasn't invited to read, but even the guilt is overshadowed by my sadness. I snatch up the hankie and head back downstairs.

I set the lantern down on the table, and we sit in its glow waiting for Pap to return. I decide not to breach Glenna's privacy any further. So, much as I want to, I don't tell Ceilly about the letter.

Instead, while we wait, I thread a needle with blue floss. Without any drawing on the rescued handkerchief to go by, I stitch scattered snowflakes, six arms each, from my imagination.

Ceilly leans over my work. She pokes me gently in the side. "Artist bones."

I shrug. "'Course, since no two snowflakes are alike, I can't go wrong."

That earns me Ceilly's bubbling laugh.

But Pap is gone so long that I have time to fill the corner of that hankie completely with falling snow before slipping back upstairs with it. I begin to worry about his safety in what's left of the storm.

Finally, when Pap stands inside the door, wet to the skin, Ceilly says, "Thank you, Mr. Tipton. You sure were gone an awful long time."

"Your aunt wanted to know all the details about Clint and the hospital," Pap says.

I interrupt. "I do too! I want to know every detail too."

"Well, Cora, perhaps we can go over those tomorrow night when your brother is home."

"Maybe I'll bring my notebook too," I say.

Pap turns back to Ceilly. "Your uncle saw me out to the porch as I was leaving."

"What did Uncle Eben want?" I interrupt.

"He inquired about my new job," Pap says. "We stood and talked a good long spell."

"What sorts of things did he ask?" I say in my best journalist's voice.

This time, he seems willing to share.

"Well, he wondered about nearly everything I've learned while working for the cooperative," Pap says. "We talked a bit about the prospects for the rural electrification cooperative way up here on Shadow Mountain. He was mighty interested in hearing about it all, Eben was."

Excitement over Uncle Eben's continued interest bubbles up my spine and into my brain. But remembering Great-Aunt Exie's dead-settedness keeps it in check. To tamp it down further, I turn my mind back to a question I haven't yet been able to answer. Once Pap sells our hankies, how will we find a way to raise the monthly payments for the school?

I sink back into the sofa to think.

"Go on and get yourselves up to bed, girls," Pap says. "Tomorrow's a big day, welcoming Clint back home."

Ceilly tugs my hand, and I resign myself to waiting for tomorrow.

TWENTY-SEVEN
A Token of Their Affection

The new morning dawns sunny, and the early light teases me awake. Glenna and Ceilly are still asleep on either side of me. I shimmy down to the bottom of the bed and slip to the window. Bluebirds swoop over the long grass, snatching up the last of the tasty bugs.

My heart soars. I'm sure as sure that the sun will dry the path enough for the nurse on horseback to ride Clint back home today. I can't wait to see their figures getting larger and larger as they ride up toward our house.

On my side of the room, I pull on my clothes, fold last night's snow-flake hankie into my pocket, and poke Ceilly awake. With my finger to my lips, I point to the stairs, and she nods.

The kitchen is warm and cozy, and it's not Mommy who's there. Instead, Pap stands at the counter, just as I hoped.

"Good morning!" Pap says. "Where's your partner?"

"Here I am!" Ceilly chirps, jumping down from the second-to-the-bottom step.

The time seems perfect, so I plunge in. "Pap, remember the idea for a school newspaper I told you about last night? Well, Ceilly and I have been doing even more plan-hatching than that."

He claps his hands once while he looks at us in turn. "Let's hear it."

I lay the completed hankie on the table.

He picks it up and turns it over. My heart thumps inside my chest.

He looks from the snowflakes on the cloth to me and then to Ceilly. "Whose stitching is this?"

"Well, Pap," I rush to say, "I stitched it, but it's not the only one. We're hoping they'll all get boughten by the men on the Stepdown Mountain crew."

He leans his head to the side as if he's asking a question.

"We're back to work trying to get three more members for the cooperative," I say. "Raising money for the school to join is still the first part of the plan."

"You mean replacing the money you raised and then gave for Clint to be treated at the hospital," Pap says softly. "I'm so thankful to you girls for that money, just when we needed it."

"We know, Mr. Tipton," Ceilly says.

"But fact is, now we have two choices. Either we need to be sure to get the five dollars you raised with those pies back into a sack for your school electricity scheme, and I'm not certain how hankies are going to do that, or we need to pay that money back to the ladies who baked those pies for the school electricity."

Ceilly's fingers graze across my arm.

"It's as though those neighbors paid Clint's hospital bill with their generosity," Pap continues. "So we owe them the value of those pies."

Ceilly turns to look me full in the face. I reckon I should have mentioned that worry to her the very first day. But it's not a problem, now that the hankies will refill the school electricity money sack.

"You two were enterprising in raising the money for the school to join," Pap says. "But it just wasn't meant to be."

"Just listen, Pap," I say. "We're not giving up, and you haven't heard about the plan for the hankies!"

Then our voices tumble over each other as we describe our thick stack—fifteen in all plus one for Mommy. We explain our pricing scheme, twenty-five cents per handkerchief times sixteen, which of course Ceilly calculates is four dollars. Only one more dollar needed for the school to join, and we'll surely raise that.

Pap stays quiet all this time.

"And who do you say will pay a quarter for these beautiful handkerchiefs?" Pap reaches out to touch a snowflake with his wide, flat pointer finger.

"Like we said—the Stepdown Mountain crew members!" I say. "It's not too much, is it?"

"Probably not, but would a delicate item such as this stand up to the rugged use those fellows would put them through?"

"They won't need them for *themselves*," I say. "They'll send them to their wives and sweethearts as a token of their affection!"

"Ahhh, a token of their affection." Pap strokes his cheek with a widespread hand, as though he were trying to hide a smile. "And I'm to bring them to their job site and collect the money?"

I grab his hand again. "Oh, Pap, *could* you?"

Ceilly rushes to add, "We'd be ever so grateful to you, Mr. Tipton."

Pap is quiet again for a long time, like he's puzzling something out. "It's more complicated than it seems, girls. I can't promise you that, not until I talk to your mommy, Cora. I promised her after the pie sale that I'd not keep such things a secret from her ever again. She is right when she says that she deserves to have a say in these matters."

My heart pounds, and an anger rises up in me as hot as the iron that scorched my dress. It fills the place in me that had begun to feel some understanding and appreciation for Mommy. I don't answer him for fear I'll say something that will make him say no right this minute.

Finally, he stands and pats my shoulder. "Let me ponder the best way to handle this."

When his last footfall sounds on the porch, I turn to Ceilly.

"She *can't* stop me. She *won't* stop me."

Ceilly opens her mouth to speak.

But I can just see her kind bones rising up. "No Ceilly, don't. She's *my* mother," I say fiercely. "And she is *not* going to stop me!"

* * *

Mommy won't hear of us staying home on Tuesday to wait for Clint, even when Glenna pleads.

She uses her firmest voice. "He'll be right here waiting when you all get home."

That adds fuel to the anger already burning inside me. I stomp out the front door and wait for Ceilly on the porch. But it's Glenna who comes out first.

"I'm sorry your mommy won't let you stay home," she says softly.

"My mother doesn't give a pickled bean what I want!" I nearly growl.

Glenna's voice is still quiet. "Maybe she does but doesn't know how to combine it with her own wants?"

I cross my arms and turn my head away, tossing over my resolve to be friendly. Why even bother to keep chasing my goals with Mommy dead set against my progress?

"Still, I am sorry." Glenna sets out down the stairs and walks across the front yard. For only a moment the words in her mommy's letter come back to mind. But it's too much to keep my cousin's concerns in mind too.

Just then, Ceilly appears next to me, holding out the pail with our lunches. "Where's Glenna?"

"Gone." I sigh.

TWENTY-EIGHT
Scheming and Dreaming

My dark mood slowly lifts throughout the day as I look forward to seeing Clint at home. Without waiting for Glenna, who is talking with Rilda in the schoolyard, Ceilly and I chase each other up the path after school under a warm sun, scattering chipmunks as we go. The ground has dried, the footing is good, and we make it faster than fast.

From down on the path, I spot Orrin perched on the top step. When he catches sight of us, he comes running. He wheels his arms as he gallops toward us.

"Clint's home! Cora, Ceilly, Clint's home!"

I grab one of Orrin's hands and Ceilly grabs the other. We swing him as high off the ground as our strength will allow without slowing our forward motion. He soars between us all the way to the steps.

When we let go, he rushes forward and then stops still at the door. He turns to us with his finger pressed to his lips. "Shhhhhhhh. Clint is mighty tired. Mommy says you should come inside on cat's paws. What *is* cat's paws?"

"Watch." I say. I tiptoe forward and nudge the door open slowly, silently. And there, right across from the door on the sofa, is Clint lying in that nest of quilts. I stop still. I draw in a breath.

His long lashes rest on very pale cheeks. His breathing is quiet and even. His burned leg, wrapped in a white bandage, rests on one of Granny's pillows. My heart swells with sadness for that poor leg but the feeling quickly turns to gladness that Clint's home.

I reach behind me and silently sweep Orrin up into my arms, squeezing him tight. He wraps his legs around me, snuggling his face into my neck. It's something that Clint would be more likely to do, but right now I imagine Orrin's heart is fixing to burst—just like mine. We steal across the room, and I let my eyes have their fill of Clint.

Mommy heaves herself up from the chair next to the sofa and heads to the stove. Then Ceilly comes close to Orrin and me. She wraps her arm around us and pulls us sideways into her. We three stand quietly like that for a good long time.

At some point, Glenna comes in on her own cat's paws. She only stops long enough to drop a soft kiss on Clint's hair. She whispers, "I'm sorry, Clint," before she heads upstairs.

When Clint finally opens his eyes, he smiles a big old smile. Mommy notices and brings him a cup of her rose-hip tea sweetened with Uncle Eben's honey, full of vitamins for healing and made from the fruit of the dog roses she grows in her herb garden. The three of us kids plop down on the floor in front of the sofa. Then Clint tells us so many things—many that we have never imagined.

His voice is halting at first. "The hospital had lights from electricity! When you sleep, they turn them off. When you wake up, they turn them on."

"How?" Orrin asks. "Do they light them with a match?"

Clint giggles. "Not a match, silly. A switch."

"What's a switch?' Orrin asks.

"It's just a knob for turning on lights!" Clint says.

"Oh Clint! What is the light like?" I ask.

"The one on the ceiling is as bright as the sun, and don't touch the bulb on the lamp. It's hot," Clint says.

"How do you know?" Orrin asks. "Did you touch it?"

"There was a lamp on the little table and I touched it twice—hot and still hot."

At that, I stop listening for a few minutes. I'm jealous that this little brother of mine got to see—and feel—electricity before I ever did. For a moment, I'm tempted to run and get my notebook and write it all down and fashion it into an article for my school newspaper. But even more important right now is just listening, and Clint's still talking.

"I slept in a bed all alone." He glances at Orrin. "I was scared to sleep without you, but the nurse showed me a trick."

Orrin bounces on the floor. "What trick?"

Clint's voice gets stronger. "The end of the bed had a crank. She could crank me up to sitting or crank me flat to lying down."

"I aim to get one of those for us," Orrin announces with a serious expression.

"I expect that would cost a lot of money, Orrin," Ceilly says.

"Well, *if* I can find some dollars...or earn some"—he pauses to look at me—"I will."

I wince. He must have overheard us when we took him to the schoolyard to start our embroidery project. I expect Mommy to scold from the stove, but she doesn't seem to have heard.

"The doctor was like Uncle Eben," Clint continues. "He had lollipops in his pocket. If I didn't pull my leg away when he took the bandages off, I could have one—every single day."

Orrin launches himself off the floor and bolts up the stairs without a word. He returns and hands Clint the lollipop he saved from Uncle Eben. "Eat this one now!"

Clint snatches the lollipop up and takes a long lick of it, his eyes squeezed shut.

I glance at Ceilly and see her taking pleasure in her connection to Uncle Eben, in Orrin's generosity, in Clint's satisfaction.

"How was the ride up the mountain with the nurse on horseback?" I ask.

"Bumpy," he says. "But she let me help her hold the reins."

Why, that boy has had a whole life full of adventures in a little less than one week's time—including electricity. I look at Orrin, up on his knees, imagining his brother's jarring horse ride all the way from the hospital and the feel of the reins that weren't Stormy's, and I realize that, for the first time in their lives, the twins have had different experiences.

I reflect on the months I've lived without Ida—well over a year's worth—growing and changing without her by my side. I'm forever different now.

We stay that way, while afternoon shadows grow longer, listening and talking. Soon we smell the sweetness of a welcome-home apple pie.

$$* * *$$

By the time Pap arrives, Mommy has gone upstairs to lie down. Orrin rushes outside again when he hears Stormy, this time to lead Pap in. Pap's nearly as lively as Orrin when the two of them bound into the room. His eyes are shining when he bends down to brush his fingers across Clint's bare toes, clean as Saturday night, on the pillow. He stops long enough to listen to Clint tell again about the horseback ride up the mountain. Then Pap heads upstairs to change clothes.

Not too much later, after I walk Ceilly out to the porch, Mommy calls down. "Cora?"

"Yes?" I call back.

"Come up here, please." Nothing in the actual words raises an alarm. But her voice surely scares me. It's as firm as a newly planted fence post and as hard as sandstone. Dread rises in me, and I drag up the stairs.

I find Mommy and Pap standing at the window in their room. I search Pap's face. His eyes look sad. They land quickly on mine before he leaves the room. Nothing good can come of Pap leaving the room.

Mommy doesn't pause for even a breath. "You'll stop this new hankie plan you and your pap have cooked up." Her voice is deep—and dark somehow. "You'll stop it *right now*."

"But Mommy, Pap says—"

"Your Pap has no more to say in this matter." Mommy reaches her hand 'round back of her waist and presses hard there. "Did you hear me? No more."

My mind scrambles to find a way around, between, through. "But Mommy—"

"Cora Mae, NO!"

My head snaps up. I've long ago grown used to Mommy's voice without the softness that I once heard there, before Ida died. But I'm alarmed to hear her shout like this.

"You will *not* take hard-earned money from the hands of our neighbors," she snarls. "Folks don't have spare change—not even a penny in these hard times—for pie or handkerchiefs or such other blame foolishness. Why, you see how often they come to our door without pennies or goods to trade for my medicines—*medicines*, Cora!"

It's like she has slapped my face, this pain of her accusing me of something I haven't done—stealing from our neighbors. I stare into her face that is red and full of accusation. Before I can protest, she's carrying on again, all the while rubbing and rubbing her back. For a moment, it occurs to me to worry about that baby.

"You're a child, Cora, but you surely aren't an infant. Think how hard we work just to raise the food we eat and to keep ourselves clean and warm and dry. Don't you dare go putting anyone in the uncomfortable position of having to say no to your begging."

"Mommy, I—"

Suddenly, Mommy swings that rubbing arm 'round front of her. She slams her palm flat on the open door.

I jump from the sheer shock of it. Her eyes on me are dark and cold.

"You listen to me, girl. I've not finished and you need to hear what I'm about to say. I *know* I can't control what our neighbors decide. If enough folks sign up for electricity, there's not a thing I can do. But *I* don't want it. I have had my fill of change. And I won't have *you* supporting it by taking hardworking Kentucky people's money."

I take a deep breath and try one last time. "But Mommy, change—"

"No, Cora! No. Every time something changes, I about lose my hold, girl. *This* is the life we are living under this roof, and you'll *stop* with your impositions and scheming and dreaming today!"

I slip around her and rush to my room. On my bed, memories of the fight we had the day I taught Glenna to make corn bread wash over me. Then, she'd shouted just as loudly, but somehow, though she stole my joy that day, she didn't steal my resolve. Now, for the first time, I'm not sure she has left me with a path forward or the will to continue treading it if it still exists.

I sob myself to sleep.

TWENTY-NINE
A New Plan

In the dawning light of Wednesday morning, I awake with the resolve I was afraid last night I'd lost forever. I dress in a hurry and slip downstairs. I plan to sneak out the door and head up to the mountain peak where I can be alone and think undisturbed.

I spot Mommy, wet strands of hair hanging in front of her eyes as she leans over a boiling pot with steam rising. Seeing her like this once flooded me with sympathy—and longing. No more. Not after last night. I've spent more than a year hoping for her to return to the Mommy I knew, but despite the glimmers of understanding and sympathy that have tickled my heart of late, now I know the truth. She is never coming back. The mother who knew me, saw me, loved me was buried with my sister.

While she's bent to her task, I tiptoe toward the door. But just then she straightens up and faces me. "You're down here early."

I freeze, trying to determine in the early light whether her eyes are still as cold as they were last night.

"The twins will be awake directly," she continues. "Until you leave for school, you keep Orrin out from underfoot and Clint comfortable on the sofa."

Of *course* she has dashed my plans for the mountain. Why would I expect anything else? "Yes, ma'am," I say in a flat voice.

I will. I will tend my brothers while I hold fast to plans to someday leave here for high school, if you by some miracle are willing to sign, or for Detroit or someplace else far, far away if you're not. I'll love those little boys with all the love you don't show us, and I'll keep them safe for now—while I'm still here.

"Cora?" Mommy snaps.

I spin around. "What?"

"I'll ask you to get rid of that attitude right now."

I say, "Yes, ma'am," and turn my back again, this time for good.

I think back on my realization that Ceilly and I are in near the same difficult situation. Ceilly's the luckier one, though. Her mother died still loving her. Great-Aunt Exie's just been a pitiful substitute.

Ceilly learned her lesson, and so will I. Don't ask. Don't expect. Don't yearn for more than is possible from Mommy.

I peek over to check on Clint on the sofa and catch sight of Glenna in the rocking chair next to him. She must have slipped downstairs while I was tangling with Mommy. I meet my cousin's eyes for a second and pause to wonder about her father. Maybe she's more like Ceilly and me than I realize. But then I look away and trudge up the stairs.

While I help Orrin into his clothes, I ponder the electricity plans I've been juggling. Mommy has stolen most all of them, from selling the hankies to finding a second cooperative member, to making sure we get connected here at our house. What's the point anymore of trying to influence other families with my newspaper? As best as I can figure, I have but two worthwhile goals left to me still—making friends with Glenna, and determining a way to leave this mountain behind while giving the twins all the love Mommy can't show them so long as I'm still here.

Orrin and I bring the Jack storybook down to the sofa just in time for Clint to open his eyes for the day. Glenna stays put to listen. Clint says he missed my singing when he was in the hospital, and Orrin claims he wants a good old tale where Jack risks his life. So I choose "Fill, Bowl, Fill," with the song we can sing while Jack takes his wild chances.

Then I eat my fried apples quickly, eyes focused down on my plate, before carrying Clint's bowl to him. I coddle him by spooning chunks into his mouth while he pretends to be a baby bird. From the table, Mommy opens her mouth to object, but I set my chin and stare right back into her eyes. She shuts her mouth again.

Ceilly raps the door in her knock-knock-tap-tap-tap rhythm, and I reflect on how she has no idea how my world has turned upside down. I dread telling her that our money-making plans are over. No handkerchief sales. No electricity at the school. No electricity up here on Shadow Mountain. All is lost—and Ceilly doesn't even know.

Glenna grabs her lunch bucket and slips out the door first. I drag my feet, not wanting to see the look of disappointment on Ceilly's face when I tell her. But when I walk outside, Glenna and Ceilly aren't waiting on the porch after all.

I check around the back of the house before I hear Ceilly's whistle. It appears to be coming from a ways down the mountain. I follow it. And there, under our beechnut tree, I find Ceilly and Glenna with their heads together. But the minute I get close, Ceilly throws her arms around me.

"Oh Cora, Glenna told me. I'm so sorry." She pats my back, and my throat swells with an ache I can't withstand.

That's when I feel Glenna nearby, her hand on my back, patting too. With Ceilly standing in front of me and Glenna behind, I'm squeezed in caring. And truly, it's just what I need on this all-is-lost day.

I give in and let my sorrow wash over me again—just as I did when I sobbed myself to sleep last night. I set to wailing.

"No, Cora, wait." Ceilly pulls back but I cling to her.

She tries again and again to interrupt, but I won't listen. I cry until I have no tears left.

Finally, the three of us collapse to sit under the tree.

I whisper, "Thank you."

Then words rush out of Ceilly as though a dam that has been fracturing for weeks has finally broken. "But Cora, Glenna has a plan! We can still get the money for the school. Every bit of it and even more than we planned. We can raise the five dollars for joining and even the three dollars for the first month's fee!"

Glenna nods.

I hiccup and wipe my eyes on the hem of my dress. "How?" I squeak. I look from my best friend to my cousin and back. They're both smiling.

"Aunt Mattie forbade you from selling the hankies to mountain folk here in Kentucky, right?" Glenna says.

I mimic Mommy in my sourest voice. "You will *not* take hard-earned money from the hands of our Kentucky neighbors."

"And we won't do that with Glenna's plan," Ceilly says.

Glenna breaks in. "*I* can sell the handkerchiefs—to people in Michigan. I bet I can sell them for fifty cents apiece up there, what with people there working in the automobile factory. That will get us the full eight dollars you need. My mommy sent me a dollar with the sweater, so I can pay the mailing costs."

"Wait," I say, digging in my satchel. "I'd kept this hankie for Mommy's birthday. It's decorated, but I can pick out the initials pretty quickly."

Ceilly looks me in the eye. "What do you want to do about that one?"

"Sell it in Michigan," I say firmly.

"Okay, I've got the other hankies with me today, so Glenna will fashion an envelope at school while you pick out those stitches. Then we'll ask Miss Bentley to mail it Special Delivery in town."

"Mail it to my best friend, Anna," Glenna adds, "with instructions."

That phrase catches me unaware. *Glenna has a best friend?* I glance at Ceilly as another thought occurs to me. *Does she miss her as much as I'd miss Ceilly if I had to live three states away—as I* will *miss Ceilly whenever I manage to leave this place and Mommy behind?*

For the first time, I really *see* Glenna.

"Thank you," I whisper. And suddenly I feel that friendship plan I've been juggling soaring high in the air—without me even trying.

THIRTY

The Editorial Team

Now that the weight of Mommy's interference has been further lifted from my shoulders with Glenna's offer to take over the hankie selling, I know exactly what I'll do next. Thanks to my cousin, there may yet be some sense to publishing our newspaper in an effort to spread the word about the advantages of electricity.

So, on the rest of the walk down to school, I fill Glenna in on my need for her to write an article about what it's like to live in a place with electricity. At first, she is nervous.

"Maybe I shouldn't. What will Aunt Mattie say if she finds out?"

"She won't necessarily find out," I say. "And besides, how could she fault you for simply reporting your experience?"

Glenna raises her eyebrows at that, and I take her point. When does Mommy ever bother to think of the plain and simple sensibleness of anything concerning electricity?

"Please, Glenna?" I say for the first time in our relationship.

"Oh, all right," she says. "I'll write it, but depending on how I feel when the time comes to publish it, I may ask for my byline to read 'Anonymous,' okay?"

Ceilly and I are both quick to agree. Though I can't think how Glenna could truly be anonymous writing about her experiences, seeing as she's the only kid around here who's ever been anywhere else.

We arrive at the schoolhouse well before the bell—time enough for us to approach Miss Bentley with the request for her to mail an envelope off to Detroit from the general store. She is quick to say yes and doesn't even ask what's in the envelope. I suspect she's so darned happy to see the three of us together that she'd agree to most anything.

After we get Miss Bentley's agreement to send our mail, Glenna heads right off to fashion an envelope for the hankies. But Ceilly and I stay at Miss Bentley's desk to break the news.

"Cora," she says. "I am so happy to see you and Ceilly and Glenna working on something together. I have been hoping you would find a way to include her."

"Then you'll be even happier about our next plan," Ceilly chirps. "It has to do with the special project we started on Monday!"

"Ah, I wondered what that Do Not Disturb sign was all about," says Miss Bentley. "What is the project?"

"I'm starting a school newspaper!" I announce.

Miss Bentley's face lights up even more. "I just *knew* you were destined to follow in Nellie Bly's footsteps, Cora! It is a pleasure to see you stretch and grow." Then she looks thoughtful. "A project like this is certain to catch the eye of the scholarship and admissions committees at the settlement school *and* give you, Ceilly, experience you can use to join the Williamsburg school newspaper if you are eventually of a mind. So, girls, how can I help?"

"For right now," I say, "could we use our reading and lunch time every day at the long table?"

"Well, of course you can. If you post a Do Not Disturb sign again, I believe it will build anticipation for your published newspaper."

"I hadn't considered telling anyone about the newspaper until we had it all written," I say.

"Why, some researchers would consider that good marketing," Miss Bentley says.

"What's marketing?" Ceilly asks.

"Basically, it is a way of informing people about a product you can supply or sell that may interest them," Miss Bentley says.

"Like the advertisements in the Louisville newspaper?" I ask.

"Precisely," she says. "Cora, I suggest you have a strategic planning meeting to discuss this marketing option after we say the Pledge this morning. Outside, if you do not mind?"

I sizzle with excitement at the phrase "strategic planning meeting," and quickly agree.

Our meeting lasts about three minutes and thirty seconds. We walk a ways from the building, so as not to be overheard, and I pose the question. "Are we in favor of announcing the newspaper to the whole school?"

"I am, except..." Ceilly pauses. "It means we have to commit to a particular date, doesn't it?"

Glenna chimes in nervously. "Do we have to tell them what we'll be writing about in this first edition?"

"Absolutely not! It's best if it's a surprise, anyway." I glance at Ceilly. "'Course we'll get it done."

We walk back inside and return to our seats. Miss Bentley looks at me with raised eyebrows. I nod.

"Class," she says. "Please put down your pencils and books for a moment. Cora has an announcement."

I stand and clear my throat. "Ceilly, Glenna, and I have a new project we'll be working on for a while at the long table."

"What is it?" Dewey shouts.

"It's a school newspaper," I announce.

"Who's writing it?" his brother asks.

Hildy snaps back at him, "Obviously, Cora is writing it, Custer."

"Not just me. Ceilly will be writing it too." I glance over at Glenna. "And Glenna is on the team as well."

Miss Bentley breaks in. "The girls and I request that you not disturb their work for the rest of this week." Then she adds, "Though I do hope that their first edition may pique your interest and, perhaps, encourage your own participation down the road. For now, please return to your studies, everyone. Cora, you and your team may begin at reading time and work through lunch each of the next three days. Will you be ready to publish on Monday?"

My heart thumps, but I nod yes.

* * *

Miraculous! That's what it is. Mommy's initials are gone from the last hankie, we have a very good start on our articles, and Miss Bentley heads off at the end of the day with an envelope addressed to Anna White in Detroit, Michigan. And Glenna even had the dollar in her pocket for the stamps.

For the first time, it seems completely natural for Ceilly, Glenna, and me to head up the mountain together. We talk excitedly about our progress on the newspaper and what it will be like to hand the full eight dollars over to Miss Bentley for the school's electricity.

"How long will it take each of you to finish a draft of your article?" I ask.

"I am aiming for tomorrow," Ceilly says. "Is that our goal, Cora?"

"My article is short," Glenna says. "So I can definitely make that deadline."

"Glenna, no! It has to fill a whole column," I say. "Besides, you're the one who has the most to say from personal experience."

"But that's the thing," Glenna says. "I don't actually know what else to write."

"Maybe ask yourself what all *does* an electrified life include?" Ceilly says.

"Well, lots of things," Glenna answers. "Light to read, or work, or *see* by, of course. But in the city, we have so many more things run by electricity than just lights. At our house, we have a washing machine that's so helpful on laundry day. Mrs. Hughes, our next-door neighbor, has an electric music-making Victrola in a wood cabinet. You plug it in, place recordings of music on round discs called records onto it, and the electricity sets them to spinning. Then a needle that travels in the spinning grooves releases the music without even need of cranking. She is now saving for an electric vacuum cleaning machine that sucks up the dirt on floors without need of a broom and dustpan. That's what Mommy and I want to get next. Oh, and my teacher even has a kettle that plugs in and boils water for her tea."

"Well, as your editor and fellow journalist, I say include all of that!"

Glenna turns quiet. "You know, though, Cora, that I'm not quite like you and Ceilly. I've told you I actually love how life is here."

"That's fine, Glenna. It's good, even. You could start your article by saying what you love about this life and then state your intention to compare it to life in Detroit."

That puts a wide grin on her face.

"By the end of our work time tomorrow, let's have revised drafts that we can swap with each other," I say. "Each of us will read the articles of the other two and make suggestions."

"Speaking of how long," Ceilly says, "how long do you think it will take Anna to sell those hankies?"

"Oh, no time at all," Glenna says. "Anna is a very persuasive girl."

"Tell us more about Anna," I say.

Glenna's smile softens. "She's just about the best friend a person could ask for. When my father would have too much to drink…" She reaches up to the cheekbone that was once traced in purple and then green and pauses. "Well, I mean, whenever I needed her, she's always been right there."

"Just like Ceilly." I smile at my own best friend.

Ceilly grins and poses in the middle of the road, fists on her hips, arms akimbo. Then she drops her arms and looks at Glenna. "You must miss her terribly."

"More than I can say," Glenna whispers.

And with that, the last little corner of my heart softens, and I know that there's no more juggling needed. Glenna isn't just my cousin. She's my friend.

✳ ✳ ✳

I slide under the covers hoping Glenna and I will talk for the first time ever in this bed. I lie waiting for her to come upstairs from the privy, pull her nightgown down over her head, and join me.

When she's settled, my first words are "I'm sorry."

"Why are you sorry?" she whispers into the darkness.

"For my selfish bones."

"Selfish bones?" she asks.

Cold tears run down both of my temples and into my ears. "Oh Glenna, I always think of what I want first, and I just can't help it, no matter how hard I try. I'm sorry for treating you so badly these last weeks."

"We each have our own burdens to carry. I bet having me here makes you miss Ida more."

For just that minute, the memory of Ida lying next to me in this bed overtakes me. The way that I always felt so protected, so safe, so loved, the way she reassured me that my different bones were *not* selfish bones. I touch my pinky to Glenna's, hoping for a dose of that kind of reassurance from my cousin.

"Glenna?" I whisper, but she doesn't answer. Her breathing is soft and steady. I fall asleep to its rhythm.

THIRTY-ONE
Nurse Bailey Comes to Call

After I score one hundred percent on the Friday spelling test, Miss Bentley gives me permission to gather Glenna and Ceilly for an extra-long work session to finalize our articles. We start by swapping them around, each of us reading the words of the other two and jotting down questions or comments for the author.

When we are done reading, I begin. "I think you've both done a good job for your very first time writing newspaper articles. Ceilly, I suggest that you expand your article a little bit beyond the contents of Jewell Roberts's article from three weeks ago. You know how she quoted Mr. Garnett Combs saying that bringing electricity to the hollers is 'an investment in possibility.' Could you write more about that? When Uncle Eben returned from his visit to Williamsburg, he told you what life was like there. Can you find some of those possibilities in what Uncle Eben saw?"

Glenna jumps in next. "I liked your article too, Ceilly. I do think, though, that you could explain the Rural Electrification Administration a bit more." She looks away for a moment, and we all remember the REA and the bee, but then she goes on. "Your article will be better than Jewell Roberts's article if you give more details."

Next, we turn to Glenna's article. "I loved reading your article, and I know all the kids will too," I say. "I like the way you list out so many of those 'modern conveniences' Mr. Combs said city folks enjoy in Miss Roberts's article. But it seems like there are only conveniences *inside* of buildings and homes. Since you started the article by talking about the quiet darkness on the mountain at night and the sounds of nature during the day, can you add some details about what electricity means *outside* in the city itself?"

Ceilly chimes in with "Everyone is going to like your article best, Glenna. I know I sure do."

Now it's my turn to listen. Glenna stays quiet so Ceilly starts in. "I don't really know too much about writing articles, but I really liked how you made sure to list all of the reasons why we really need electricity up here on Shadow Mountain. I noticed that you also included some of the reasons the ladies gave us when we were collecting pie promises, like Mrs. Hudgins saying that electric stoves have even heat in the oven."

Glenna starts softly. "Yes, it's good to quote those ladies, but maybe it's not the whole story? Like you thinking I could talk about my experiences both in the city and here on the mountain? I think Miss Bentley is right when she says that the purpose of a printed newspaper article is to *inform* the reader. And informing means you tell everything you know, both sides if there are sides. Otherwise, she says, it's an editorial."

I pause to think on the truth of that. Looking over my work, I realize that while I may have had Walter Lippman's advice for objectivity in my mind the day I was doing those interviews, I clearly didn't have it in my heart while I was writing. Otherwise, I would have done a better job of informing in the piece I wrote. I try to keep my face from showing how disappointed I am that Glenna doesn't just love my article.

"You're the editor in chief, Cora," says Ceilly, turning to Glenna. "So she can certainly publish an editorial, right?"

"Yes," Glenna says. "But do you mean to, Cora?"

I tap my pencil on the table. Of course, I didn't set out to write an editorial. Three articles—that's what we agreed to. But Ceilly makes an important point. I *can* publish an editorial in this first edition of the paper. If I do, it sounds like I won't even have to revise what I've written. But then I think of Miss Bentley wanting me to stretch and grow.

"Okay," I say. "I've got some work to do too."

Ceilly pats my arm. "Brave bones!"

✳ ✳ ✳

A warm October breeze blows through the open windows after lunch, and kids start teasing Miss Bentley about letting us go home early to enjoy the sudden return of summer. But it surprises us all—and maybe even Miss Bentley—when she agrees.

Glenna, Ceilly, and I find a horse tied to the fence out front of the house when we arrive. Orrin pops his head out the door and calls, "A nurse is here!"

We follow him inside. A tall woman in a uniform, just like the one the last nurse on horseback wore, is bending over Clint on the sofa. She turns to us and then asks Clint, "Are these your sisters?"

From his place behind the sofa, Orrin rushes to answer for Clint. "Mostly." He points at each of us in turn. "Cousin-sister Glenna. Friend-sister Ceilly. Sister-sister Cora." Then he drops below the back of the sofa again.

The nurse laughs. "I'm Nurse Bailey. Pleased to meet you three!"

I take a moment to look closely at Ceilly, hoping that Orrin's claiming her as a sister is balm to her lonely soul. And the bright and happy smile I see on her face assures me that it is, for now at least.

Mommy brings a kidney-bean-shaped metal bowl of steaming water nestled in a towel and sets it on the floor next to the nurse.

The nurse pulls out a red-and-white-striped bag from her leather satchel and removes a long, rolled bandage.

She unwraps Clint's leg and inspects it, poking around the area of the burn, but not touching it directly. Clint squeezes his eyes shut. My stomach turns sour, and I look away.

When the nurse is done cleaning the wound, applying the salve Mommy brings her, and rebandaging the leg, she talks directly to Clint. "You are a very brave boy. I'm not sure I would be as brave as you. And all of that bravery and your mother's good salve have added up to faster healing than I expected."

Orrin jumps up onto the back of the sofa. "He's brave, and I'm brave too!" He throws himself at Clint.

Mommy snaps, "You be careful of your brother, Orrin."

"I think it'll be fine now to let the boys play," Nurse Bailey says gently. "I'm giving Clint official permission to get off this sofa today." She keeps her eyes on Mommy and reaches out to touch her arm. "And how are *you* feeling, Mrs. Tipton?"

"Mighty dragged out, but I wager, now he's up and about, I'll perk up," Mommy says, with her hand on her back again, like it has been so often lately. And just like that, I'm struck with a lightning bolt of worry. I tell myself it's for the baby. But deep down I know that despite my anger and frustration with her, or maybe even because of them, my heart remains tied to this complicated mommy of mine.

At the door, the nurse tells Mommy, "Clint may be tired for many weeks still, and you'll need to keep the wounded leg clean, dry, and dressed. But I know you need no reminders. Your reputation as an herbalist is strong on this mountain, Mrs. Tipton. Why, some of the other nurses and I were talking about how we would be pleased to have a jar of your salve in each of our saddlebags. That is, if you have time to make extra before your new baby arrives." Once again, she sets her hand on Mommy's arm. "I know you'll continue to take good care of your boy. I hope you'll also take good care of yourself. I'll be back next week."

And that one comment about Mommy's salve opens my eyes, all the way, to some knowing that has been growing inside of me, behind my anger and disappointment and frustration. My mommy has a whole store of knowledge and ability for healing that I have always taken for granted, even when I have helped her to grow the herbs and find and harvest the roots for her remedies.

Then I'm struck by another bolt. Miss Bentley told me that I'd need to know botany for my exams. Starting next July, she's planning to tutor me twice a week on all those subjects I don't yet know. But all of my whole life, I've had my own personal botany tutor. I'll wager that Miss Bentley doesn't know half as much about plants and how and where they grow as Mommy does. She'd likely be the first to admit that.

Mommy may not agree with me about electricity or moving forward into a different future. She may want to stand in the way of my plans. But she carries deep and important knowledge from the past, from Granny and Granny's granny and all of the healer women in my family, probably even back as far as our early mountain settlers—and all along, she's been passing it on to me. Maybe that's an important reason she longs to protect our way of life.

I chew a bit on what I now understand, in a deeper way, of Mommy's opposition. It hasn't been comfortable hearing opinions contrary to my own, especially coming from Mommy, who's keeping me from my own wishes and desires. But as I watch Nurse Bailey ride down the mountain that Mommy is so desperate to keep unchanged, unharmed, I reckon it hasn't been comfortable for Mommy either.

And with that, I get to wondering if maybe comfort isn't always the most important thing. I surely know by now that listening with open ears, even when it causes me discomfort, helps me to see more sides of a situation. Helps me figure out what *I* think and believe. It's not always easy to take all those sides in. But my mind feels a mite bigger for trying.

As the afternoon sun heads toward the mountain, it is warm enough that I'm able to sit on the porch with the boys, waiting for Pap to ride on up while Glenna stays inside to help Mommy. I sit holding Clint, who's just so happy to be out of the house. He's wrapped in one of Granny's scrap quilts and snuggled with his back against me.

When Pap rides up the path and spots the twins out front, he shouts from atop Stormy, "There's my boys!"

Orrin charges toward him while Clint wriggles in my lap. I keep my arms locked tight, not wanting him to run on the uneven ground.

In a wink, Pap has grabbed Orrin up in one arm and walked to the porch. The next moment, he gently scoops Clint up in the other arm, quilt and all. His smile is as wide as the little boys' grins. I let out a long, slow, happy breath before I head off to tend to Stormy.

* * *

The weekend is busy, practically overrun with harvesting chores. The first killing frost isn't something anyone can predict for certain. But despite the high temperatures yesterday, Mommy knows in her bones when the freeze is getting near, and her bones are singing loud and long this weekend. We fill bushel baskets with most every tomato, green bean, butterbean, beet, carrot, pepper, pod of okra, stalk of Brussels sprouts, cob of corn, and head of cabbage, leaving the potatoes for harvesting after a hard freeze and the parsnips and turnips to winter in the ground.

The blue fall grapes are finally as sweet as ever they'll get. As a late-afternoon treat on Saturday, Pap talks Mommy into letting all four of us kids, all alone, go down the path halfway to Spruce Lick and then deep into the woods to the old clearing where the grapes grow. Pap has told us that when he was a boy, there was big competition to harvest those grapes, but now most folks have forgotten the whereabouts of the fruit.

As we enter the clearing, loaded down with empty tins and handled totes, I say, "These grape vines are the Tipton Family Secret."

"But Glenna's last name is Huffaker," Orrin says.

Clint tugs at my hand. "Can it be the Tipton *and* Huffaker Family Secret?"

"It surely can, so long as she pledges an oath of secrecy," I say smiling at my cousin.

Glenna raises her right hand. "I do so pledge."

＊＊＊

We skip Sunday services as we work from sunup to sundown getting most of the harvest into canning jars and the carrots into sand beds under the house. I volunteer to help Pap with that task so that I can ask him a few questions for revising my article.

"Pap," I begin as we dump the buckets of sand we've hauled from the creek bed into the waiting trench. "I'm revising my school newspaper article about the cooperative to make it more balanced."

"Puts me in mind of us carrying a bucket of water on each side— balance!" he says. "Always a worthy goal."

"I know some of the reasons that Mommy is against the cooperative are hers alone. She just doesn't want a single thing to change."

Pap puts down his shovel and looks me straight in the eye. "Yes, Cora, and I'll ask you to remember the reasons I explained to you that Saturday before your cousin arrived. And much as your mommy welcomed Glenna with open arms, that further change to her life and our family was just about the last one she can bear."

I listen patiently without a single argument bursting out of me. "I know, Pap. I'll try to remember. But what I really want to know is the truth about her argument—and Mrs. Strickler's and other people's too—that bringing in those power lines will destroy our whole mountain landscape. Is that *true*?"

Pap takes his time to answer. He rubs his cheek as he thinks, then dusts off the sand he's deposited there. He picks up his shovel and leans on it. "Does stringing lines harm the landscape? Yes, it does. Because trees must be harvested to make the poles. Because strips of land must be cleared to erect those poles for those wires. Because crews can't always be careful as they do their work. But does it mean that *all* of our gardens and trees and wild plants are destroyed? No. Remember, a cooperative is formed by a group of people who are members making decisions for themselves in their own best interests."

"Does Mommy know that?"

"Sometimes knowing and believing don't tread the same path, Cora, especially when other life worries weigh heavy on a person. But your mommy does have some cause for concern too, because the electric lines may well open a door for other changes. Maybe not right now and maybe not for a long time to come, but we never know the future. I can assure you, though, that this mountain will continue to offer us every bit of green and growing glory it always has, electricity or no, so long as we care for it as best as we can."

"Thanks, Pap, I'll put that in my article."

"Good! But not before you've got these carrots covered and the green beans strung and hung to dry, or your mommy will have reason enough to lay into us," he says with a smile.

When Glenna comes out to the porch after setting the jars of tomatoes to boil, she finds me with a darning needle and a bucket of beans. "You're sewing again?"

"Yep," I say, holding all the strung-up beans aloft. "See! We call them leather britches."

I wonder whether Great-Aunt Exie has Ceilly busy with a needle too and how many other classmates are home doing the same. Certainly, everyone who has a mommy with frost bones, bones that claim to know exactly what is coming.

THIRTY-TWO
Waiting for Mail

When Monday arrives, the morning air is sharp and the ground deep now with fallen leaves that release the sad perfume of autumn underfoot. But one thing isn't sad at all. Today is the day that we do what Miss Bentley calls "debut" our newspaper.

After the Pledge, Miss Bentley asks everyone to be seated, then invites Ceilly, Glenna, and me up to the front of the room to take turns reading our articles aloud from the big sheet of paper we pass back and forth.

After Ceilly reads her article about the hows of electricity coming to Shadow Mountain, Miss Bentley asks, "Are there any questions for Ceilly?"

No one raises a hand, and I hope that Ceilly doesn't feel badly about it.

"None?" Miss Bentley asks. "Ceilly, that certainly means you did a very thorough job of explaining the electric cooperatives concept. Thank you. Next, Cora will read her article."

Last night in bed, I thought I might be a bit nervous about reading it aloud, but instead I find myself calm and proud. I read through to the end, then look up.

"Questions for Cora?" Miss Bentley asks.

Custer Strickler immediately raises his hand and says, in a not-very-friendly voice, "I thought you were one hundred percent for electricity coming up here on Shadow Mountain. How come your article talks about the reasons some people, like my mommy and yours, don't want electricity? Shouldn't you just be telling us why we need it?"

I put on a smile before I answer. "I thought the same thing, Custer, and that is actually how I wrote the first draft of the article, from my personal perspective—that electricity coming here is a mighty good thing. But then my cousin"—I gesture toward Glenna—"who is a staff member of this newspaper, had some really interesting comments about what Miss Bentley calls 'impartiality in journalism.'"

I look over at our teacher, who smiles back at me. "Glenna reminded me that I was not writing an opinion piece, which is called an editorial. So, I rewrote it to show both sides of the story, which I certainly know, thanks to our mothers. But then I remembered that your mommy told me, 'We're like to lose our ability to pursue our whole way of life if those citified people get their way.' I realized that she and my mommy and the others like them are worried about who will be in charge of what life is like here. That's why I pointed out in my article that a 'cooperative' means that we—the people of Shadow Mountain—will always be in charge."

"Cora," Miss Bentley says, "that is an excellent explanation of your revision process, what necessitated it, how you revised to include the other point of view, and a further analysis of those claims. Are there other questions for Cora, or shall we move on to Glenna's article about what it is like to live with electricity?"

Unlike mine, Glenna's hands are shaking a bit as I hand her the paper. But she reads her article in a loud, clear voice. She has barely stopped speaking when Rilda has her hand up.

"Glenna," she says. "I wonder what you mean by 'streetlights' in your article? And also, can you explain what a 'streetcar' is?"

"Of course," says Glenna, flushing red. "I didn't mean to mention things you wouldn't know about without explaining what they are. I've only been here living on Shadow Mountain for three weeks today, and sometimes I forget that you haven't all lived in a city too. Streetlights are electric-powered lamps on posts along roads or streets where people are likely to be walking, like where they live or shop. At the top of the pole is a fixture that holds a lightbulb that comes on at night."

Dewey Strickler raises his hand but then shouts out before he's called on, "What happens when the lightbulb breaks?"

Glenna says, "Oh, we have a public works crew that comes out and replaces the broken or burned-out bulb."

Viney practically yells, "Burned-out! You mean there's a fire up on the pole before that?"

Glenna shakes her head. "No, no fire. There is something called a filament inside the bulb that just stops glowing, and then it is time to replace it. I don't know why we say burned-out, actually. As to streetcars, Rilda, if you've seen automobiles, or photographs of them, you know that they have rubber tires and drive anywhere they want. Well, except maybe here in the hollers."

Everyone laughs.

"Streetcars are different. They have metal wheels like a railroad car. The wheels run on metal tracks that run right down the middle of a street. The streetcar is connected up above to a wire powered by electricity. Streetcars hold lots of people, and where I live in Detroit, it is the way most people get to work in the factories and back home again."

Even though there are a few more hands raised, Miss Bentley says, "It is time for lunch, boys and girls. We shall leave the newspaper on the long table for anyone who wants to take a look. But first, can we say thank you to Cora, Glenna, and Ceilly for this wonderful first edition of the *Shadow Mountain School Gazette* and for answering our questions?"

Voices ring out from all around the schoolroom with thank-yous as we head out into the sunshine. Kids come to sit around our blanket and pepper us—especially Glenna—with more questions. As Glenna provides answers, I see kids getting more and more excited about the possibility of electricity in their own near future. Before long, many are declaring plans to tell their parents what they've learned, in hopes of convincing them to join the cooperative. When I'm not answering questions, I sit back and listen, reflecting on how well this newspaper plan of mine seems to be working.

* * *

For the entire week, Miss Bentley lets school out two hours early so we can help with putting up the harvest. She apologizes to Ceilly, Glenna, and me but tells us that for just this week we'll have to forgo our work on the next edition of the paper. I'm just as glad, as I have an idea for a special article, but I'm not sure that I can rise above my swirl of feelings to do the interview I'd need to write it.

Every day, Glenna and I hurry home from school with kitchen work foremost on our minds. We bid Ceilly goodbye at Clayton Fork as she rushes home to help Great-Aunt Exie with the same tasks. I reflect on how much lonelier her afternoons must feel than ours, now that Glenna and I are working together.

Meanwhile, we pass the full week at school without expecting mail. It'll take time for Anna to receive the letter, time for her to sell the hankies, time for her to mail the money back to us. But that doesn't stop us from worrying and wondering about all of the details. We take turns asking the same questions over and over again on our way to school.

"Do you think she got the envelope yet?"

"Did she start selling the hankies right away?"

"Is fifty cents apiece too expensive?"

"How should we give Miss Bentley the money?"

Every morning before school starts, Ceilly, Glenna, and I follow the cozy smell of woodsmoke into the schoolhouse. Every day, Miss Bentley shakes her head sadly. No mail for Glenna, in care of Miss Bentley, has arrived at the Spruce Lick general store.

But today, such a warm, sunny Friday morning that no fire is required, Miss Bentley greets us at the schoolhouse door holding a bright white store-bought envelope. She hands it to Glenna with a smile. It's much smaller than the brown homemade envelope filled with hankies that Glenna sent to Anna ten days ago. Yet there, in the upper left-hand corner, in beautiful blue script, is written "Anna White." We thank Miss Bentley and follow Glenna out to the schoolyard.

Her hands shake as she tears off the end of the envelope and tents it open. We lean over her shoulders and peer inside with her. From the edge facing us, we spot a white piece of paper wrapped around some green. Green! All three of us gasp aloud.

Glenna drops to sit on the damp ground, and we do too. She draws the paper out of the envelope, leaving the money resting inside. She opens the letter and reads aloud:

Dear Glenna,

I was so excited to get a large envelope from you. Goodness! I was surprised when I pulled out those pretty hand-stitched hankies.

Your cousin and her friend are very talented for eleven-year-olds and I imagine that they are also friendly and kind. But I sure hope that you aren't already better friends with them than you are with me—your best friend in the whole world.

I didn't have one bit of trouble selling all sixteen of those hankies. I just stood at the automobile factory gate after school for two days. Before I knew it, the hankies were gone, and the factory girls were begging for more. It almost makes me want to take up sewing myself so I could earn the money to come visit you in faraway Kentucky.

I don't see your mother very often in the neighborhood, but I did see her hurrying out of the factory gate when I was there to sell the hankies.

As for your father—

Glenna stops reading aloud, but I see her mouth moving for a few seconds, silently reading something too personal to share. Then she resumes.

I went to the bank with all of the quarters and changed them to dollar bills. I am wrapping them up in this letter. I hope that they get to you without anyone stealing them. And I hope that your school, and maybe even your aunt and uncle's house, will soon have electricity. I can imagine how a city girl like you is missing it!

> *Love,*
> *Anna*

P.S. Say hello to Cora and Ceilly even though they don't know me. And tell them how much I loved their hankies, especially the snowflake one. Maybe they could make one for me sometime? I'll save my allowance just in case.

> *Love again,*
> *Anna, your best friend in*
> *the whole world*

"What's an allowance?" I ask Glenna.

"Ummm." She ducks her head and pauses. "It's money that parents give to their children for helping around the house."

"Money?" I yelp. "For *chores*?"

Just then, the school bell rings. Glenna stuffs the letter and the envelope of money into her pocket. We run.

At lunch, we three go off by ourselves to discuss how we should proceed.

"I think it's safer to take this money home and share it with your pap first," Glenna says.

Ceilly nods. "He can advise us about what to do next to get the school directors to agree."

"Absolutely not," I say. "Mommy told me that I should forget electricity for good. And much as I don't want to upset her, I won't forget it. So let's just give Miss Bentley the money before we talk to Pap. That way, it's already in her hands before Mommy knows anything." *And I can't back out,* I add silently.

I can see that Ceilly will go along with me. But Glenna crosses her arms.

"What?" My tone with Glenna is sharp for the first time in so long.

"I'm afraid of Aunt Mattie too, Cora."

"It's *me* who has to be afraid," I say. "In fact, maybe if you tell her that your best friend Anna sold those hankies, she'll be just dandy with the eight one-dollar bills." I know, sure as anything, that this isn't true. So does Glenna.

But in the end, this is what we decide to do. We'll hand the money over to Miss Bentley and let Glenna tell Mommy the truth about the money, whenever Mommy finally hears tell of it and brings it up herself.

THIRTY-THREE
The Muck of Hopelessness

In the little time after lunch, Miss Bentley works with Hildy, Rilda, Custer, and Glenna at the big table on a kind of arithmetic she calls algebra, part of a subject she calls mathematics. I'm in no particular hurry to learn anything more about it. Meanwhile, in the front row, Ceilly and I help the youngest ones with their counting. That I can manage.

Just before the early dismissal, Miss Bentley gives us a writing assignment to complete at home, due in one week. All of us except the littlest ones in the front two rows must identify a topic that we'd like to learn more about and write a report about it. She says with all of the time we have missed for harvesting, there's just not time to complete it in class.

Of course, I immediately ask Miss Bentley if Ceilly, Glenna, and I can count the articles we'll be writing for the next edition of the newspaper, and she agrees to that plan. Best of all, we will earn extra points if we interview someone for part of our information. Ceilly is planning an article about modern transportation, including planes, of course, as well as automobiles and streetcars, now that she knows they exist, and she can interview Glenna, Miss Bentley, and Uncle Eben about them. Glenna is writing a follow-up article to her first one, this time comparing her experiences with electricity to Uncle Eben's in Williamsburg. As for me, I've still got the same idea bubbling that I've had for a few days, but my feelings about it are still complicated so I don't share it aloud.

When Miss Bentley rings the bell, Glenna locks eyes with first me and then Ceilly and nods. The other students dash out. Together, the three of us head to Miss Bentley's desk. When Miss Bentley looks up, she opens her eyes wide. "Why, what is keeping you three glued to the floorboards when harvest tasks await at home?"

Ceilly steps forward. Glenna and I move up to stand on either side. Together, we hand Miss Bentley the envelope. She opens it and shakes the eight crisp, green dollar bills onto her desk. I silently count them.

Miss Bentley wrinkles her forehead.

"It's money—for the electricity!" Glenna says.

"And this time there's enough for joining the cooperative *and* for the first month's bill," I say.

"Count it," Ceilly encourages her.

"I have counted it," Miss Bentley says. "But Cora, your pap told me about the pie money and how it went to hospital bills. Of course I understood, and so I put off my discussion with the school directors about the cooperative because I knew there was no longer any money."

I nod.

"So…how on earth did you girls manage to get the money again?"

"Glenna and her best friend Anna in Michigan helped us!" Ceilly chirps at the same time as I blurt, "Handkerchiefs!"

"Well!" Miss Bentley says, tucking the money and the envelope under a book on her desk. "Girls, do you think we can sit and talk for a few minutes more about this before you head up the mountain?" She steps to the side of her desk and reaches for my hand. We head out to the front porch, Ceilly and Glenna trailing behind us. Miss Bentley sits carefully on the edge of the porch, and we flop down on the sun-warmed earth below.

"Now tell me everything," she says, and we rush to fill in the details about what was in the big homemade envelope she mailed for Glenna and how that turned into the little envelope with eight one-dollar bills.

"Miss Bentley," I say, "now you really can have that conversation with the school directors."

"Don't you think they'll be glad to have the joining fee *and* the whole first month's payment?" Ceilly asks. "Remember, before, we only had an extra fifty cents!"

"I do think so, yes," Miss Bentley says. "But as before, girls, I cannot promise anything. You understand that, right?"

We all nod.

Miss Bentley stands up and smooths her skirt. "I will have a talk with your father, Cora, and get all of the information I need to take to the school directors. I don't know whether connecting the school, versus a private home, entails different planning or materials, for instance. Maybe he will even come with me to present the idea to them."

A wave of worry rolls through me, but then I say, "I bet he would, now that he works for the cooperative."

"Glenna," Miss Bentley says. "I am so grateful to you and your friend Anna for your part in all this. Please tell her that for me. And girls, I want you to know that it is a great privilege to have come to Shadow Mountain to be your teacher."

"And we three are so lucky to have you—and each other!" I say.

"Yes," Glenna says in a voice just above a whisper. "I am so lucky."

My heart swells with something I don't quite recognize. It feels like a mixture of pride and gratitude and something even bigger. I glance over toward Glenna, and there she is, smiling right back at me. That's when I know what it is. And I can't help myself. I give her a hug.

* * *

We chatter our way out of the schoolyard and up the path. But the glow I'm feeling doesn't last past the beechnut tree.

As we get closer to that tree, I can't help but think about the pie money we'd stored there before Clint's accident. I reflect on how glad I am that we had that money to help Clint. But that feeling is stirred into the pot that also holds my unease about Mommy finding out we've raised the money—and more—again.

I stop right below the tree, thinking hard. It takes a minute for Ceilly and Glenna to notice I'm not with them.

"Cora?" Ceilly calls to me.

I look up.

When I don't answer, the two of them circle back to me.

"You're thinking about Aunt Mattie finding out?" Glenna asks quietly.

I nod.

Ceilly chimes in. "Remember that it's Glenna who's going to tell her when the need arises."

"But *what* are you going to tell her?" My voice rises.

"You're right," Glenna says. "We should make a plan. I've been thinking I could start by telling her all the things I miss about having electricity at home, the things I put in my newspaper article. I haven't wanted to do that because it seems so ungrateful when she's given me food and shelter, and besides, she knows how I love the mountain. What do you think?"

"I already know Mommy will be dead set against every single one of those newfangled inventions. She doesn't even want a lightbulb."

"But it wouldn't hurt for Glenna to say it, would it?" Ceilly asks.

"It absolutely might. It could make her mad all over again to think of wasting all that money and, with a radio, of bringing the outside world in. No, Glenna, please don't. It's not worth it." And, I think to myself, *I don't want her* forbidding *anything else.*

Glenna ducks her head. After a minute or two, she says, "Okay, then what *should* I say?"

By now, my heart is as heavy as the willow laundry basket full of wet clothes Mommy must have carried back and forth five times today. "I don't know there's anything you *can* say that'll make her see that we've done a good thing in raising that money."

"Shall we make a plan anyway?" Glenna asks.

"Not now. Not yet. I need time to think," I say. Fact is, I'm uncertain that a useful idea will come to me anytime before I'm a fully grown woman.

THIRTY-FOUR
A Spilled Willow Basket

I trudge the rest of the way home without a word, thinking my own thoughts. Every one of them leads to dread.

I glance at Glenna. Now worry shadows her face too. Likely she is trying to imagine how to tell Mommy that she was involved in this sneaky scheme to raise money.

But I know what she doesn't know. The blame won't stick to Glenna. No. Mommy will see through it all. She'll know that the blame lies with me—my plan, my disobedience, my fault. She's going to blow up at me and me alone, and I will have to bear it with the strength of my commitment to my plans.

Of the three of us, only Ceilly has a lightness to her step. Of course, it's not her mommy or even her aunt. Ceilly isn't going to have to live with the consequences of Mommy's anger in the same way I will.

Still, how can I envy Ceilly for that now that I understand a little of how she feels being an orphan under Great-Aunt Exie's thumb? No, maybe it's Ceilly I need to learn from—to step more lightly into adversity, to be prepared to try to turn hardship into honey, as she does, in order to face the next bit of hurt.

As we climb the last rise in the path up to the house, Ceilly reaches out to take my hand. But the minute we reach our fence, I let go.

Something's not right.

The harvest having taken priority all week, Mommy had water boiling in the black kettle for laundry when we left this morning.

But I don't hear sheets snapping in the wind!

Instead, when we enter the yard, I see a spilled willow basket and wet clothes strewn on the ground beneath an empty line.

My heart starts in to pounding.

I break into a run even though I am afraid of what I'll find. Ceilly and Glenna's footsteps pound behind me as I cross the porch and fling the door open.

The downstairs is empty and cold.

I race up the stairs. Mommy's bedroom door is open, and the twins are curled in the doorway across from each other, each with a toy automobile in one hand, Clint with his thumb knuckle in his mouth.

"We were waiting for you," Orrin sobs.

I say, "Shhhhhhh," as I look past them to Mommy lying on her side on the bed, her eyes squeezed shut. As I step over the boys, I hear her soft quick pants, like a dog in summertime, but so much quieter.

I reach for her hand, and her eyelids flutter. "Mommy."

Clint whispers from the doorway. "Mommy dropped the laundry basket. She says the baby is like to come."

That can't be true! The baby's coming should be near three weeks away at least.

From behind me, Glenna and Ceilly swoop in and grab up one twin apiece. They clump down the stairs.

"Cora?" Mommy pants. Her eyes are open wide now.

"Yes, Mommy."

"Your pap...walked down to Spruce Lick...to catch a motor ride...for a meeting today. I need...you to help me...birth this baby."

She closes her eyes again and sets to panting, noisier this time.

My heart's just as loud as it can be, nearly as loud as Mommy's breaths. "I don't know how, Mommy! Maybe Glenna can do it. She's thirteen."

"Yes but...you are my—"

"I can ride for the nurse."

"No time...for that."

My mind chases around.

I search my memory from four years ago when the twins were born. Then I rush to the top of the stairs and call down, "Glenna, get the stove blazing. Set a pot of water to boil!"

When I'm back in the room, Mommy sends me to wash my hands, then, when I return, starts rattling off tasks in a raspy voice. I can tell she's rushing to get them out. She gulps a breath between each.

"Fetch two diapers...a gown, booties...a hat. Bottom...dresser drawer."

"Three baby blankets...from there too."

"Two clean sheets...from the hall shelf."

"Kitchen shears."

"Have Glenna...boil them...separate pot."

"Wrap them...clean dishcloth."

"Bring sterilized string...wrapped in brown paper...above the stove."

"Tell Ceilly...feed boys...take them home...with her."

I scurry around gathering things and passing on orders.

Each time Mommy sinks down into the deep panting, it gets louder.

For a long time, I don't have a moment to feel anything. I just do what Mommy orders me to do.

But when the orders stop, I stop too. Fear drenches me like the torrential rain did on the day Clint was due home from the hospital.

I've heard about stuck babies, babies coming the wrong direction, feet first, or with one arm down and one up. More than anything, I want to dash from the room, the house, the mountain.

I picture the nurse-midwife who came last week. She told Mommy the baby was still small and wouldn't come for a while yet. I wish she were here, with her full saddlebag of supplies, instead of me.

"Cora Mae...help me...sit up." Mommy's barking voice scares me.

I hurry to pile pillows against the wall.

I slide my arm under the shoulder that's nearest me. With the other hand, I reach over her for her other shoulder.

I feel nearly useless, tugging her.

I'm not strong enough to do it right.

Still, I move her up, inches at a time. Together, Mommy and I work to slide her back up against the wall. Somehow, we manage it.

I stand by the pillows. The lantern is on the bed table, drawn up near. But the rest of the room is mostly in late-afternoon shadows. I long for even one single lightbulb, somewhere nearby, helping me to see well enough to aid the baby's way into the world.

Mommy looks up at me and touches my cheek, and just like that my heart opens, like the evening primrose buds in her herb garden startled into bloom in the heat of August mornings. Before I can even think, I whisper, "I love you, Mommy."

"Oh, my onliest girl, stay right here and help keep my spirit hopeful."

How? My mind races to find something hopeful. Then I get a mental image of those rascally twins and how we all love them, more now than ever, since Clint's accident. And I think that living, breathing children might keep a mother hopeful.

"Imagine those twins right now with Ceilly," I say, "begging—dearly *begging*—to stay out in the near-dark and play hide-and-go-seek."

Mommy nods. Then she grasps my hand tight. She is panting hard. I wait for her to stop panting and open her eyes. Then I try again.

"They are just the sweetest boys. Why, yesterday Clint said to me, 'Cora, you are my star in the sky,' and Orrin chimed in, 'Star and moon too!'"

Mommy tries to smile but can't seem to.

"You'll rock this little one in Granny's rocker and sing—"

She interrupts me and barks, "Give me your hand. I need to push this baby out. Squeeze back as hard as you can."

And I do.

THIRTY-FIVE
Saddle Up Stormy

The baby girl comes into the world, and I catch her wet body in my open hands just the way Mommy tells me to. She lets out only one small cry. She is tiny, and so quiet. I quickly wipe her off, my fingers shaking. "Her skin is so cold, Mommy," I whisper.

"Cora, string and scissors," Mommy says. "Tie a tight knot around the baby's cord two inches from her belly and then another two more inches farther away."

I set the baby down on the sheet and tie the knots as tightly as I can.

"Hurry, cut between those two knots so I can warm her."

I'm surprised at how tough the cord is. The scissors finally slice through it.

I place the tiny body on Mommy's chest. Mommy talks softly to her. I pile blankets on top of the two of them, leaving a slice of space for air to reach the scrunchy little nose.

I rush to the top of the stairs. "Glenna, go out for more firewood. Burn the fire hotter. Heat the house up as hot as you can."

I set to cleaning up, again according to Mommy's precise instructions. After a time, Mommy encourages the baby to nurse, but maybe it's too soon. She won't latch on. Mommy tries again and again. But the baby is quiet, and the last time Mommy tries, her little head flops back.

Mommy turns to me and whispers, as if she doesn't want the baby to hear. "She's too little, Cora. Too small and too weak."

My breath stops in my chest. *What is she trying to tell me?*

"No, Mommy. She's fine. See? She's just sleeping."

"No, Cora." Mommy's voice is shaking now. "She isn't fine."

My mind buzzes, empty of ideas. Then a picture forms again of the nurses who have ridden up the mountain to us. They come from the hospital where Clint stayed, about five miles down and over.

"Mommy, I can help," I say.

"How?" she whispers, tears running down her face.

I take a deep breath, scared of the words I need to say next. "I can ride her down the mountain to the hospital."

"Oh Cora, no!" Mommy holds the baby closer. Her face is full of struggle.

"I can do it, Mommy."

"I can't let her go, Cora. It's too risky," Mommy cries.

I gaze into her eyes, feeling helpless. This is Mommy's decision alone.

Finally, she lifts her hand from where she's held it against the baby's back under the covers. That hand is soft and warm when she reaches out for mine.

She nods. "Yes. You must take her."

My heart pounds, but I nod.

✳ ✳ ✳

Glenna appears outside the bedroom door, as if she knows the moment I most need her help.

"Saddle up Stormy, right away," I say.

I go back toward Mommy's room, not sure of the next steps until I realize I will need another layer of clothes on the ride down.

I turn on my heel and head across to my room. My hands shake as I try to lift an extra sweater from the shelf, and a small pile of clothes falls to the floor. I leave them there and run back in to Mommy.

Glenna calls upstairs that Stormy is hitched up out front.

"Good. Please come up here and help me!"

Glenna stops at the door to Mommy's room. In a quivering voice she says, "How?"

I draw her into the room. "We have to hurry."

Mommy instructs us in a tired version of her no-nonsense voice. As quickly as we can, we uncover one part of the baby at a time, careful to keep the rest of her covered and touching as much of Mommy's skin as possible to keep her warm.

Finally, the baby is dressed in a knitted hat, two pairs of tiny woolen booties, and a double diaper. The rest of her soft skin is bare and touching Mommy.

"Take your shirt off, Cora," Mommy says.

I don't question her. I unbutton my sweater and then my shirt and take both off.

"Now lean over me," Mommy says. She moves the baby from her chest to mine, along with all of the extra blankets I'd piled up on them. When the baby's skin slides against mine, and I feel her heart beating as I stand, I know I will do whatever it takes.

Mommy tells Glenna how to tie the baby around me using torn strips of a sheet. This will leave both of my hands free for Stormy's reins, she says. When the baby's tied up tight, I button my blouse partway up over her and then my sweater.

Next, I try to pull the extra sweater I grabbed from the shelf over the top of the baby, me, and all of my clothes. It doesn't fit. Glenna runs back to our bedroom and returns with her blue sweater—the one her mother knit and sent to her from Michigan. She slips it over my head and tries to pull it down. Even though Glenna is bigger than I am, it is still too tight and will smother the baby.

Glenna reaches for the scissors, and I yelp, "No, Glenna!"

She ignores me and slices into the sweater. Then she pulls it down over my head and arranges it so the baby can breathe. Our eyes meet for one second.

Then Mommy interrupts. "Should I send the lantern with you?"

I look to the window and see that the daylight is nearly gone. But it's not like Mommy to ask me to decide what should happen.

"I could take the barn lantern," I say. "But I don't have an extra hand for it. Stormy and I can manage."

"Go quickly, then," Mommy says. "Glenna, can you help Cora get up on Stormy and then come stay with me? I need you to help me. It's too soon for me to be left alone."

Glenna's eyes open wide, but I can't add one more worry to my swimming brain—not even a worry about Mommy. I walk carefully down the stairs and out the door. Glenna helps me climb up with my precious bundle tied to my chest.

* * *

At first, as Stormy and I begin to pick our way down the mountain path, I hold my breath. But Stormy goes slowly. I trust his footing, but I don't trust that I've got enough time to get to the hospital. I squeeze the stirrups into his sides.

"I'm sorry, Stormy," I say. "I know you're trying to keep us safe."

He shifts into a careful trot, but I wish I were flying on Pegasus instead.

Where the path is open, it's still dusk, with a few last glimmers of daylight to help guide our way. But when we ride beneath a canopy of trees, the route becomes evening-dark. I've never ridden down the path in the dark. I remind myself that I only need to make it to the hospital. There will be someone who'll untie the baby from me and use medical knowledge to save her. I move the reins to one hand and pat the bundle on my chest with the other to calm myself, trying not to count the long minutes passing by.

Every time Stormy stumbles, I clutch both the reins and the baby tighter, terrified to lose hold of either of them.

When I hear running water up ahead, I picture the rocky stream we have to cross. Stormy steps confidently down the embankment. When we reach the streambed, I let him put his head down to look carefully at his footing. Step by cautious step, he carries us safely across.

But the embankment on the far side is much steeper. I hold the reins in my left hand. Just then, I feel the baby wriggle in her cocoon, and I worry whether she is still snug. But I have to trust that she is tied tightly and won't shift. I let go of the bundle and grab a big handful of Stormy's mane with my right hand to keep my balance. I stand in the stirrups so that I'm just above the saddle. Then I give Stormy all the slack he needs.

Twice he puts a front hoof on the slick embankment and falters. I squelch the terror I feel so that neither my horse nor the baby will sense it.

Finally, slowly, carefully, he climbs back up to solid ground.

On the far side of the stream, the high-pitched scream of a bobcat fills the night. I move the reins to my right hand and wrap my left arm tightly around the helpless baby tied to my chest. I feel her tiny heartbeat there against me. My breath comes in gasps as I urge Stormy to go faster now.

Stormy picks up his pace, and we ride down and down—off the mountain and through the hollers. As I recall the details that Pap recounted to me of the ride from there to the hospital, I also count on Stormy remembering the way.

We come to a clearing, and I remember my Papaw's words once again: *In darkness we can better see the stars.* As Stormy canters across the open expanse, I hold the reins in one hand, my other hand on the bundle on my chest. And I look up at the spangled sky, now so full of stars we three are engulfed in their magnificence. I reflect on Mommy's fears of loss, and for one moment I pray, *Please, may I have the light of electricity and this glory too.*

The path leads us back into the trees and up a steep and winding trail that gives me pause, but I keep the picture of the stars inside me until at long last, ahead, I spot several windows glowing brightly in the night. It can only be the hospital.

When we reach the front gate I lower myself carefully to the ground and tie Stormy to a hitching post. Then I rush up the five steps to the door, where I pull the bell rope several times and set up a clanging.

A tall nurse in a uniform throws the door open, and I am washed in relief. It's Clint's Nurse Bailey.

"Cora Tipton! What's wrong? Is it Clint?"

"Not Clint. It's Mommy! The baby has come, and I've got her right here." I pat the bundle on my chest. "Please, please help her."

THIRTY-SIX

A New Sister

Nurse Bailey sweeps me inside.

She pulls the door closed and draws me into a room off the foyer, closing the door behind us. The room is so bright after the dark of the night, I squint.

Quickly, Nurse Bailey lifts Glenna's sweater up over my head. The beautiful blue yarn unravels even more where Glenna sliced it open with the scissors. When I try to unbutton my own sweater, my fingers shake so hard that I can't.

"Here," says the nurse softly, "let me help you."

She loosens the blankets around my bundle and peers inside. She holds her first two fingers against the baby's neck and says, "Good, a strong pulse." Then she lifts the baby's left hand and peers at the fingernails. She nods. Finally, she circles her right thumb and pointer finger as far as they can reach around the baby's head and nods again.

She points me to a chair, then wraps two more blankets around both of us. "We'll keep that baby right there for now. Boy or girl?"

"Girl," I say. I realize for the first time with a jolt—I have a sister again.

"How is your mother?" she asks.

"I don't know!" My voice rises at the end of the sentence.

She lays her hand on my shoulder. "We'll figure that out. Did she help you tie on the baby?"

"No, Glenna did. But Mommy told Glenna what to do."

"Glenna?" she asks.

"Remember? My cousin?"

She nods. "Was there a great deal of blood?"

I remember stains on the sheet beneath Mommy and small streaks of blood on the baby's waxy skin. "Not too much."

"Oh, that's a very good sign," she says. "I'm going to send two other nurses right up to her, so you can rest easy."

She rings a bell on the wall. As we wait, I finally look around the bright room. White cupboards line the walls. On the metal counter below them sits a little steaming pitcher on some kind of metal ring. And sure enough, a lightbulb, just like the ones in the magazine, hangs from the ceiling.

Another nurse in uniform opens the door.

Nurse Bailey says, "Mattie Tipton, up Shadow Mountain. Premature delivery of infant girl. Seemingly fully coherent. No reported immediate postpartum bleeding."

"Wait," I say. "Mommy told my cousin she'd need help."

Nurse Bailey turns back to me. "That is exactly right, Cora. Your mother has had plenty of experience birthing babies." She lifts up my chin with her hand and looks into my eyes. "Nurse Clark and Nurse Robbins will soon be with your mommy, and I think she'll be just fine. Now we need to see about this baby."

"My sister," I say, and feel a little smile creep around the corners of my mouth.

A tall table in the center of the room is covered with something like a white paper sheet. It crinkles as she sets blankets down to make a nest. "You rode down the mountain?"

"Yes, on Stormy."

"How long ago do you think your sister was born?" She doesn't turn around.

My mind races to figure that out. "I . . . I don't know. I had just gotten home from school, and it was still mostly light, I think. I helped Mommy birth the baby not long after that. But then by the time I left, it was starting to get dark." The fear rising in my chest is coming out as a squeak.

She pulls a rubber bag she calls a hot water bottle from a cupboard. She unscrews its cap and pours in some hot water from the pitcher, then fills the bottle with water from a jug on the counter. She nestles it beneath the blankets on the tall table.

"This will do for now," she says quietly. "But we'll create an incubator as soon as I take a closer look at your sister."

An incubator? "What's that?" I ask.

"I'll show you soon," Nurse Bailey says, coming over to where I'm sitting. I startle and look down, realizing that I haven't heard any sounds from the baby. All the way along the ride, I'd noticed her every movement. But now, I'd forgotten to check on her the whole time the nurse was talking.

The nurse pats my shoulder and pulls the blanket farther away from the baby's face. "You've done a wonderful job keeping her safe. Now we're going to untie these sheets and put her into this little bed I have made that will keep her warm while I examine her."

I stand so that Nurse Bailey can work on the ties.

"I want you to keep her close against your skin while I untie her. And when I'm done examining her, I'm going to ask you to put her right back in the same spot. She needs the warmth from your body."

She needs me. My new little sister needs me.

When the last of the strips of cloth are untied, the nurse lifts the baby from my chest. She flings out a little arm but doesn't make any noise.

I feel cold and a little shy. I find my shirt, but even as I slide my arms into the sleeves, I know that my shivers are from more than the cool air on my skin. I leave the shirt unbuttoned, jump to my feet, and hurry over to the table.

The nurse has pulled something next to the table. It's a long pole with a metal shade, like a wide cone. Inside is a lightbulb, shining brightly down on the baby. I let out a little gasp.

"This lamp will help me see the baby clearly as I examine her," she says. "But more importantly, it will help keep her a little warmer until we can get her into an incubator."

There is that word again. But the nurse is leaning over the baby, examining her carefully, and making notes on a pad. I stand quietly at her side, but I surely wish that I had my notebook and a pencil too. Instead, I have to be satisfied with taking mental notes about all that I am seeing and hearing.

Even from where I stand, I feel the warmth from that bulb. It's as though a small sun is radiating in the darkness, warming my sister. She has her little eyes squeezed tight against the brightness. But as the nurse examines every inch of her body, I keep mine wide open.

THIRTY-SEVEN

The Incubator

At last, Nurse Bailey looks over at me. "Your sister is perfectly formed and has a strong heartbeat."

She pauses, and I drop my shoulders. "Thank you," I gasp, tears sliding down my cheeks. I had tried not to let myself feel any worry beyond her size, but now I release my hidden worries in a whoosh. I'd only thought about getting us both here safely and handing her over to someone who was smarter than me, if my sister even survived the trip. But truth told, I carried many fears for her on that ride.

"However, Cora," Nurse Bailey continues, "since she is small, regulating her temperature is a problem."

I slip my hand inside the blankets to my sister's back and feel the warmth that's coming from the bottle the nurse filled with kettle water. Now I understand what that was for. I bite my lip as she points me to the chair again. She settles the baby back on my chest. This time my hands support both the water bottle and the blankets right next to my sister's skin.

"I know it seems frightening—and it *is* serious—but it is not unusual. Premature babies, like this little one, do not have much body fat so they have a hard time staying warm enough, even when they have a hot water bottle below them, blankets all around, and someone with warm skin to rest against. So...let me show you how we can make an incubator."

She walks to a shelf against the far wall of the room and takes down an oval basket, smaller than a laundry basket and about a foot high. She lays a pillow in the bottom and then lines the sides with fluffy wool she pulls apart from a ball of what Great-Aunt Exie calls roving. On top of all that, she lays a thin blanket. I begin to understand what an incubator is—a basket for a baby.

But what Nurse Bailey does next amazes me. She goes to a cupboard and fetches several thin strips of wood, like narrow hoops of a barrel, but cut in half. She fits them into slots along the top edge of the basket, forming the beginnings of a curved roof.

Next, she turns off the electric lamp that was pointed at the table where she examined the baby, wraps the bulb in a towel, and unscrews it. Then, she removes the long cord from the lampshade and stand and reattaches the bulb to the cord, so I think maybe the cord has electricity even though she turned if off. But I'm just guessing, really.

Nurse Bailey comes to take the baby from me then. When I lift her from my chest, she lets out the tiniest little cry, like a kitten. It reaches deep into my heart, and I almost refuse to give her up.

The nurse must notice because she says, "We'll leave those two diapers on her for now. But would you care to dress her in this little garment we call a premature jacket?"

I lay the baby on my legs and tuck her tiny arms into the sleeves of the jacket, which seems to be two layers of a light fabric with a thick layer of cotton between. It has ties and a little hood. Dressing her feels a little like taking care of the twins, but because she's so little, so fragile, it feels completely different too. I whisper into her ear, "I am your sister Cora. I'm right here with you."

Nurse Bailey tucks a pad of cotton under the baby's chin and over her chest to close the gap the jacket leaves, then asks, "Would you like to put her into the incubator?"

I carry the baby over to the basket, slipping her in through one of the gaps between the bent strips. One of the strips at the edge of the gap has a clip. Nurse Bailey clips the bulb in, turns it on, and covers the whole contraption with a light blanket.

She turns to me then. "What we've learned, Cora, is that a forty-watt lightbulb radiates enough energy to keep the incubator at a constant temperature of ninety degrees. That is just right for premature babies like your sister."

I stretch my neck forward, and I'm sure I look like a cross between a goose and an owl. Finally, I chirp, "You're using electricity!"

"Yes, to make a basket that keeps a premature baby warm," she says. "That's why it's fortunate that you rode to us here."

I'm near bug-eyed with excitement when she smiles and asks, "Would you like to learn more about incubators, now that you've seen one?"

When I nod, she says, "I have just the thing for you to read later."

Just then the baby starts to fuss.

"But we have another priority right this minute," she says. "Did the baby nurse after she was born?"

"No," I say. "Mommy tried and tried but she wouldn't, and then I rode her down here."

"That's not uncommon for a premature baby. She may be crying for a little feeding soon, though."

"Oh no!" I say. "What can we do? Mommy—"

"Cora, please don't worry. Once Nurse Clark makes sure that your mother is well, she will help her to express her breast milk. Then Nurse Robbins will ride it back to us as soon as she can."

She motions me over to a big chair with tiny blue flowers on a white background. When I settle into it, I sink a bit in a very nice way.

It feels like the chair is holding me in soft arms, like Granny used to when I was small.

The nurse goes out and returns with a cup of something steamy. When I sip, I taste chamomile, teaberry, ginseng, and honey. The flavors make me think of Mommy, who grows chamomile in her own herb garden, harvests wild teaberry, digs ginseng, and trades herbs with Uncle Eben for jars of his homegrown honey.

Nurse Bailey watches as I take several large sips. Then, she hands me a magazine from a nearby shelf. The cover says *Kentucky Medical Journal*, Volume 19, November 1921. Why, it's older than I am! There is a small white card sticking out of the middle. "If you read the article I have marked titled 'Care and Feeding of Premature Infants,' you will understand even more how electricity can save lives."

My heart speeds up. "I am very interested in electricity and the electric cooperative. It's about all I think of most days."

She smiles. "Well, electricity—and light in particular—certainly helps us here at the hospital."

I pause to formulate my response. No sense in letting this nurse know about the struggles with Mommy.

"My family hasn't signed up for the cooperative yet. But my best friend and I raised enough money for our school to join. If that works, we'll only need two more members up on Shadow Mountain above the school."

"That's wonderful!" she says. "The Frontier Nursing Service is very excited about the arrival of electricity for our families."

I immediately ask, "Why?"

"Oh, there are several reasons," she says. "Electric lamps in homes don't release smoke and soot into the air, like lanterns do, so people breathe cleaner air. Lamps are also much brighter than lanterns, as you see." She motions around the room. "That means eye health is improved. And in time, we are hoping that the number of house fires will drop significantly with fewer woodstoves and open flames in fireplaces."

At the thought of fire my mind, which usually flashes to memories of Ceilly's house and parents, now includes an image of poor Clint. I long for my notebook, but I trust that I will remember all Nurse Bailey is saying, to write down when I get home.

I think so hard on what she's just said that it takes me a second to realize what Nurse Bailey is now telling me is that my work, for the moment, is done. "But for now, Cora, I'll keep watch over your sister while you go upstairs for a nice, long sleep."

"Oh no, I have to stay with the baby!" I say.

"Cora, you're exhausted. You must go upstairs to lie down."

"Mommy wouldn't approve of me leaving the baby." I know that's true.

She squeezes my hand. "I promise I'll wake you if I need any help."

I can't help but smile at the thought of me helping this grown-up who seems to know everything, so I agree. First, I walk over to the incubator and take one last peek under the canopy. I'm quietly proud of myself that I got this baby to safety and warmth.

Then Nurse Bailey leads me upstairs to a room with a hospital bed and an electric lamp on a little table nearby. I lie down on the bed and wonder if it might be the one Clint was in when he was sick, but I forget to look for a crank.

I pull out the magazine and set in to reading the article. It's not long before I'm again longing for a pencil and paper. I go back downstairs, and Nurse Bailey is more than happy to supply a sharpened pencil and many sheets of paper, along with a reminder to rest.

As I read and jot down facts and questions, I grow more and more tired but I shake myself awake and keep working. I feel a story taking shape, and as I do, I let go of my other idea for Miss Bentley's writing assignment, with all my complicated feelings that go with it, and settle into this new idea about incubators. I feel in my bones that it's going to be my very best piece of writing ever.

Finally, I slide into the comfort of the blankets and of knowing that someone else—someone very nice and very smart—is taking care of everything, and I needn't worry about a thing. I wonder if Mommy ever wishes for this. Now I truly understand how tiring it can be sometimes to have the weight of caring for others on your shoulders.

Right this minute, I'm grateful to lay my burden down.

THIRTY-EIGHT
The Interview

I must have slept the night through because it's dawn when I'm startled awake by the thin wail below me. By the time I rush into the downstairs room, Nurse Bailey is bending over the incubator. She is shush-shush-shushing my sister with a hand inside, under the canopy. The baby's cry gets louder.

Just then, Ceilly darts in from the hallway, followed by Mommy! Ceilly's cold hand grabs mine.

"Oh Cora!" she whispers, shrugging out of her coat. "You're the bravest girl in the world."

At the same time, I hear Nurse Bailey talking to Mommy. "Mrs. Tipton, it must have been a difficult trip down the mountain and across country for you so soon after giving birth." She leads her to the blue-flowered chair and says, "Let me get your baby for you right away."

Still holding hands, Ceilly and I watch as the nurse uncovers the gap in the canopy, reaches in, and lifts the baby. Ceilly squeezes my hand as Nurse Bailey hands the little bundle to my mother.

"I'm so glad you're here to feed this hungry girl in person," Nurse Bailey says.

My heart skips a beat when I spot tears streaming down Mommy's cheeks. Goodness! I had not seen her cry since we buried Ida, and now I've witnessed her tears twice in twenty-four hours.

In a moment, the baby's tiny whimpers have turned to little sounds of sucking in the silence of the room.

Nurse Bailey sets her hand on Mommy's shoulder. "As I told your exceptionally capable daughter earlier, Mrs. Tipton, your baby is perfectly formed, with a strong heartbeat. Now she only needs the warmth of the incubator."

Mommy's glance moves from the nurse to me across the room. And in that moment, I know that she sees me—really sees me. Then she turns her gaze back to my sister.

For a while the room is quiet, everyone listening to the baby's tiny gulping sounds.

The minute the baby stops making noise, Nurse Bailey swoops in and carries her back to the basket. Mommy struggles a minute getting up from the chair. But then she follows and watches the nurse tuck the baby inside and close the blanket over the top.

Mommy reaches out a finger to touch the basket and says in a quiet voice, "Tell me about this incubator."

Nurse Bailey turns and asks, "Cora, would you like to explain?"

I go to Mommy and tell her everything I learned from Nurse Bailey and from the medical journal last night too, about premature babies and how they can't regulate their temperatures. I explain how a hot water bottle doesn't give a steady, even temperature to all the air surrounding a baby. But a lightbulb radiates just the right amount of heat.

Mommy's eyes are looking straight into mine again. They are soft and warm, the way they once were, so long ago.

"Oh Cora Mae, you saved your baby sister."

I want so badly to smile and keep her gaze. I want so much to accept her praise. But I haven't earned it.

"No, not really, Mommy," I say, looking at the incubator. "The electric lightbulb in that incubator is what is saving her."

Mommy looks down at the incubator too, and I worry that she's just so tired of the word "electricity."

"Cora, your efforts last evening were heroic, as your mother points out," Nurse Bailey says, smiling. "But your daughter is also right, Mrs. Tipton. Electricity is going to keep your baby warm and healthy until her body can do its own job of that."

"I can't take her home today?" Mommy exclaims.

"Not yet," the nurse says. "We'll need to keep her here at the hospital with us until she gains some weight and is big enough to regulate her temperature outside of the incubator. That might be two weeks or so."

Mommy sucks in her breath. "Two weeks! Why, I've got the twins back home, only four years old and also needing their mommy."

"I know." The nurse pauses. "You can decide whether to stay here with us so that you can nurse the baby or whether you'd prefer to collect your milk and send it down the mountain to her."

I watch Mommy for her answer. I can usually read her face and body as well as her voice. Only this time I can't read either. She seems uncertain of what she wants. It's as though she is a new person standing here.

"Take your time," Nurse Bailey says. "Settle in for this morning, at least. You may need attending to as well, after birthing this baby and riding down the mountain. You can rest on a cot right here near little ... well, goodness, does this baby have a name?"

"No," says Mommy, "I don't believe she does, does she, Cora?"

I'm confused. How the heck would *I* know what Mommy and Pap had in mind for this new baby's name?

"Not that I know of," I say.

That's when Mommy sets her hands on my shoulders. "Cora Mae, your ride in the dark last night has, at the very least, earned you the privilege of naming this new sister of yours. I'm sure your pap will agree."

My heart starts in to pounding like a woodpecker in the spring. It's a wonder everyone doesn't notice.

✳ ✳ ✳

Nurse Bailey sets us up with ham biscuits in the upstairs room. There, Ceilly and I ponder a name for the baby as we sit atop the hospital bed. But we fail to land on the perfect one.

Suddenly, the quiet rumble of Pap's voice from the foyer below rises up to us. We hop off the bed and scramble down the stairs.

"Cora Mae Tipton, the heroine of the day," Pap says as I fling myself into his arms. "I hear you and Stormy flew down the mountain with the wings of Pegasus to save your sister!"

I don't correct him the way I corrected Mommy. He'll understand the role electricity is playing. It's enough just to be held in his warm arms.

"How'd you get here, Pap?"

"Why, I borrowed Scout from your sidekick's uncle," he says, pulling Ceilly into our hug, which feels just right to me. "I hear that you kept our twins safe and fed and happy during it all, Ceilly."

"That's usually pretty easy," Ceilly says. "But they were so excited, I couldn't get them to sleep for hours. Even in the pitch dark."

Looking serious, Pap lets us both go. "Speaking of, there may be a lot more light up on Shadow Mountain. I've got some news that will please you two planners and schemers."

"What, Pap?"

"Your Miss Bentley insisted on a meeting of the school directors last night. It seems they decided to accept eight dollars from three enterprising young ladies. They are using it to join the electric cooperative and pay the first month's bill."

That mention of *three* enterprising young ladies jolts my brain. "Pap, where's Glenna?" I hadn't thought of her since I climbed up on Stormy last night. "And Pap, I forgot all about Stormy!"

"Don't you worry about Stormy. I tended to him when I arrived. As to Glenna, your stalwart cousin is with those twin scamps. I left them climbing all over her when I headed down this way."

"Does she know about the school?" I ask.

"'Course she does!" Pap smiles. "She's near dying to talk to you both about it."

Ceilly's grin is as big as a slice of melon. She hops from foot to foot on the foyer floor.

But then I whisper, "What about Mommy?"

Pap pats my head. "Don't worry about Mommy. I'll fill her in when the baby isn't so much on her mind. I'm holding out hope she might be a bit proud of you three girls, in her own time."

"And, Miss Ceilly," Pap continues, "you'll be glad to hear that your Uncle Eben has also signed on to the cooperative!"

Ceilly's eyes grow big. "Electricity? At my place? Does Great-Aunt Exie know?"

Pap nods. "I reckon it'd be well nigh impossible to keep it from her. Eben says they have reached what he's calling a truce."

Ceilly yelps, "What in all the known world did he have to promise her to get electricity in our *house*?"

Pap chuckles. "Your uncle is a wily man. Seems he's starting with a light socket that will be installed in the *barn*."

Even though Mommy and the baby are trying to sleep right on the other side of the door, I can't help myself. When Ceilly grabs my hands in hers, we jump together and squeal until we hear the baby's cries in the other room.

We take that as an invitation to skip inside to introduce Pap to his new daughter.

✳ ✳ ✳

By the time Mommy chooses to stay at the hospital with the baby after all, I've changed my mind yet again on my homework assignment for Miss Bentley. I've decided to write *two* pieces—one for homework and a separate one I'll publish as my school newspaper article. Seems that those tangled feelings I had have loosened themselves up, here in the hospital. I just need to arrange to question an important source for the homework piece. After checking with Nurse Bailey about it, I go to speak with Pap, who's still smiling over the covered incubator.

"Pap," I explain, with Ceilly standing at my side, "I've got a report to write for Miss Bentley, and it requires an interview of Mommy."

"You don't say!" Pap says. "And what exactly are you interviewing your mommy about?"

I grin up at him. "What she knows better than anyone in these parts—herbs and plant medicine."

"That she does," he says. "But I need to head back now to relieve Glenna from care of those twins, and I also suspect Nurse Bailey has her hands full enough without the addition of another Tipton girl in this hospital."

"I asked her if I can stay just now, and she says it's fine—and Ceilly can stay too!" I crow.

"She did, did she?" he says. "And how do you plan to get home?"

"I figure Stormy and I just need to retrace our steps all the way to our front yard. And Ceilly will ride right up behind me."

233

At last, when he's sure of Nurse Bailey's consent to my plan, Pap heads out on Scout and we go upstairs to talk to Mommy.

Nurse Bailey has moved Mommy and the incubator to the room I slept in last night. She ushers us in to join them and closes the door behind her when she leaves.

"Girls," Mommy says, from the pillows she's propped up on.

"Mommy, are you sure you're not too tired for this?"

"How in blue blazes could I be too tired in this comfortable bed with this kind nurse tending to me?" she asks. "I've heard tell of people taking something called 'vacations' from city life. I wager I'm taking my own vacation right here."

Ceilly giggles and so do I.

"Mommy, we have a homework assignment to interview someone and write a report, and I would like to interview you."

I guess Pap didn't tell Mommy why I was staying, because her eyes grow round. "Interview *me*? Whatever questions can I answer for a school report? Now, before you get ahead of yourself, know that I will *not* be entertaining questions about that basket yonder," she says, pointing to the incubator across the room.

"No, Mommy, Nurse Bailey told me all about that, and I aim to write about that too, for my article in the *Shadow Mountain School Gazette*. But this report will be about you being an herbalist!"

She raises one eyebrow, but then a smile crosses her face, a smile I haven't seen for a very long time. It's the smile that I remember from before the flu, the smile she wore when she was sure that I loved her and I was sure that she loved me.

I commence to asking my questions, taking notes all the while.

THIRTY-NINE
A Beautiful Writer

After that first day, Pap goes to visit Mommy and the baby when his work schedule allows. He tells me that even though he wishes they were both home, he's glad that he and Mommy have had time for some uninterrupted discussions in her hospital room. But when I ask what all they are discussing, he says I'll have my answer in due time.

"Remember what your mommy says, Cora," he reminds me. "Patience is a virtue."

Glenna, Ceilly, and I take care of the twins after school each day while Pap is working, tucking them in on the nights that Pap is late. But what's most surprising of all, in these days Mommy is gone, is our daytime arrangement. Every school morning, Glenna and I walk up from Clayton Fork to pick up Ceilly—and drop off the twins with Great-Aunt Exie! Never in a universe's worth of stars would I have imagined her agreeing to watch over our rascally little boys. I wonder whether Great Aunt Exie is changing too, even just a hair, in the direction of genuinely generous bones, without needing to impress others in the Christian charity department.

Of course, I also never would have imagined her agreeing to electricity. Which isn't to say that she's happy about electric lights, even in the barn. I think she just realized that one area where her son does take after her is stubbornness, and he had more energy than she did for a long battle. Plus, she is saving face by not saying "over my dead body" anymore.

But it seems this generosity on Great-Aunt Exie's part, particularly where Clint and Orrin are concerned, has done something for Ceilly too. She says it's helped her to see that Great-Aunt Exie can have generous bones, and maybe even a loving bone or two, even if she doesn't express that love in ways that most people—especially Ceilly—can readily understand.

One morning, on the way to school, Ceilly tells Glenna and me that even though she vowed never, ever to pick up an embroidery needle again, she's decided to finish that God's graces sampler she'd started under Great-Aunt Exie's tutelage so long ago and gift it to her. Of course, Ceilly couldn't help but embellish the finished piece with a little monoplane, using her new stitching skills. Still, when she presented the finished sampler, Great-Aunt Exie said, "This is beautiful" and "Thank you."

"What do you suppose has come over her?" I ask.

Ceilly shakes her head. "The other night, Uncle Eben commented on how much like my mother I was starting to look. I wonder whether she's seeing the same resemblance and longing for the niece she lost to the fire."

For once, I am hopeful that Ceilly can find some feelings of comfort when she is in her home with her great-aunt. As Ceilly says, "Will wonders never cease?"

As for me, most nights I even have some quiet time near the lantern now that it's not always up in Mommy's room. I write up my reports, first the one about Mommy being an herbalist. When it's done, I ask Pap if I can take it for Mommy to read before I hand it in to Miss Bentley.

"I think we can arrange that, Cora," he says. "Will you read it to me first?"

And so we sit across from each other at Papaw's pine table, by lantern light, and I begin to read.

Mattie Tipton, Herbalist of Shadow Mountain, Kentucky

Mountain mommies grow gardens, gather eggs, put up food for winter, sew clothes, make quilts from those clothes when they get too small, knit hats and sweaters, and darn socks. They feed their families, dress their families, love their families, and keep them warm. They also come to the aid of their neighbors whenever they are needed. All of that takes a lot of hard work.

But my mommy, Matilda Nadene Tipton, isn't like every other mountain mommy. She does do every one of those things the other mothers do. But my mommy is also known as the Shadow Mountain herbalist. She learned about healing herbs and plants from her mommy, my Granny Palmer. Granny Palmer learned from her mommy, my Great-Granny Robinson, and so on and so on, back as far as anyone can remember. As my Mommy says, "Through all of those names written in the family Bible, plant knowledge has been passed down in the quiet and protected shelter of the mountain."

Mommy says, "Plant healing is a gift and a responsibility." She notes that an herbalist has to know each plant from root to leaf to blossom. Has to know which plants heal and which plants poison. Has to know when to harvest each part of each plant too. Be it digging ginseng, which my Granny Palmer called 'sang,' or harvesting her home-grown coneflower blossoms and leaves at their peak, my mommy keeps a watchful eye over all the plants on this mountain that she uses to heal, wanting no disruption to any of them. She makes teas, tonics, medicines, balms, and salves that heal the sick and wounded and revive the weary. Mommy says, "I care for the plants, for the mountain where they grow, and for the people I treat."

Nor does she sell her medicines, but gives them freely, except for sometimes an exchange of some fleece for spinning, or a jar of honey, or a small bucket of syrup boiled from the sap of someone's maple trees. She is that generous with her gift of healing. Soon even the nurses on horseback will be carrying in their saddlebags the salve she used to treat my brother Clint's badly burned leg.

I am proud to be the daughter of Mattie Tipton, herbalist of Shadow Mountain, Kentucky.

When I look up from the last line, Pap's eyes are filled with tears. He rises slowly from his seat and takes my cheeks gently in his hands. He looks straight into my eyes with his pale blue teary ones. "And I am proud to have Cora Mae Tipton, journalist of Shadow Mountain, Kentucky, as my daughter," he says. "Your mommy is too."

While Pap is visiting Uncle Eben to arrange for him to ride me over to the hospital on Scout tomorrow, I write my article on incubators for the school newspaper, using all of the notes I have transferred to my reporter's notebook. And after that, I start to work on a new birthday hankie for Mommy, made from an extra piece of cotton lawn Ceilly got from Great-Aunt Exie.

＊＊＊

When I arrive in her hospital room, Mommy is sitting with the head of the bed cranked up, nursing the baby. She looks startled to see me. I give her and the baby each a quick kiss on the forehead and then sit down to watch them from across the room. I wonder how it feels to be a newborn. I wish I could remember being held in Mommy's arms like that when I was so new.

After a while, Mommy tucks my sister back into her incubator and returns to the bed. She pats the mattress and motions me over. There isn't room next to her in the narrow bed, but I settle myself at the end, cross-legged and looking right at her.

Mommy smiles at me. "Now, Cora, tell me how you come to be visiting me today," she says in a quiet voice.

I explain about Uncle Eben riding me down on Scout. But then a sudden shyness washes over me. I look away and whisper, "I've written a report from our interview last week, and I wanted to read it to you before I hand it in."

She pauses a moment. "Why, Cora, I don't believe you've read any of your writing to me since the twins were born."

"No," I say. "Not until today."

With that, I unfold my pages and set in to reading aloud.

When I come to the end, I look up, just as I did with Pap. And like Pap's, Mommy's eyes are full of tears.

"Oh Cora, daughter of my heart, I have never been so honored in my entire life. When Miss Bentley returns it to you, promise you will give it to me to keep. I'll treasure it always."

Unsure of my voice, I just nod.

She reaches out her hand and I scoot up closer to her on the bed. She squeezes my hand, then lets go. "We've had some mighty hard times this autumn, you and me. I feel as though we've been on opposite sides of a big boulder, unable to see or hear each other clearly. But it is such deep comfort to know that you *do* see me and appreciate who I am and what I do."

"I do, Mommy. I meant that last line most of all."

Mommy sighs. "I don't suppose you've felt that way most of the weeks since the electric cooperative was announced. But I'm glad you do now."

With her fingers, Mommy worries the edge of the white woven blanket that covers her lap. "I've been in such a dark time these last months, Cora. The thought of any change has completely overwhelmed me." She pauses, then continues. "As a girl I was raised on Shadow Mountain, just like my own mommy and her mommy before her. So the mountain fills my heart with comfort and love—just the way it is. But I love it even more than most because I don't simply live there. As its herbalist, I feel I am a partner with the mountain in protecting and tending and growing its plant medicines." She looks up and meets my gaze. "Do you understand better, Cora, why I don't want to lose any of it—not the plants, not the way of life, not the mountain? And more, do you appreciate why I'm so afraid when the dark time threatens me?"

As Mommy says all this, tears slowly slide down my cheeks. And after she falls silent, they continue. Lord knows I don't have humble bones, but right this minute, I am again humbled by the responsibility she carries even as the demon-catfish threatens her too. And I am embarrassed to realize how little I have understood all of the reasons for Mommy's resistance about electricity coming to our mountain.

"I know so much more now, Mommy. Thank you for telling me," I say. But as I say those words a struggle arises within me. Should I lay down my promise to myself to bring electricity to the mountain? Should I even bother to say more?

But then Mommy says, "I'd like to hear what you have to say now, Cora. I promise I'll listen as well as you have."

I start out slowly. "Mommy, I do think I grasp more now. How the dark time makes you feel. How afraid you are of what electricity will do to your mountain—our mountain—its plants and its quiet, protected way of life. But I wonder whether we can have both, electricity *and* your plant medicine and mountain living. And whether having both might help keep the dark time away somehow."

Now I hear my voice getting a little louder and a lot more certain. "With Pap working for the cooperative, we will have his voice to speak up for where the lines should run and how much they should disrupt the mountain. And remember, in a cooperative we'd be joining with other families to make decisions. We can use our voices to make sure that we get electricity and its advantages for those of us who want them without costing you the things you are worried you'd lose. And maybe that would help keep the dark times at bay too."

Mommy sighs. "Cora Mae, my fear is awfully strong, as you well know. So I'm still not sure that I would even be willing to do what I think you're suggesting. But let me ponder all of this during these last days I'm in the hospital. Then we can talk some more when I get home."

I nod, contented that we understand each other a little better.

"For now," Mommy says, "isn't Uncle Eben waiting for you downstairs?"

I hop up. "Yes, he is. I nearly forgot!"

When I lean over to kiss her goodbye, she whispers in my ear, "Cora Mae Tipton, you are a beautiful writer."

✳ ✳ ✳

Miss Bentley is quick to mark the class's reports this week, and both Ceilly and Glenna get an A. I'm the only one who gets an A-plus— and another A-plus because I handed in both a report and an article, both chock full of quotes, from Mommy and from my conversation with Nurse Bailey. In fact, Miss Bentley calls me up to her desk the day she hands our papers back.

"Cora, would you allow me to keep your incubator report for just a little while?"

"But it's for the next issue of the school newspaper," I say.

"Perhaps you could copy it out tonight?" she asks.

"Why?"

"I would like to share it with my college friend at the *Courier-Journal* newspaper in Louisville, if you will allow me," she says.

I'm surprised that Miss Bentley hasn't ever mentioned this Louisville friend before, and can't help but wonder if the friend is a man and whether she has romantic ties to him and that's why she's kept him a secret.

For once, though, I keep my questions to myself and just say, "You may." I smile all the way back to my seat, just thinking about how lucky I am to have a teacher like her, even if she does keep secrets.

✳ ✳ ✳

Every single day on the way down to school and back up to Ceilly's, the three of us girls keep busy talking about possibilities for a third cooperative member. Electricity is within our reach—at school and even way up at Ceilly's house—if the cooperative can only find one more household to join. Trouble is, we don't have any good ideas.

"Are you sure we shouldn't talk to Aunt Mattie one more time about your house being the third member?" Glenna asks me.

"*Our* house, you mean." I poke my elbow into her side, and she smiles.

I consider whether Mommy might have changed her mind. But I say, "No, Glenna, we mustn't. All Mommy really wants right now is a healthy baby in her arms at home by lantern light. She's spoken her piece on this subject many times. I need to accept it and to respect her reasons."

That doesn't make me mad like it did in the past. I've set aside my hopes to make the Tipton house the third cooperative member.

I'll be satisfied with the light around me—especially considering some of that light would be at my own school—if we can find a final member. Knowing that I, and so many other kids, are benefiting so much...that'll be enough.

Besides, I've got a new task at hand—finding a name for my baby sister. I page through the books at school searching for an unusual name I might not have thought of yet. But each time I settle on one and get ready to announce it, it starts to feel not quite right. So I keep my silence. Ceilly and Glenna are kind enough not to pester.

Miss Bentley has promised that once the school has electricity, we can stay after school to read past dark sometimes—and for the tutoring Ceilly and I'll get starting next year. We'd need Mommy's permission, of course, and maybe she won't give it for either reading or tutoring. But if not, Ceilly, Glenna, and I'll just gather up Clint and Orrin—and maybe even the baby when she's older—and pay a visit over to Uncle Eben's barn for reading among the animals.

As for the third cooperative member, we finally decide that we'll have a lunchtime talk with the children of each school family not yet signed up, except for Dewey and Custer Strickler. We'll learn whether they've been able to open their parents' minds, even a small crack, using the information in our first newspaper issue. Then we'll go door to door to any hopeful homes to bolster the argument with the addition of Uncle Eben as an example and an impetus to change people's minds.

It's the last and only idea we have left.

FORTY
An Equal Say for All

After thirteen days, well into November, Mommy and the baby come home. We all wait on the front porch for them to come riding up the mountain with Pap. He has taken two horses—Uncle Eben's Scout, plus Stormy—down to get them. We hear them before we see them.

"Let us go! Let us go!" Orrin tugs, trying to loosen my grip on his hand.

"No. Orrin, stay put," I say. "You'll startle Scout. He doesn't know you as well as Stormy does."

When they finally come into view, Mommy is sitting sidesaddle on Stormy with the baby in a sling on her chest. Pap quickly ties Scout to the hitching post, then helps Mommy down. Finally, I let the twins loose from my grasp. They gallop off the porch yelping their hellos, hugging Mommy around the legs and jumping up to try to peek at the baby.

Ceilly and Glenna corral them while I walk with Mommy into the house. Pap and I settle Mommy on the sofa with the baby in her arms.

"Clint! Orrin!" Pap calls. "Come meet your new sister."

The boys rush inside, crowing and dragging Ceilly with them over to the sofa. Their voices tumble over each other.

"Mommy, we went to visit Great-Aunt Exie again and again and again!"

"Orrin crashed his automobile into Great-Aunt Exie's table. She scolded."

"But we remembered 'Sorry.' And then she *smiled*!"

"Yep. She has crossed teeth!"

"Uncle Eben gived me a red lollipop, and he gived Clint a green lollipop!"

"And we remembered 'Thank you!'"

"Does this baby like automobiles?"

The weight of responsibility to listen to every single one of their words lifts from me. Mommy listens to them, nodding and smiling and asking questions, and I feel like I can think my own thoughts for the first time in two weeks. Which is why I remember that Glenna hasn't met the new baby yet.

She stands quietly just inside the front door where the twins left her. My heart aches seeing her standing apart and alone.

I go to her, take her hand, and lead her to the rocker. "Come. Sit."

Then I lift the baby from Mommy and carry her to Glenna. As I lower her into Glenna's arms, I say, "Meet your new sister."

She looks up at me. "*Your* sister," she says.

Pap hears her. He clears his throat. "Glenna, your aunt Mattie and I had a letter from your mother this week. She's asked us to talk to you about staying on here on Shadow Mountain. She likes knowing you are settled—and safe."

Mommy catches my gaze and holds it a moment before she turns to Glenna and says, "Your mommy knows that I have my hands full with the new baby and these lively twins. I've told her what an enormous help you've been, what with our Ida gone..." Her voice trails off.

At almost the very same moment, both Ceilly and I cry, "Please stay!"

"This is a big decision for you, Glenna, for so many reasons," Pap says. "For one, up in Detroit, you'd have continued right on into high school nearby after finishing eighth grade. Here in the Kentucky mountains, when the time comes, you'd have to board at the settlement school."

I let out a small gasp at the mention of high school. My eyes quickly search out Ceilly's. I wonder if her heart is pounding as hard as mine.

Pap hears and gives me the tiniest wink. "Cora, what with your A-pluses on herbalist and incubator reporting, your mommy and I have discussed whether your cousin might need time to consider whether she'll *precede* you to the high school."

I can't hold down my squeal at this news.

That's when Clint pipes up, "Sister-cousin, you mean!"

"Right, young man. Sister-cousin." Pap ruffles his hair. "So, daughter-niece, I recommend that you take the time you need to decide."

Ceilly pipes up. "But don't keep us waiting too long."

And right then and there, I determine to enlist Pap to help Uncle Eben overcome Great-Aunt Exie's resistance to high school in Williamsburg for Ceilly. To help Uncle Eben realize his own dream *through* Ceilly. My parents have just given me the greatest chance yet for my dreams to come true. I want Ceilly to have that same feeling of an opportunity waiting.

Glenna stands up from the rocker and motions me to sit down. "Why don't *you* rock her for just a few minutes?" She puts the baby in my lap.

Then Mommy and Pap come to stand right close to one another behind the rocker. They call Clint and Orrin and Ceilly and Glenna to gather 'round too.

"There's one other decision that needs to be made in this family," Mommy says. "And everyone needs to have an equal say."

"Could be this will be a tough one," Pap says, rubbing his cheek. "So listen closely, and carefully consider your opinion."

I tip my head back to glance up at him, and catch a twinkle in his eye and a lopsided grin.

The twins start hopping up and down, chanting "What? What?"

"As you know," Pap begins again, "our electric cooperative needs but one more member to join."

I sit up straight and look right at Mommy. She's looking back at me. She's not smiling, but her eyes are soft. "Given as how," she says, "with Cora's brave help, it was *electricity* that saved the life of our new baby..."

"...we were wondering," Pap says, "whether any of you might think the Tipton household should be that final cooperative member needed."

We hardly let him finish before we set into a chorus of "Yes! Yes! Yes!" which wakes the baby, who lets out a cry.

"Well," Pap says, looking down at the baby, "looks like it's unanimous."

In that moment, the love in my heart feels as vast and shining as the starry heavens. And that is when I know. The voice inside is as clear as the baby's little cry.

"I've made a decision too," I say, as I look right down into my sister's face. "This little baby's name is..." I glance around at each member of my family. "Radiance Grace."

The boys set to chanting "Radiance Grace! Radiance Grace!"

Mommy moves to where I can easily see her. A big smile lights up her face as she looks deep into my eyes and holds my gaze.

Finally, she reaches to rest her hand on the tiny head. "Radiance Grace, may you grow up to be as brave, and as strong, and as *generous* as your big sister—who is bringing light to Shadow Mountain."

FORTY-ONE
A Forty-Watt Lightbulb

The late-November wind whips my curls as it chases me up the path that leads to the peak of Shadow Mountain. It's been a good long while since I've had a moment to head off here alone. But today, I find myself with time that's my very own. And I am in possession of a newspaper clipping that's like to burn a hole in my pocket.

Down below, Pap is hard at work chopping winter wood, while the twins help Glenna stack it. Mommy, who shooed me out of the house to tread this path, has soup beans simmering on the stove with Radiance tied to her chest. Ceilly is with Uncle Eben today, putting the bees to bed for winter and conspiring to get Great-Aunt Exie to open her heart to electricity *inside* the house—and maybe even to high school in Williamsburg.

As I settle on a sun-warmed rock in the clearing, it fills me with comfort to know everything that is unfolding below. Still, it's exciting too, to ponder all of the changes ahead.

I gaze out over the neighboring mountains and the beautiful vista that surrounds my mountain home. I think upon the transformations this fall has wrought, in me, in my family, in these mountains. Then I reach into my pocket and pull out the clipping Miss Bentley handed me yesterday with a smile brighter than a forty-watt bulb. And I start to read.

THE COURIER-JOURNAL

November 12, 1937

Opinion: Electricity Saves Lives

By Cora Mae Tipton

Electricity saved the life of a baby born on Shadow Mountain on October 29, 1937. I know this because that baby, Radiance Grace Tipton, is my newborn sister.

Only one year ago President Roosevelt signed the Rural Electrification Act into law because he knew that those of us living in the mountains and other rural places in America were living in more darkness than most of America. But what even President Roosevelt may not have known is that electricity would do more than take away that darkness.

My baby sister, Radiance Grace, was born late on a dark and cold October afternoon at our home on Shadow Mountain, three weeks earlier than we expected her. She was tiny and very weak. As hard as my mommy tried, she couldn't get Radiance warm, and the baby wouldn't eat. That's when I knew I'd have to ride my sister down Shadow Mountain on horseback—and all the way to the hospital—to get help.

Shadow Mountain does not have electric lines, but luckily the hospital does. The staff member on duty at the hospital that night, Nurse Florence Bailey, kept Radiance warm in an incubator—"an incubator that could only be made with an electric lightbulb," she said. As Nurse Bailey explained to me, "The biggest challenge for babies born early is regulating their temperature." The problem is, those babies just don't have

ENOUGH BODY FAT TO KEEP THEM WARM. BUT ELECTRICITY CAN DO THAT WARMING FOR THEM!

HERE'S HOW: LINE A LOW BASKET WITH BLANKETS AND WOOL ROVING. FIT WOOD STRIPS INTO THE TOP EDGE OF THE BASKET TO MAKE A CURVED FRAME OVER THE TOP. CLIP A FORTY-WATT LIGHTBULB TO THIS FRAME. COVER THE WHOLE FRAME WITH A LIGHT BLANKET TO CREATE A CANOPY. "THAT LIGHT WILL BE STEADY, RELIABLE, AND SAFE," NURSE BAILEY SAYS. KEEP THE BABY IN THE INCUBATOR AS MUCH AS POSSIBLE WHEN NOT FEEDING UNTIL SHE GAINS A SATISFACTORY AMOUNT OF WEIGHT.

FOR ANYONE PONDERING A MEMBERSHIP IN AN ELECTRIC COOPERATIVE, THE COST IS $5. THEN EVERY MONTH THEREAFTER THERE IS A $3 FEE. AS EXPENSIVE AS THAT SEEMS, IT'S NOT VERY MUCH TO SAVE THE LIFE OF A BABY!

———————

AUTHOR'S NOTE

Cora's story came to me down a long and winding road of discovery that I didn't, at first, realize I'd set my foot upon. More than two decades ago, I was working as a school librarian when Rosemary Wells's book *Mary on Horseback* fell into my possession. Oh, how I loved that lyrical book with its musical language and stories based on the life of nurse-midwife Mary Breckinridge. I learned about the important work that Mary did in the mountains of Eastern Kentucky establishing the Frontier Nursing Service. The FNS brought professional medical services to so many people who had none, while also incorporating and respecting the importance of the natural folk and herbal medicines that were widely used in those mountains.

My long-standing interests in nurse midwifery and herbal medicine added to my excitement in learning about Mary Breckinridge. After reading her autobiography, *Wide Neighborhoods: A Story of the Frontier Nursing Service*, I felt compelled to discover even more, and over the next dozen years I became convinced that I would someday write a book featuring the nurses of the FNS.

Three years after *Mary on Horseback* was published, Kathi Appelt and Jeanne Cannella Schmitzer published *Down Cut Shin Creek*, about the intrepid librarians of the Pack Horse Library Project who delivered books to the homes and one-room schoolhouses scattered across the mountains of Eastern Kentucky. When I was young, my own neighborhood was served by a bookmobile, so I had a personal appreciation for the magic of book delivery. And now, as a librarian myself, my heart raced to learn these pack horse librarians were traversing the same mountains during some of the same years as the nurses of the FNS. I set out to learn more about this brilliant service.

As I researched both the nurses of the FNS and the PHLP librarians, I became aware of a fact that startled me. Until 1937, residents of Eastern Kentucky did not have electricity, although most of the country had been electrified some decades before. As I dug further, I learned about the law President Franklin D. Roosevelt signed creating the Rural Electrification Administration in 1935 to bring power to rural areas of the United States. By 1937, the first pole in Eastern Kentucky was raised by a rural electric cooperative, the start of many years of bringing electricity to those mountains.

Now I had three essential historical elements of the story I'd grown committed to writing. As I continued to learn more about each, I spent as much time as possible immersing myself in the world of 1937 Eastern Kentucky in books and film. This was the home of Cora Mae Tipton, the feisty young heroine who emerged as the main character of a picture-book manuscript I wrote in 2011. My wise editor, Kelly Loughman, suggested that Cora's story needed room to grow, that it was not picture-book-sized, but novel-sized. And as you see here, she was entirely right!

I began to imagine a time, three-and-a-half decades into the twentieth century, when rural Kentuckians like Cora lived without electricity. Even though cities were bright with lights and modernized in so many ways, Cora, her family, and her neighbors lived differently. I knew that once a child was exposed to the idea of electrified life, as Cora was in the newspaper article Miss Bentley shared and the *Life* magazine Pap brought home, she would spin dreams of what her own life with electricity might be like.

And I knew something else about Cora. I knew that she would have strength, will, and resolve in the face of her mother's opposition, but also acquire a willingness to listen, allowing both Mommy and Cora to benefit from the light they create through mutual understanding.

Cora's power to stand for what she believes in, while learning to truly listen to other points of view, and her mother's willingness, in the end, to acknowledge her daughter's wisdom are all important aspects of the story. I wanted to model for my readers what isn't always true in childhood: that children can have independent ideas, different from those of their parents, and that they can make a difference in their world by exploring those ideas and working to bring them to fruition, particularly if they have the support of loving adults to guide them in their pursuits. In this regard, Cora is the child I wish that all children might be.

MORE TO KNOW

What was the Frontier Nursing Service?

Before 1925, when nurse-midwife Mary Breckinridge started the Frontier Nursing Service in the isolated mountains of southeastern Kentucky, there were no trained nurses or doctors nearby. But by 1928, Breckinridge had ordered and overseen the construction of the very first hospital in the area, Hyden Hospital and Health Center, in Hyden, Kentucky (the hospital upon which the one in this story is modeled). The hospital and the brigade of horseback-riding FNS nurses, like Nurse Bailey who comes to tend to Clint after his hospital stay, supplied rural mountain communities scattered over seven hundred square miles with trained nurse-midwives. The nurses worked alone, attending births and providing general health care that had been lacking in the region until then. They visited remote cabins carrying saddlebags packed with all the medical supplies they needed to help deliver babies or care for sick or injured patients like Clint. While the nurses brought modern medicines and techniques with them, they also honored the knowledge of wise herbalists, like Cora's mommy, who cared for their families and neighbors with plant medicines.

If you're interested in learning more about the Frontier Nursing Service, read *Mary on Horseback: Three Mountain Stories* by Rosemary Wells (Dial Books for Young Readers, 1998). You might also want to listen to some of the 212 audio interviews in the Frontier Nursing Service Oral History Project (over 100 of them with nurses themselves) at https://

kentuckyoralhistory.org/ark:/16417/xt7kwh2dbt7n or enjoy watching the film *Angels on Horseback: Midwives in the Mountains* at https://www.pbs .org/video/angels-on-horseback-midwives-in-the-mountains-qqr9tt.

What is herbal and plant medicine?

Medicines made from plants, particularly herbs, that are used to treat diseases and injuries or to keep people healthy are called herbal medicines. These plant medicines can be used on the outside of the body, like Mommy's healing salve when Clint is burned, or inside the body, like Mommy's feverfew tincture when Clint develops an infection resulting in a fever. The plants used in herbal medicines may be grown specifically for that purpose, as Mommy does, or harvested in nature, as Cora helps Mommy to do. Herbalists like Mommy are people who have studied the medicinal uses of plants and their preparation. Often, in the isolated mountains, this knowledge was passed down from generation to generation of herbal healers, as in Mommy's family.

If you'd like to learn more about herbal medicine and even try concocting a few remedies of your own, read *A Kid's Herb Book: For Children of All Ages* by Lesley Tierra (Robert D. Reed Publishers, 2018). And for even more fun, visit Herbal Roots zine, an online publication and learning center dedicated to kid-friendly herbal learning at https:// herbalrootszine.org.

What was the Pack Horse Library Project?

The Pack Horse Library Project was an amazing service of the federal government's Works Progress Administration from 1935 until 1943.

Over those nine years, the librarians (often called "book women"), horses, and books of the project reached one and a half million people in rural Eastern Kentucky. While early Depression-era WPA projects employed men like Cora's pap in heavy manual labor constructing roads, parks, schools, and buildings, the PHLP primarily employed women in forty-eight Kentucky counties to deliver books! But their work too, was hardly easy. These PHLP librarians—nearly a thousand of them—rode their own personal or borrowed horses or mules from a headquarters library up steep mountain trails and across streams, as far as eighteen miles a day, to schoolhouses, post offices, community centers, and individual homes. Books and magazines that the librarians carried—one and a half million by the end of the program—were donated through PTAs and were also purchased new through donations to a Penny Fund Plan. The PHLP ended in 1943, but not long afterward, bookmobiles like the one I visited as a child were rolling on the roads of Kentucky.

You can learn much more about the PHLP and its librarians in the same nonfiction book where I first encountered them: *Down Cut Shin Creek: The Pack Horse Librarians of Kentucky* by Kathi Appelt and Jeanne Cannella Schmitzer (HarperCollins, 2001). You might also enjoy two fictional picture-book stories of children who got books from the book women: *Books by Horseback: A Librarian's Brave Journey to Deliver Books to Children* by Emma Carlson Berne (Little Bee Books, 2021) and *That Book Woman* by Heather Henson (Atheneum, 2008). And if you'd enjoy a listening experience, tune in to *The Pack Horse Librarians of Eastern Kentucky,* which features Kathi Appelt, Jeanne Cannella Schmitzer, and Heather Henson, at https://www.npr.org/2018/09/13/647329067/the-pack-horse-librarians-of-eastern-kentucky.

What was the Rural Electrification Administration?

In 1935, only ten percent of farms in the United States had electricity. This was at a time when the cities of America were completely electrified. But ten years later, nearly all of the farms were too. How did that happen? To begin, on May 11, 1935, President Franklin Delano Roosevelt signed an executive order creating the Rural Electrification Administration (REA). Then, in 1936, Congress followed up by passing the Rural Electrification Act, which was signed into law on May 20, 1936. Under the REA, the federal government made low-cost loans to groups of farmers for the formation of rural electric cooperatives like the one Cora's family joins. Over time, many Kentuckians, like the families on Shadow Mountain, banded together to form twenty-six electric cooperatives. Over the next decade, these cooperatives changed rural Kentucky forever, providing electricity for girls like Cora Mae Tipton to read by, study by, and stitch by, and enabling adults like Mommy and Pap to use modern electric appliances such as refrigerators, washing machines, electric irons, and radios.

To learn a bit more about electric cooperatives, both how they began and how they continue to run, check out the video *The Electric Cooperative Story* at https://www.electric.coop/our-organization/history.

What was a settlement school?

Settlement schools were first established in Eastern Kentucky in the early 1900s with the purpose of educating students who had no access to local schools. Over time, some settlement schools became boarding high schools for students like Cora, who had no local option to continue their schooling after eighth grade. Settlement schools gave students educational opportunities they might not otherwise have had. The schools were largely started, staffed, and managed by young, educated women from central Kentucky as well as from farther away in New England. The campuses first included schoolrooms for learning and dormitories for housing the many boarding students. In time, they grew to include extensive gardens and dairies for raising much of their own food and even workshops for making their own furniture. Some schools also started health clinics, shops for selling traditional local arts and crafts, and cooperative stores.

To learn more about settlement schools, watch the documentary film *Settlement Schools of Appalachia* at https://education.ket.org/resources/settlement-schools-appalachia.

Is Shadow Mountain a real place?

No. As so many historical fiction authors do, I created Shadow Mountain and the little town of Spruce Lick based on many such lovely places in Eastern Kentucky.

Is the *Life* magazine Pap brought Cora a real issue?

While the issue of *Life* that Pap brings home to Cora is not an actual issue, *Life* magazine was a reading staple for many households for decades. As a child I regularly read my parents' issues of *Life,* learning about important topics of the day through its photographs and brief text. When I thought about how Cora might first encounter information about modern schools, I imagined her reading an issue of *Life* too.

You can visit the *Life* website at life.com to see its many photographs categorized by subject.

Was there an actual "eye health study," like the one Cora worries about?

Yes! A study titled "School Illumination" was published by the American Educational Research Association in October 1938. The study emphasized the importance of adequate school lighting to health and made specific recommendations for the amount and type of light required in various rooms. I took a bit of liberty in having Cora encounter this information a year earlier in *Life* magazine.

Is the article Nurse Bailey gives to Cora about incubators a real article?

Yes again! Dr. James W. Bruce published an article titled "Care and Feeding of Premature Infants" in the November 1921 issue of the *Kentucky Medical Journal*. Dr. Bruce didn't note who first constructed a makeshift incubator, using a forty-watt lightbulb to maintain a consistent temperature for babies born before their due dates, nor did he credit the inventor of the "premature jackets" used to keep those babies warm, but he did advocate for the use of both.

Who made up the songs and chants in the book?

The songs and chants in this novel are all traditional and authentic to Eastern Kentucky, where music has long been a vital part of daily life. Many are traceable to their English, Scottish, or Irish sources. If you'd like to hear these songs performed, simply enter the title (in quotes) at youtube.com. For the musical scores and lyrics of "Pretty Polly," "Noah's Ark," and eighteen other traditional tunes, check out *Twenty Kentucky Mountain Songs*, collected and arranged by Loraine Wyman and Howard Brockway.

ACKNOWLEDGMENTS

The lights on Shadow Mountain might never have been illuminated were it not for my editor, Kelly Loughman, who, like Cora, practices the magic art of seeing "what could be" in "what is." Not only did Kelly steer me to the novel form when my way was dimly lit by lantern light, but she shone her own steady light deeply and thoughtfully upon every character and event in the book, helping me to locate the truth in each. For that, I thank her and Holiday House editor in chief Mary Cash, as well as associate editor Della Farrell, who supported the journey Kelly and I were on.

Like most writers, I do not always write in isolation, and so across many years I have had support, critiques, and endless rereadings of this novel from many other writers. Foremost among them have been members of my critique groups. In Maine, my dear partners, Cynthia Lord and Terry Farish, read drafts and gave input on the early picture-book manuscript. Thereafter, Florida Writer Babes Dianne Ochiltree, Linda Shute, and Sara Pennypacker read chapter after chapter of my early attempts at the novel with patience and wisdom and guided me toward this finished work.

In Massachusetts, Hive Mind members, Alison Goldberg, Ellen Mayer, Heather Lang, Jane Sutton, and Sara Levine also lavished years of attention and careful scrutiny on each chapter. I extend extra thanks to Kerry Madden for reading the picture-book version and Dorian Cirrone, Erin Dionne, and Sara Pennypacker for full novel manuscript readings at crucial times.

Retreats are this writer's salvation—time away to focus on the work. In fact, I started the picture-book manuscript and its research at

Kindling Words West in Taos in 2011. I also turned to my autumn High Test Girls retreat group, Franny Billingsley, Jacqueline Briggs Martin, Jane Kurtz, and Nancy Werlin, year after year. Since then, I've attended many retreats with a host of writers, particularly Swinger of Birches on Lake Champlain and both the Breakout Novel Intensive and the Breakout Novel Graduate Learning Retreat with Brenda Windberg, Donald Maass, Henry Neff, Lorin Oberweger, and Veronica Rossi, all of whom offered timely and invaluable developmental input. Finally, both Dorian Cirrone and Kathy MacDonald deserve medals for critiquing and moral support both at the Break Out Novel retreats and throughout the process of finding my way through to the end.

For additional support—practical, literary, and emotional—"Mildest" group members Ammi-Joan Paquette, Diana Renn, Erin Dionne, Jacqueline Davies, Julie Berry, Kim Harrington, Loree Griffin Burns, and Nancy Werlin stood by me when, in grief, I could not write a word and also when I first managed to commit words to the page once again. They are with me still.

My research files for this book stretch all the way back to May 2011, and thus I have many people to thank for the information, wisdom, and experience they lent me. It is all reflected in the pages of this book. Any errors in accuracy are strictly my own.

Angelica Estrada and Dr. Karin Molander of the Sepsis Alliance helped me to understand the enormous threat of sepsis and how it might have taken Clint's life without help from the FNS nurse on horseback and the Hyden Hospital. And Dr. Tammy Horn Potter, the Kentucky state apiarist, answered my questions about Uncle Eben's beekeeping and honey harvesting in early twentieth-century Kentucky.

I am exceedingly grateful to Rick Childers of the Loyal Jones Appalachian Center at Berea College for his careful reading of the novel. And both Dr. Jennifer Cramer, associate professor and chair of the Department of Linguistics at the University of Kentucky, and Phoenicia Miracle, principal of Miracle Strategies Fundraising and Marketing, provided excellent guidance about the geography of hollers.

As a librarian myself, I always go to libraries and librarians as my initial research sources. To Trenia Napier at Eastern Kentucky University Libraries I owe a deep debt, for it was she who found the key to the story—the article by Dr. James W. Bruce about the incubator that ultimately saved Radiance Grace's life and changed Mommy's mind. In concert, Carla Townsend of Frontier Nursing Services University supplied information about the presence of electricity at Hyden Hospital, making use of such an incubator feasible.

For help with the politics, mores, and specific practices of journalism in 1937 Kentucky I owe thanks to Dr. Erika Engstrom, director of the University of Kentucky School of Journalism and Media, and David T. Thompson, executive director of the Kentucky Press Association. Librarians Carla Cantagallo and Laura Hall at the University of Kentucky Libraries and librarian Dan Forrest at Western Kentucky State University Libraries were especially helpful in this pursuit.

The Pack Horse Library Project posed some unanswered questions in my research, and once again I turned to librarians for the information I needed, notably Marcal Turner, library assistant, and Sarah M. Coblentz, research services specialist, at the University of Kentucky Libraries.

Additional thanks for help in understanding whether coal mining should play a part in my story go to Renda Morris at the Exhibition Coal Mine in Beckley, West Virginia, who offered clarification about electricity in coal mining towns. I obtained further clarification about the prevalence of coal mining, specifically in southern counties of Eastern Kentucky, from Sue Smith, engineering librarian at the

University of Kentucky Libraries, and Director Clifford Hamilton, who connected me with librarian Kenny Pace at the Leslie County Public Library for further answers.

For his deep commitment to accuracy and the lending of his personal knowledge, I'd like to thank copy editor George Newman. And no book comes into the world without a whole team of dedicated marketing and publicity folks. This book is lucky to have had careful shepherding from my Holiday House crew: Terry Borzumato-Greenberg, Michelle Montague, Sara DiSalvo, Bree Martinez, Mary Joyce Perry, Elyse Vincenty, Alison Tarnofsky, Darby Guinn, Melissa See, and Annie Rosenbladt.

Finally, I owe thanks to the friends who asked every single week for three years about the progress on my novel—my beloved BBTJS, Basia Lebow, Beryl Benacerraf, Jan Wall, and Susan Backus—and to Zia Conedera, who gave me four decades of support while I found and then used my authorial voice.

Thank you to my upstairs family, Topher Cyll, Caitlin Walsh, Camden Cyll, and Elsie Cyll, who are right here to celebrate every victory. And to Ken Cyll, who was there when the very first wisp of a story flew into my heart; how I wish you were here to celebrate with me now.

ABOUT THE AUTHOR

Toni Buzzeo is a *New York Times* bestselling children's author of many picture books, including the Caldecott Honor–winning *One Cool Friend*, illustrated by David Small. A former elementary school librarian and writing teacher, Toni has loved stories of all kinds since she was very young—and, like Cora, she still covets every quiet moment she's able to spend with them. Toni lives in Massachusetts, and you can visit her online at www.tonibuzzeo.com.